J.S. Morrow, action thriller and non-fiction author, has had several stories from his book of shorts, *Mystic Bloodnight*, appear on the Edge of Darkness horror podcast. His script, *The Trap Door*, was used in a Hunter College, CUNY student video production, and his poems *Push, Bus Pass,* and *Soap and Silk*, were published in the poetry anthology Rhyme and Reason. Non-fiction work includes *Hokkaido Bound* (with Narayan Akbar), published in Commotion Magazine, and *The Ultimate Road Trip*, which appeared in the Jet Journal. Originally from the USA, J.S. lives in Kumamoto, Japan where he teaches, writes, rides motorcycles, and plays bass in a rock band.

Scapegoat Protocol

J.S. Morrow

ESCARPMENT PUBLISHING

CHAPTER 1

**SIX KILLED IN MASSACRE AT
GREENSBURG WOMEN'S CLINIC**
Greensburg Evening TribLIVE
World News Service / Tuesday, October 3, 2017, 7:17 p.m.

On Tuesday, October 3 at 9:37 a.m., women waiting for scheduled abortions packed the Greensburg Women's Abortion Clinic when a man entered and started shooting aimlessly.

Mary McDeen, a witness who managed to escape, said, "He wore a tan coat, carried a briefcase under his arm, and had a Halloween eye mask on. And there was a big purple mark on his neck." McDeen also said that while in the bathroom she heard a window shattering and peeked out the door. "I saw blood spurt on the wall, and everybody was screaming."

Activists have been active at abortion clinics since President Frederick Flood announced plans to ban abortions nationwide. Soon after the shooting, dozens of pedestrians and office workers gathered around the shot-out building. Fire trucks and ambulances arrived quickly, and the police were on the scene in minutes.

Police Lieutenant Dominick Darrera said in a briefing, "This type of thing is a first for our area, but it's been happening across our country more frequently now than ever. But make no mistake, we will catch these assailants."

Steve Bailsworth.
Bailsworth can be reached at sbailsworth.facebook.com

~

The next morning, a beeping alarm clock pulled Brad P. O'Connor out of a deep sleep.

Man, what a sleep; my mind is numb.

Morning light streamed in through the blinds and fell across his face. He cracked open his eyes, brushed aside his shaggy hair, and silenced the clock with an open palm. Several blinks dissipated the dream of the naked young woman strolling down the beach.

Brad cocked his head towards the ratty chair in the corner of the room where he'd hung the clothes he needed for the day. His gaze passed across a group picture of twelve twenty-two-year-old trainees at the Wildlands Outdoor Experience School where Brad had completed the six-month survival training course. In the picture, they wore camouflage clothing, hiking boots, machine guns, and black backpacks. In another picture, Brad and his best friend, John Talford, posed holding their rifles and smiling.

Those were the days.

Shortly after the picture was taken, though, things had gone sour for Brad.

Couldn't have made it without that guy. I made a huge faux pas. Sorry, John.

Finally able to wrench his eyes fully open, Brad noticed the time: 8:10.

Shit, better get up!

He had a 9:00 a.m. interview with Tallen and Kline, a local public relations firm that Arrow Employment had arranged for him. He either made it to the interview or remained jobless.

Gotta get out of here by eight thirty.

Brad rolled over and perched up on his elbows. His hand flashed over unshaven stubble. Why was he so out of it? He didn't even drink last night.

He stumbled into the bathroom and caught a view of his five-foot eleven-inch frame in the mirror. *I think I gained a pound.* After a shower, Brad looked at the blue shirt and blue and red striped tie waiting on the chair and changed his mind. He threw on a dress white and a simple red tie, brown Dockers, and a blue blazer. The collar, he pulled up as far as possible, and he flattened his hair down behind his ears to try to cover the curse: a large purple birthmark on his neck that started under his left ear and flanked half of his cheek and the left-hand nape of his neck.

At eight thirty-three, Brad grabbed his phone and sped out the front door, closing and locking it in one fluid motion. He jumped in his green 2003 Honda Accord, backed out of the driveway and headed off to his interview. On the way, he stopped at a 7-11 for a Big Gulp coffee, adding milk, no sugar. He glanced up and noticed the clock on the wall: 8:42. He still had some time, but he had to hurry.

Brad jumped back in the Honda and started the worn engine; it turned over twice and conked out. He tried again. Success! But when pulling out of the 7-11 parking, he nearly crashed into a young woman pushing a baby carriage down the sidewalk. She glared at him and then hurried up to cross the street.

"Sorry." Brad nodded and waved.

The woman didn't wave back.

He drove a little more conservatively towards the A-1 Parking on Vine Street. When almost there, he noticed a garbage truck at Image Makers, a ten-dollar hair salon. Brad frowned. *Why are they there on a Tuesday? Wednesday is garbage day.*

Having no time to think of it further, he parked and strode into the Brinmann building, a Pennsylvania colonial structure that looked like it was still locked in the 18th century. Nervous, he pushed the up arrow twice, hoping it would make the elevator come faster. While he waited, he pulled up his tie, checked his blazer, and straightened his curly hair in the reflection from the elevator doors, then pulled out his phone. He got as far as logging on, but the elevator came too quickly. He shoved his phone back in his pocket.

The elevator stopped, and he accidentally followed a short bald man off the elevator at the sixth floor.

Damn, wrong floor! I don't have time for this!

He turned around and jammed the up arrow several times in panic. The next elevator finally came, and he made sure to push number fourteen. Brad watched the floor numbers tick by ever so slowly: *six, seven, eight, nine … finally.* Tallen and Kline, a midsize public relations firm, sat on the left side of the fourteenth floor. The detailed, brass nameplate on the center of the large wooden door made him feel intimidated. He hated job interviews.

He opened the door and entered meekly, letting the door rest upon his left leg while glancing at his Citizen's Reguno Classic model: eight fifty-eight.

In the nick of time.

The receptionist, black office phone crooked under her chin, eyed him as he approached the desk. "Yes. That's right, we've changed it to tomorrow at 4:30 p.m.

Bye, now." She dropped the phone back in its holder, wielded a pen upon the open notebook, then peered over the top of her granny glasses as if she'd done the same thing on a thousand other occasions.

"Good morning. May I help you?" she asked with a forced smile.

"Well, yes ..." He read her nameplate. "Yolanda ... I have an appointment with Robert Hoskins. Um, Brad O'Connor."

"Okay, just one second, please." Yolanda looked down at the office's appointment book, scanning her pen over the times and names. She looked back up with a frown. "Hmm, I'm sorry; did you say O'Connor?"

"Yes, that's right."

"Hmm, Mr. O'Connor, you're not in the appointment book."

"Really? I know I have an appointment for today."

"Okay, let me just check again ..." She continued to scan the book, then her pen stopped on an entry, and her eyebrows rose. "Ah. Mr. O'Connor? We have you down for an appointment yesterday." She looked up for a response.

Brad squinted, his brain trying to process her words. "Huh?"

"Yes. Here it is." She pointed to the spot in the book. "Your appointment was yesterday. I'm sorry for the mix-up."

"But that's impossible ... Betty Smith from Arrow Employment made my appointment for Tuesday, October third at nine, I'm pretty sure, and here I am."

A puzzled expression formed on the receptionist's face. "Well, yes, you're right. She did. But, Mr. O'Connor, Tuesday, October third, was yesterday."

"Huh? Nah, come on." *She's mistaken.* "You're kidding."

She shook her head. Not kidding.

His brain finally registered the information, and a sudden rush of panic flew up his spine as he looked into Yolanda's piercing and dead serious eyes. "Really?"

She nodded in confirmation. "I'm sorry, sir, but yes, really." She pointed her pen towards the calendar perched on the edge of her desk. It displayed the numeral four in bold.

"Oh. Right. Okay." He shook his head. "I ... I lost track of time. I just got back from a business trip, and, you know, just tired." He feebly attempted to fake it, trying not to sound like a sorry soul.

"That's okay. But we called Betty Smith to tell her you weren't here for the interview, and she was a little upset to hear that." Yolanda's lips curved into a patronizing smile that said, *I'm glad I'm not in your shoes, fuckup!* But she said, "Are you okay?"

He nodded. "Yes, I am. I'm fine. Thank you." He wanted nothing more than to retreat, to take off and run down the street, far away from this place. He turned and looked down at the appointment book, dazed. The receptionist glared at him with her beady eyes.

Jesus, what's going on here?

He couldn't think straight from the shock. "Is it possible to make another appointment?" he asked.

"Mr. Hoskins is in a meeting now, but I'll check his availability and let Arrow know later." She stared at him with pursed lips, as if maintaining control. "That's the best I can do."

"Okay, thanks." *Is she in on this? Is this a big joke?* Brad tapped his middle finger on the front desk three times, wondering what to do now. He let his legs make the decision, and they took him to the car.

CHAPTER 2

The ride home took a long time. He purposely drove slowly on the familiar route, trying to recall the day before, but he couldn't remember anything that said Thursday the third. He played with Sally's kids, Justine and Christopher, on the Santa Maria ship on Saturday. They'd looked cute, and he'd looked like a complete fool because he didn't know how to behave around kids.

Saturday had been crisp and chilly, fall in October. It had reminded him that Christmas was coming. Sunday afternoon he'd had lunch with Sally at Donnelly's at noon on 6th Street while her kids were at their grandmother's. He remembered that Sally looked gorgeous that day. He'd had a steak sandwich on rye, and she'd had ... a Caesar salad. Monday, he'd just watched TV cooked up some chicken and broccoli, and then he'd gone to bed and fallen asleep.

He had no other memories; nothing for Tuesday the third.

Today when he woke should've been Tuesday. But he'd just discovered that today was Wednesday.

He felt weird, hot all of a sudden, and even thought he might faint. Everyone else knew the day, but not him. Why did he feel as if he had a big black hole surrounding him? Sucking him in.

Back in the apartment, he ran his hand through his knotted, messy hair and plopped down on the folding-futon couch in the living room—at only eight-by-six the couch and coffee table took up most of the space. He felt much better and told himself that everything was okay.

Just a strange mix up. Maybe I stepped into the twilight zone?

With dexterity obtained from much practice, he scooped up the slippery remote and clicked on the TV. *Blane Hart,* a local NBC talk show host, appeared in the middle of an interview with Candice Bergen, the actress. He clicked to Channel Four, ABC; it showed a commercial for Exeldone, a natural laxative.

Steve Barson appeared. "Welcome back to News Today. It's Wednesday, October fourth, and Thanksgiving is right around the corner. Next week at Greensburg-Salem High School—" Date confirmed, Brad clicked off the TV.

He stood and paced, terror welling up again, and pulled and twisted the mid-length hair on the back of his head—a nervous habit he'd developed in college during exam time. At that moment, average-build, brown-haired Brad P. O'Connor accepted the fact that he had no recollection whatsoever of the previous day. Today was supposed to be Tuesday, and his mind had trouble comprehending that he'd just been told it was Wednesday.

This can't be happening! What the hell happened to Tuesday?

He tried to retrace his footsteps, but found it difficult. The interview experience indicated that he was indeed missing a day, which meant that the last day he felt sure of was Monday. A day couldn't just disappear into thin air. There had to be an explanation.

He'd scheduled a meeting with Tom after the job interview. What if he hadn't shown up for that either? At ten twenty, he grabbed his phone, quickly thumbed through his contacts for Tom's number, and punched the call button.

"Hello, Ratner Construction." Mandy, the receptionist, answered the call with her usual sing-songy tone—too cheerful for Brad.

"Hi, is Tom available? This is Brad O'Connor."

"One moment, please."

Tom came on in the next three seconds, speaking with a gravely yell as usual—it suited his six-two frame and lumberjack-style tan. "Hey, Brad, what's up? I thought we were supposed to meet yesterday. Sorry I didn't remind you about it—"

"No, that's okay. Yeah, we were supposed to meet. Uh, did I show up?"

Tom paused for several seconds. "Uh, no, you didn't ... whaddaya mean? Don't you remember?"

"Actually, no. Did I call you? I mean, did we speak at all?"

"No. What's up? You really don't remember? I wish you had called, by the way. I hate being stood up!"

"Sorry, but I've got a little problem. I'm missing a day. I don't know what happened to yesterday."

"What? What are you yacking about? Doesn't sound like a little problem to me."

"Yeah, it's not really. I can't remember anything about yesterday." Brad pulled on the skin under his chin.

"So you're saying you're having a mental mind-fart?"

"Yeah, a big one."

"Oh, shit. That doesn't sound good. Come on, you probably got drunk and forgot about it. Slept the whole day. And if that happens, you don't deserve the job!"

"No, that's the whole thing. I had a job interview, so I didn't drink! I went there today thinking it was yesterday."

"Right, the third was yesterday."

"Thanks, I know that now."

"Hey, you might have some kind of problem, like amnesia."

"Yeah, maybe. I don't know if I'd call it amnesia, just a missing day. I remember Saturday and Sunday and Monday. I thought today was Tuesday; then when I went to that job interview, I was told I was mistaken. So I don't know. You tell me."

"Maybe you just have twenty-four-hour amnesia."

Brad scratched his head. "Is there such a thing?"

"There's this thing called transient global amnesia. People suddenly can't remember the recent past, you know, but most memories usually come back soon. They usually remember personal identities, but little things ... maybe not. Causes are unknown."

"Really? Who made you the expert?"

"Chalk that one up to a documentary on the Discovery Channel."

"Anyway, I don't know what to do. Am I friggin' goin' nuts?"

"Maybe you should give it a little time. I would. Then see someone like a neurologist ... or a psychiatrist, or something ... if nothing comes back. I mean, it could be something brain-related. It might be serious."

"Right, okay, thanks. I'll do that." Brad ended the call.

How could this happen? Is it really that big of a deal? I blacked out for a day, so what?

His thoughts didn't help eradicate the terror that enveloped him—the terror of not knowing. Not knowing was the worst part.

After finishing his conversation with Tom, Brad called Sally. He doubted she'd be home, since her teacher's conference in North Carolina went until Friday. The kids

10

stayed with her mother, a common occurrence since Sally's messy divorce.

The answering machine came on, and Brad left a quick message: "Hi, Sal, it's me. I know this might sound weird, but I can't remember yesterday. I know it sounds crazy, but I'm drawing a complete blank. I don't know what happened, but I've a bad feeling about it. I don't want to worry you, but could you call me when you get home? Thanks."

At one o'clock, Brad called Arrow, the search firm he'd been with since he lost his job as the director of the media center at Weston College six months before. *Can't believe they cut out the media center completely. What a waste of time and money—making a deal with Geneva College! Unreal. I hate administrators! I wouldn't be in this mess if I still had that job.*

"Thank you for calling Arrow. May I help you?" A high-pitched voice screeched into the phone.

"Hello, this is Brad O'Connor. Betty Smith, please."

"Oh, yes, Mr. O'Connor. One moment, please." Brad could tell by the receptionist's condescending tone that she knew he hadn't shown. They probably all did.

He felt bad about it. Betty Smith had always stuck up for him, and she went the extra mile for this one. "I raved to Tallen and Kline about you," she'd told him. "They're really interested. They're looking for a director of their new in-house media center, and the pay is great and benefits are equally great!"

That conversation he remembered. He ground his back molars. *I don't believe I missed that interview.*

Betty's voice on the phone pulled him from his thoughts: "Hello, Brad. What happened yesterday? Can't wait to hear this one."

"Well, uh, I kind of have some amnesia or something. I'm missing a day. It's been wiped out of my memory. I know it sounds crazy. But it's true. I went there today thinking it was yesterday."

"Well, all I can say is that I went out of my way to set this thing up. I practically sold them on you, and you didn't show up. I could kill you!" Betty Smith, a large, intimidating lady, who dressed in bright colors, was extremely outgoing and had an air of professionalism. The moment you met her, you felt her power. "Don't be surprised if they give the job to someone else!"

"I know! I'm really sorry. It won't happen again."

"I hope not!"

"Really! I promise. It won't happen again."

A deep breath enveloped the phone. "Are you serious? You really went there today, instead?" she said in a lighter, calmer tone, much to Brad's relief.

"Yeah."

"You dummy." Her voice now had the same casualness that Brad had begun to like so much. "You can't remember anything?"

"No, not a thing. I remember Monday, but not yesterday. I hope I can soon."

"Oh my God, that's horrible ... All right. Call me later. I'll try to set something up for later in the week. I have to call Mr. Hoskins from Tallen and Kline and let him know. What do I say?"

"I asked them to try to arrange another appointment, so they'll probably call you. The receptionist knows I messed up the days. Tell them the truth. I'm really not lying; I know it sounds ridiculous, but I want this job. I need this job."

"Okay. Keep in touch. And don't do this to me again!"

He replaced the phone on the hook. *Oh, God, I hate this!* What happened yesterday? Was he awake? He didn't remember even the slightest detail. Maybe it was a prank, a cruel joke, but who would do that and why? He wanted to sleep and forget this whole mess.

He did—for a little while.

At three o'clock, he walked outside to get some fresh air. He even considered smoking again. He'd quit seven years ago, and for what? Smoking calmed his nerves, and right then he missed that calming feeling. *That's what I need right now.*

The air felt good: cool, not too cold, not too hot. He visited the little grocery on Tartan Street, picked up a paper, a turkey hero, some chips and a bottle of water. *I'll skip the cigs.* On his way out, he noticed the *Latrobe Press* newspaper in a pile by the cash registers. A majestic headline sprang out at him:

MAN WANTED IN MURDER OF SIX AT LOCAL ABORTION CLINIC.

Under the headline, a photo and a story captured the details. Brad looked closely. Something caught his eye. *Wait, what the ...?* He picked up the paper and started out the door.

"Hey, that's a dollar fifty!" The clerk called.

"Oh, right. Here ya go." Brad yanked a crinkled dollar from his right-front pocket, flipped it on the counter, and tossed two quarters after it.

The man in the picture had his back to the camera. He wore a brown Aspentrail jacket identical to one Brad owned, and the leather case he carried looked a lot like Brad's case. It had the same brass clasps.

Of course, a thousand other people probably had the same briefcase and jacket, but he noticed another surreal and unbelievable connection: the man had the same hair

13

as Brad, and that wasn't all. He seemed to be running away from the camera—off to the right while looking back over his shoulder to the left—and though his direction concealed his face, the angle of his neck exposed quite a large, purple birthmark on the nape of his neck, a birthmark the same as Brad's.

He grabbed the paper, shaking. Since he couldn't see the man's face, Brad couldn't be sure, but he had a deep, dark feeling that the man in the photo was him. But it couldn't be him. Surely, he would remember something like that. What if he didn't, though? What if he did that during the amnesia or whatever it was?

On his way out of the store, he spotted a man in a baseball cap—chubby and with the hint of a beard—leaning against a fence across the street. He looked in Brad's direction, almost staring right at him. His suspicious behavior gave Brad a jolt and raised his paranoia level two-fold. He stared at the man for a few seconds, but the man didn't flinch. His head moved as Brad walked off, seemingly tracking Brad with his beady eyes, but he couldn't be sure.

Brad's thoughts raced: *Is that me? Did I do that?* The questions were endless and the answers unknown. He grabbed his hair and gritted his teeth in frustration. He had to find out what had happened. What was lurking behind that photo in the newspaper?

The items in the photo looked similar to his, but that's not what worried him. The clear shot of the birthmark was the most unmistakable feature of the photo and also the most troublesome. It was definitely Brad's.

Shit, that thing is like a huge fingerprint. Fuckin' birthmark! I shoulda had it cut off.

Since his face wasn't in the photo, he figured he'd be safe for a little while, so once back home, he called the supermarket and ordered some provisions to be delivered. He planned to piece together every part of the mystery until he'd solved it, and the newspaper was a good place to start.

He tapped the number in his phone while continuing to pore over the damning newspaper article. The antiquated ringtone of the newspaper office surprised him; shouldn't that size newspaper have more up-to-date phone lines?

"Latrobe Press." The voice sounded like a New York City telephone operator rather than a small-town newspaper receptionist.

Brad read the name of the journalist and photographer at the end of the article. "Von Roberts, please."

"Hang on."

Brad heard muffled voices and squeaks and squeals in the background. It sounded as if the man had covered the receiver. "Who's calling, please?"

"Steve Simons. I'm covering the story about the abortion clinic shooting for Channel Thirty-seven. Out of Holyoke. I'd like to speak to Ms. Roberts about some of the details. It's a professional matter, of course." Brad tried to sound legitimate. This initial contact would be a very important link in the whole mess.

"One minute."

After what seemed like an eternity, Von Roberts picked up the line: "Hello, this is Von Roberts. You're from Channel Thirty-seven?"

"Yes. Steve Simons here. I'd like to ask about—"

"Steve Simons? Hmm. I know Don Harold, the station manager."

"Really?"

"Yeah! I interned over there for a year and a half. Harold never gave me the time of day. 'Cause I was a girl, I guess. Wouldn't send me out to cover anything. Small world, eh? What did you say your position was?"

Brad's heart sank. Did she know he was fibbing? Caught off guard, he had to improvise. He thought he'd picked a small enough station that no one would know anyone else in the business. In the media circle, reputation gets around. He hoped he could still bluff his way through. All he needed was information. He didn't care what happened after he got off the phone.

"Well, actually, I'm a freelance documentary writer and producer, and I was hired by Don to help out with a new piece on the abortion issue. I'm not actually on staff." Brad sighed when he'd finished that line. He thought he'd sounded pretty convincing. Maybe being in the media business would come in handy.

"Oh, okay, what do you need to know?"

Green light. *Don't sound like an idiot.*

"I wanted to know exactly what happened at the clinic the other day. Did the person in the picture have the gun? And how many people saw him? Were there more people involved?"

"A witness I spoke to said he heard gunshots around opening time, made a call to Greensburg Police, and ran to see what was happening while giving the police a play-by-play of what he saw. John Wilhelm and I were driving through Greensburg at the time, on our way to an interview for an article. We had the police scanner on, as usual, and heard the police calling in cars in the area, so we made a quick detour. As it turned out we were only a couple of blocks away, and we arrived along with the first police car. We were walking up the street on the other side of the road to the clinic when suddenly some guy with an machine gun came running across the road towards us."

"Uh huh."

"John started snapping pictures and kept taking them as he ran past us. We got a ton of shots, but this one was the best. Pretty good, huh?"

"Yeah, I'll say."

"I was kind of frozen, you know, scared he might see the camera and rip it off us, but if he saw it, he didn't care. Some cops chased him, but he disappeared down an alley, and we went to cover the carnage and talk to survivors and witnesses. Apparently, there were some pro-life protestors hanging around outside and some women waiting to get in. Just as the doors opened, a single gunman ran up and started shooting—protestors *and* clients; no discrimination."

"Does anyone know why this happened? Why this particular clinic?"

"Who knows? It's just one of those things. Greensburg is one of the clinics with the guts to withstand two-sided issues: pro-abortion, pro-life. People are so concerned with human rights these days. But women need a place to go, too. That guy in the photo better watch his ass, that's all I can say. I hear the cops are moving in. There were some witnesses who saw him: two, I think. I don't think anyone else got any good looks."

Brad didn't want to hear that news. Sheffield, his street, was most likely being combed, and chances were good that he'd be seen, recognized, and taken in. He didn't even want to think about that unnerving possibility.

Though unsure if it was him in the photo, he couldn't ignore the terrible feeling that it might be. He had to handle things rationally now and keep his wits about him. He had to discover the key to unlock this web of confusion. If it weren't him, fine; a little wasted time, a little paranoia. But what if it actually was?

"Okay, thank you, Von. I appreciate your help."

"Just act cautiously covering this story. It sounds like it might get a little dangerous."

Brad frowned. "What do you mean?"

"Well, you know; these days we have gang warfare, random drive-by shootings, the opioid epidemic, terrorism, who knows? I just tell everyone to watch their butts, that's all."

"Yeah, okay, I will. Bye." Brad hung up, more nervous than ever, but also intrigued and more driven to find out what was going on.

To be safe, he'd have to clear out of his home, at least until things quieted down. He thought about sneaking far away, into the woods where no one would ever find him. He'd not turn himself in for something he knew nothing about, although several times he considered it just to gain some piece of mind, to put an end to this nightmare. But would they believe him? And does memory lapse stand up in court?

Brad's gut advised him against tearing up his past just yet, and he thought it best to listen. He didn't think he'd done it. But he didn't know for sure that he hadn't done it either. He vowed he wouldn't let his side down.

~

Lieutenant Dominick Darrera swung around on his leather Drexel swivel chair and banged his coffee cup down on the mound of papers covering his desk, splashing liquid onto the stack. John Paxton and Greg Stone sat in his office.

"Damn it." He yanked a few small swabs of Kleenex from the box next to the landline phone and dabbed at the coffee. Dom Darrera, a bulky man of six feet five inches and fifty-two years, had trouble being neat. He tossed the Kleenex onto the desk in front of the computer. It landed next to a broken pencil, a stained coffee mug and another stack of papers—a typical scene in Dom's office.

"I just don't know what to believe about this case," Dom said. "The witnesses said they saw the guy take off and head towards the south side. One guy in his late thirties, early forties got a good glance at his face, but you know how eyewitness IDs are, and we can't find the witness now. He talked to Deverone, and then Deverone took his name and number. But he's not around today. Don't know where he is. We've had cars over at the witness's and at the clinic all day. Nothing."

Stone flexed his upper-arm muscles under his too-tight, short-sleeve dress shirt. "I had guys over at the clinic last night talking to everyone and anyone. These creeps are pros. My guys took prints, but so far? *Nada*." Greg Stone's favorite tag words lately were all in Spanish: *Hola, nada, gracias*. "I'm sure we'll be able to negotiate with whoever is doing this—when we find them."

"Well, you're the expert with terrorists, Mr. Hotshot detective," John Paxton said, his eyes scanning the room. "Not to mention gang warfare."

"For the most part," Stone added, then he turned to walk out. His foot caught the bottom of the door, which bounded off his foot with a hefty *booomp!* "Ah, shit."

Paxton emitted a muffled laugh from the corner.

Dom frowned. "John, try to track down those witnesses again. Also, we gotta get to everyone at the clinic. Anyone who saw anything."

"But we did, boss." John Paxton, who was busy chewing on a piece of gum, didn't hurry to get up. Dom hoped he could shape the greenhorn into something, but sometimes it didn't look hopeful. "Everyone we talked to told us all they know."

"So they said, right? That's why we have to do it anyway." Dom explained slowly and clearly, like a teacher over-annunciating his words. His bottom jaw moved out at each stress point. "Just go to all the offices and storefronts in the area. From Chestnut down to Fourth."

"But, Dom ..." John raised his hands in a questioning gesture.

Dom glared at him. "John, goddamn it, just do it, all right? We don't have shit on this one. So just do it?" Dom narrowed his eyes as he spoke.

"Okay, okay, I will!" John shrugged, a crease forming on his glistening brow. "Fuck." He turned around and rolled his eyes.

Stone stared, speechless, at his commander.

"What the hell are you staring at?" This broke the silence.

Paxton found the doorknob, turned it, and he and Stone walked out. The door closed, leaving Dom in silence.

He picked up a pen and clicked the ballpoint in and out repeatedly. Dom noticed a ray of sunlight reflecting off the roofs of the cars in the parking lot beneath his window. *Abortion clinic, six people dead, no leads ...*

CHAPTER 3

The next morning, after an incredibly light sleep filled with paranoia and restless dreaming, Brad began his quest. *Gotta change my identity and then get the hell out of Dodge.* Over the next two hours, Brad shoved everything with his name on it, everything traceable to the old Brad O'Connor, into a small lockbox and stuck this in the hole in the back of the closet. His college diploma went in, along with his driver's license, credit cards, DVDs of all his productions, and two books he'd written for the media studies curriculum. He also put in his phone. If they were looking for him, they could use it to trace him. He hoped pay phones still worked. He wasn't sure how he'd beat this or get out of it, but he had to try—somehow. If he got busted, all that work and effort at achieving some kind of success would be instantly obliterated. But if he got out of it without a scrape, it'd be the best media story in years.

He put some gel in his dirty brown hair and shaved off his graying beard, then pulled a box of old sunglasses out of the closet and shoved three of them in a brown paper bag. He grabbed a blue-nylon duffel bag with a yellow Weston College logo on the side and added a toothbrush, deodorant, several pairs of jeans, and two T-shirts: one a Green Bay Packers and the other the Eiffel Tower. He also threw in his professional Zoom H5 digital field audio recorder, a microphone, a pair of headphones, an SD card, a flash drive filled with various media, and $750 from the hole in the closet. Several months prior, he'd started the kitty to save for a rainy day. It looked like his rainy day had arrived. Other important items, like some snack food, vitamins, fingernail clippers, and a notebook, went in. Then he hefted the bag over his shoulder and walked to the front door, where he pulled on his new Goliath hiking boots.

The landline phone rang. Brad paused. The answering machine clicked on, but no one responded, even though the line was open. He heard static, scratchy noises in the background, and then the phone went dead and returned to the annoying dial tone. He recalled the staring stranger in front of the supermarket. The phone call confirmed something was out of sync. He'd better get out of there fast. He left his apartment with a feeling that he might not return, but he kept both the front keys just in case.

Trusting his gut, he exited through the back of the apartment complex, flanked on the left by a huge trash receptacle and on the right by an ancient, noisy air-conditioning unit. Between those, a road led down to Route 66 and out of Greensburg.

Generally a happy-go-lucky, even-keeled person, Brad felt his nervousness and paranoia deeply. He'd taken an outdoor survival course, so why was he so nervous now? Sometimes his kindness opened him up to being taken advantage of, but never in big ways. He'd learned how to be just tough-skinned enough to keep himself out of trouble, yet retain his usual supportive calm. Through all his fantasies and writings, Brad never thought he'd be in the middle of a far-fetched story such as this.

The old adage is convincingly true: truth is stranger than fiction.

~

The phone rang at Ratner Construction's front desk, startling receptionist Mandy, who was reading *Soap Opera Digest*. Tom watched her jump slightly and pick up the phone on the second ring.

"Hello. Ratner Construction. ... Brad O'Connor? ... Uh, okay. Hold on a sec."

She was about to transfer the call when Tom yelled, "I'll take it in here, Mandy."

"Okay!" she yelled back.

He lifted the receiver. "Hey, buddy. How's it goin'? Where are you?"

"All right," Brad replied. "Listen. I need to talk to you. It's about Tuesday."

"Really? You're starting to remember something? I knew it was only temporary." Tom Ratner, America's charming brute, prided himself on being in control of everything. He wanted to comfort Brad, since his friend's base wasn't as solid as it usually was.

"Not exactly. I just need to talk. I have something to show you."

"Okay, sure. Hey, Brad, you okay? You know there's a logical explanation for all of this. Why don't you come up to my office? We'll do lunch and talk it over."

"No. Listen. Come and pick me up. I'm at the 7-11 near Sheffield. I'll be waiting here. Just hurry up."

"Okay, okay. Just hang loose for a couple. I'll be there."

"All right ... thanks."

"No problem." Tom hung up the phone and looked quizzically down at the receiver. Something was going on, but what? He twirled a pen in his fingers, thinking he wasn't so sure about his friend. Brad had sounded as if he were falling off the deep end. Amnesia? Maybe he was trying to avoid something. Tom grabbed a sheet of paper and scribbled a possibility:

Brad has Alzheimer's?

Tom had never seen Brad so unsure of anything. *It must be a fucking nightmare for him!* His life until this point had been smooth, almost like clockwork, except for some small things like the divorce. Maybe his pedestal was crumbling. Tom hoped his friend could stand long enough on this crumbling pedestal to make it through alive. And sane.

Twenty minutes later, Tom Ratner's dark blue 2003 Toyota Tercel pulled into the parking lot of the 7-11. Tom saw Brad, and Brad came over, pulling open the door even before Tom came to a complete stop.

"Hey, Braddy, what's the hurry? Don't break the door, okay?"

"Sorry." Brad climbed in and let out a sigh.

Tom noticed that he gripped a newspaper tightly. "What's that? And look at you; you're a freakin' mess ..." He pointed at Brad's dirty pants and shoes.

"Yeah, I know ..."

"So what's going on? Why the urgency?"

"Well, like I said. I'm kind of ... I don't really know ... going crazy with this thing. I don't know what's up. But I found this. Here, take a look." He handed Tom the newspaper.

Tom looked at the headlines and photo for a minute, and then replied, "So what's this supposed to prove?"

"Well, the guy's got a similar coat and bag to me. But that's not it. Take a look at this." Brad turned his head and pulled down his collar, exposing the birthmark. "See, that's exactly like mine. I should know; I've lived with it all my life."

"I know your birthmark." Tom looked more closely. "Wait, lemme check that out." He pored over the photo with greater scrutiny, then looked at Brad's neck and back at the photo, alternating these gestures about four times before stopping. He paused for a moment and stared off into space. "Holy shit. I admit it's ... pretty strange. But the bottom line is, it's not you, right? So don't worry!"

Jesus, what has this guy gotten into?

"All right; I'll try not to. I don't know, though; it looks so much like me. And this feeling I have. Things don't add up. I'm missing yesterday; now I see this photo. And not only that; I saw this ominous-looking bearded guy outside of that Korean store today. I had a feeling he was there looking for me."

"You're paranoid; you can't be sure. But you can't see your face in this photo, so it's probably not you."

"But this was big. There are witnesses who saw the guy in that picture. Somebody saw whoever it was."

Tom frowned. "Wait, how do you know that?"

"I heard it through the grapevine, from the paper. I called to see if I could get some information. I was doing my own digging."

"Okay, well, let's say you get questioned. *If* you get questioned, then you just deny it. They can't prove it. So you're in the clear."

"Well, yeah, but I didn't do it. I don't even know what's going on."

"Just hang in there. Take things as they come. I'll help you look into it. But just to play it safe, you should stay at my place for a couple of days, until it all works out. You're gonna be all right. I'll take you to my place." Tom thumped his palms on the wheel and spread his lips in a wide, forced smile while clicking his tongue—a habit he had when things went wrong, signifying his thinking mode. He stared out the front window for a moment, as if in a daze, then he turned the car around and headed for his apartment on the other side of town.

They slipped effortlessly inside and settled down for the evening.

~

Brad lay on the sofa in the huge living room in Tom's apartment and mindlessly picked up a magazine from the coffee table. Flipping through, he noticed an article, "Nuclear Engineer calls for Chimerton Nuclear Plant to be Shut Down." Eleven years ago, Brad had written a news report on a leakage at Chimerton, something mentioned in the article:

7/13/2017 MidTRIBLive
Nuclear Engineer calls for Chimerton
Nuclear Plant to be Shut Down.

Josh Sweetwater.

On Forbes Avenue, in Middlebury, Pennsylvania, sits the Chimerton plutonium extraction facility, a huge, sleeping giant piece of architecture. This plant is used to extract plutonium from spent fuel rods for use in nuclear weapons. Plutonium is a highly volatile, highly dangerous substance, and everyone knows that the Chimerton plant could be just as volatile, just as dangerous. Needless to say, the residents of the area are not happy with the operation; they staged a demonstration in late 2001 to have the plant shut down. The authorities were adamant that the plant stay open. That was, until a small leakage occurred there in 2002.

Mr. James Hattaway, manager in charge, had these comments at the time: "The plant is as safe as ever at this point. After the accident, inspectors came from near and far to make check-ups of the surroundings and all the operational procedures. We are confident that our facility now meets all the safety standards of the ANEA."

The facility lies on fourteen acres of land south of Bedford, Pennsylvania. Four different sectors are contained there: the meltdown, the extraction, the ionization, and the initialization segments, and in each, incredibly reactive conditions are present. In the meltdown, noxious fumes can be emitted from the ore; the extraction also can cause vapors and slight radioactivity, but the ionization and initialization processes are the most toxic. Once the molecules are ionized, extreme amounts of radiation can be emitted. It was at this stage that the leak occurred.

Ionization takes place only under meticulous precaution, and although no one is permitted in or out of the sector during these last two phases, it appears that a control staff may have opened a sealed door prematurely. An alarm was sounded and the facility locked down for forty-eight hours after the surroundings were checked for radioactive contamination. Since a small breech occurred, the crew was rushed to the medical unit and into the first aid showers where their bodies were scrubbed until raw. Once contamination occurs, there is not much one can do to remove its effects. There is no medicine to take, no shots, no pills. No operations.

The crew and area were closely monitored for six months following the leakage, after which nuclear engineers determined the area to be once again safe, so operations continue.

However, Phil Malterese, level two nuclear engineer, had reservations then and still has them. He contacted me saying that despite his efforts to maintain standards, staff were growing lax, and he feared another breach could occur.

"Radiation is a sightless, odorless, tasteless poison. It's Mother Nature's secret weapon. And it can, and will, kill. And this is precisely why nuclear energy facilities should not be located near populated areas," he said when interviewed. "And this one is growing old, increasing the danger that something might fail. It's time the plant was shut down. It's simply best for all concerned."

Josh Sweetwater is a reporter for Action News. He can be found using #joshsweetwater and Facebook Action Josh

CHAPTER 4

On Broadway, in Kingston, a small town in upstate New York, where The Edge of Darkness called home, a '97 black Cadillac Seville with black tinted windows lumbered along the pockmarked road. In the back seat sat Juan Gabriel, businessman, martyr, and top gun. A large man of six feet, his longish hair was graying on the sides, but his curly mustache remained as black as his car. To Juan's right, Carmine Brant, an Italian-American with big lips and a round face, sat with an M16 sub-machine gun on his lap. His six-foot, five-inch, two hundred and twenty-two-pound frame kept most people from messing around with him and anyone with him. Pedro Catorso, short but also in good physical shape, was the designated driver, and beside him sat David Carmichael, a muscular American with a crew cut, small eyes, thin lips, and black stubble that masked sharp cheek and nose bones—classic Anglo-Saxon features.

Juan Gabriel looked at the iPad in his lap and then at the MacBook Air on the floor in front of him. On the screen:

Number 14.

Check Initiate.

Sequence go.

Name: Bradley P. O'Connor.

Marital status: S
Military status: N/A
Medical Status: a-1
Job Status: 0
Arrest Record: 0
Scores on College-Level Entrance Examinations: Average-Average-Average
Categorization for use in other-than-average missions: Perfect Candidate.

Juan Gabriel not only knew of Bradley P. O'Connor's past life but also his present one. All his friends, activities, lifestyles, and all happenings, no matter how minute were seen and recorded at the EOD headquarters. For this enormous undertaking, Juan Gabriel had recruited Steven Suardino as their main watchman. Suardino had been following O'Connor constantly for weeks.

Juan reviewed his crew's portfolio. Suardino had always been a pro at this kind of work—an expert at tailing people, planning, revising, informing. He'd worked privately with the terrorist elite. Juan had needed someone to do this uniquely specialized job and knew Suardino had what it took to put him right there in the front with the top players in the world. That's why he'd recruited him and trained him long and hard. Time to give him a call. Juan picked up the cell and tapped his number.

"Yeah."

"Number One here. What's happening?"

"I've been following our man O'Connor all day. I saw him as he walked to the 7-11 and I think he made a phone call, probably to his friend, Tom Ratner."

"Yeah?"

"Yeah, and then I watched them both drive off in a burst. I think they're on their way to hide somewhere;

Ratner's apartment? They took Ratner's car. Whattaya want me to do?"

"Okay. Just keep tabs on them, and stay with them. Check in around the wee hours."

"Okay," Suardino replied.

Juan hung up the phone and trained his eye on the driver. "Let's get over to the HQ. We need to find a good warehouse to put our plan into action. Any news on that, Catorso?"

Catorso, the other of Juan's right-hand men, was responsible for finding the warehouse to build and house the mole, an underground dozer they'd use to put their next phase of action into effect: kidnap the president and blow up the White House.

"Yeah, actually, I did find a place in Pennsylvania, in the woods of the Laurel Mountains. A little far from here, but very secluded. It might be the perfect place. Used to be an old hospital, and it's got several concrete block floors, a basement, and a sub-basement with a huge opening out to the woods. Rooms for whatever we need, it looks like."

"How much?"

"Three hundred thou."

"Not bad. Get it done, then."

"Okay," Catorso replied. "I'll call them on Monday."

"Yep, and then get down there to check it out."

"You know I will."

~

Suardino punched the red hang-up button on his phone and set off after his marks in his blue 2001 Ford. As soon as Brad and Tom turned left onto Route 4, he knew his inkling that these two were going to hide out was right. Suardino would follow and sit patiently for hours; the waiting game would begin.

He tailed them as closely as possible without them getting suspicious. When they got gas at the Shell station, Suardino parked on the side of the road nearby. Their next stop was Walmart.

"What the hell are they doing at Walmart?"

Their car stopped in the parking lot near the store's main entrance. Suardino stopped, turned off the motor and pulled his binoculars from the glove box. He trained them on the car, but couldn't see Brad inside. Probably hiding under the seat. Smart. Tom disappeared through the doors alone and emerged thirty-three minutes later with several bags of goods piled in the cart.

"What did this boy buy today?" Suardino asked himself.

The car started and took off. Suardino dropped the binoculars on the seat next to him and followed down the road. Next, they stopped at the Waffle House, where Tom again disappeared alone and came back with bags of food.

"Dinner tonight, eh?"

His marks drove further and stopped at a red light. Suardino sat two cars behind them. When the light turned green, Tom didn't go. Suardino craned his neck to see what the holdup was, but couldn't see past the car in front.

Shit, maybe they're on to me.

The car didn't move. Suardino put his hand on the Colt 45 in his belt holster, just in case. He was about to get out of the car and make a run for it, but just then an elderly woman appeared in the middle of the crosswalk. Suardino let out a sigh.

Ah ha, can't hit the elderly.

The cars moved slowly. Suardino stayed back and kept following. At eight-thirty p.m. the car stopped on Fourth

Street and parallel parked. The two got out and walked up the entrance to a three-story brownstone.

"Okay," Suardino said to himself. "Must be Ratner's place."

~

The next morning, On Friday, October Sixth, Brad woke up on the sofa, yawned, and stretched his arms as the sunlight peeked in the open window. He got up and stumbled into the vast eat-in kitchen, where he saw the morning paper sitting on the counter.

At eight-thirty a.m. Brad stirred his second cup of coffee and stared blankly out the modern bay window down onto already bustling Fourth Street.

Something caught Brad's eye in the front window of Jerry's Diner across the street. The same man in a baseball cap that had watched him from outside the Korean store the day before sat at a window table facing outward.

Wait; he's looking directly at me!

Brad quickly stepped to the side of the window. Hearing footsteps behind him, he turned as Tom walked in, tucking a flannel shirt into some tan chino pants.

"Hey, Braddy, what's up? You look like you just saw a ghost."

"Come over here." Brad motioned towards the window. "Remember that strange guy I told you about yesterday who was near my place? Look, he's down there in the coffee shop."

"Yeah, I remember. Where?"

"He's looking up here, right? Trying to see in the apartment?"

Tom looked at the man. "I can't really tell. Maybe." He squinted and moved closer to the window. "Actually, he might be. Why?"

"I have this feeling he's looking for me."

"Hmmm, try not be paranoid, Brad. You don't know what this guy's doing. Sorry, I have to get to work. Just hang here," Tom said, never breaking eye contact. "You know, just make yourself at home. Just don't answer the door if it makes you feel better."

"Yeah, all right, thanks."

Tom stepped closer and took hold of Brad's lower arm. His fingers dug into Brad's flesh, and he stared into his eyes. "Listen, it'll all work out, man. I know that picture is unnerving. And now you're paranoid. But there's no use jumping to conclusions. Let's wait and see. You know I'll be with you through this."

"All right; you're right. I don't know anything yet." But there was something strange going on. He felt it. He looked out the window again at the man in the restaurant. He didn't do much of anything besides taking a sip out of a coffee cup every once in a while. Though a little far away, Brad could tell that the man's overall weight was the same as the man who'd watched him the day before, as were his movement and gestures. *It's the same guy; I know it is.* He heard Tom in the distance saying goodbye, and then a door slammed. Footsteps disappeared down the hall, and then it was quiet once again.

The man slowly rose to his feet and disappeared from Brad's view. Brad left his post at the side of the window and sat on the couch, feeling increasingly unsteady. He attempted to mentally put the pieces together, but the task seemed too large to comprehend. He'd woken up with no memory of the previous day, seen a disturbing newspaper article with an even more disturbing photo, and noticed a man who appeared to be watching him. He sighed and decided on another cup of coffee. Just after nine am, the landline phone rang as Brad walked to the kitchen.

He hesitated, unsure, then yanked it up and tried to sound confident—he didn't think he succeeded. "Hello."

"Yes. Please do not hang up the phone, Mr. O'Connor." The voice, ominously deep, sounded as if its owner spoke through a mouth full of marbles. Obviously changed by a vocal effect, it had a strange, humming quality to it. "Mr. O'Connor, are you listening?"

"Uh, yes." Whoever it was knew his name. Was it the guy watching him?

"Good. Let me explain why I'm calling. I'm from an organization called The Edge of Darkness. We know who was responsible for the abortion clinic murders."

There was a long, intended, uncomfortable, pause. Finally, Brad managed, "Oh, really?"

"Yes. And we know you know who was responsible."

That confirmed something for Brad, but he didn't want to let on too quickly. "What do you mean? I don't know what you're talking about."

"Oh, yes, you do. We know you saw the newspaper article, Mr. O'Connor. And that photo. Do you know who was in that photo, Mr. O'Connor?" The voice sounded steady, convincing, unwavering.

All of a sudden, Brad felt the world closing in on him. He didn't know what to do. His vision darkened, and Brad thought he might collapse, but the next line brought him back to reality.

"We know you know. That man in the photo was you. But that will be our little secret. Now here's what we're prepared to do. We won't mention any of our knowledge. But you must do something for us. Are you listening carefully?"

"What? What do you mean? You're wrong! I have nothing to do with that photo. That day I was ... I was ..."

"Can't remember, can you?"

"I know I didn't have anything to do with this!"

"Actually, you're right, you didn't. It wasn't really you. We did it; we did a little make-up trick to look like you! But it's just a matter of time before the authorities come looking for a middle-aged man with a birthmark on his neck!"

"Wait a minute. What are you saying? Are you telling me you purposely put on a disguise to set me up? Why the hell—"

"Now wait a minute, Mr. O'Connor. You just have to do one thing for us, and we can insure your safety. If you comply, you will not be blamed for this crime, nor will anyone ever find you. But you must not tell a single soul what I'm about to say! Agreed?"

"What? This is ... I don't believe—"

"Just listen. We are The Edge of Darkness. We deal in ... let's just say ... covert operations. But we need to obtain something for a certain purpose. We know you can get us what we need, so you were picked to do the job for us."

"What! What is this *something*?"

"Weapons' grade plutonium Pu-239. You know; the by-product material from nuclear reactors."

"You need me to get plutonium? I don't know anything about plutonium!"

"We know that's a lie. You did a report on TV a long time ago. As a matter of fact, we have a copy of it. So don't lie."

"Why did you pick me? Jesus Chri—"

"We wanted someone who is inconspicuous, single, and in no trouble with the law. Basically, someone who doesn't stand out in the crowd. Someone exactly like you,

Mr. O'Connor. You're a crucial part of our business. Just think of it that way. If you agree to do this, you'll be rewarded handsomely. But if you don't, well ..."

Brad did know of the Chimerton nuclear facility through doing his investigative report of it in the early 2000's. He knew about the reputation of the crew who had habits of playing cards and napping on the job. He knew much about the place: the entrance security code, the security system, the floor plan, the locations of all the storage rooms, and, most importantly, the storage room where the steel and lead cases of plutonium were kept. It was no accident they'd picked him. And now it was time to do or die.

Brad felt sweat beading on his brow and blood hitting his skull in rushes. He grasped the handle of the coffee mug so tightly that his fingers turned red. Where had his life taken the wrong turn? Where had he begun to sink? *One moment I'm fine, the next, jobless, and then the next, hounded by some strange outfit that's about to ruin my life.* He'd had enough, and he let out his anger, directed at the marble-sounding voice over the telephone:

"Listen, you bastard! I don't know who you are, but I'm not doing anything for you! Do you understand? Call somebody else if you want them to play your measly game! I have the police and people on my side." He slammed his fist down on the phone table.

"Mr. O'Connor! You seem to not hear me at all. I don't think you know who you're messing with! You'd better come back to reality. I think—"

But it was too late. Brad let the phone receiver drop from his ear back into its cradle. Rage and hostility had built to boiling point. *They can't do this! They can't! Forget it!*

Brad slowly assimilated the new knowledge that every thought, fear and feeling he'd had in the last two days was true. And they wouldn't like being hung up on at all. But the terrifying phone call had confirmed his worst fear—that he was in this thing deep. Phone call or no phone call, Brad wouldn't let himself be the carrier of such a heavy burden. *I'm going to fight back!*

He paced around the apartment, pulling his hand through his hair, rubbing his face, and wringing his hands together. The muscles between his eyes tensed up. Gritting his teeth, he punched his open palm. *Bastards!*

At around eleven a.m., about one and a half hours later, Tom bounded through the door, his usual happy self, but he stopped abruptly, taken aback upon seeing Brad in this unruly state.

At the first sight of Tom, Brad was ready to pour everything out. Everything. "Tom! Oh, man!"

"Brad! Hey, take it easy! What's up?"

"I got this phone call, and they said they set me up! Everything is true! They had a guy who looked like me shoot those people in the clinic, and now they want me to get them plutonium!"

"What? Plutonium? What do they want that for?" Tom scratched his head. "Holy shit, Brad. That sounds unbelievable. I don't know; it just doesn't happen like this in real life, does it? Plutonium, set-ups, phone calls, abortion clinic murders. It's crazy."

"I agree, it is crazy, but these people really did call. You do believe me, don't you?" Brad asked.

Tom frowned thoughtfully. "You know, there is a certain degree of disbelief we're talking about here. I mean, you're asking me to believe that there's a whole plot that's weaving here, right in front of our eyes? A game that's being played out right on you. Why you, though?"

"I've been asking myself the same fucking question, Tom. They said it was because I was inconspicuous. A normal guy, one who doesn't stand out in a crowd."

"Oh, come on. That sounds ridiculous. It's right out of the pages of a Ludlum novel. Government conspiracy! Sometimes our minds have ways of deluding us, Brad. You know, our minds can play tricks on us."

"So you don't believe me."

"I didn't say that. I just ... I mean, are you sure this is what happened?" Tom put his hands on his hips.

"Of course, I'm sure! I saw the guy, and I got the phone call, to your apartment, by the way. It wasn't a call for you. That means someone knows I'm here. Someone's watching me."

"How did they get this number anyway? Brad, what've you—"

"Do you think I know?" Brad grabbed Tom's arm and stared him directly in the eyes. "You have to try to believe me, and not question it. If I'd just had a goddamn tape recorder ..."

Tom was right; the story sounded far-fetched, and minds can be deluded, but Brad knew he hadn't been hallucinating. He'd seen the man with his own eyes and heard the telephone call with his own ears.

CHAPTER 5

Suardino stared at the dead phone receiver in his hand; he couldn't believe that the tame O'Connor had done such a thing. *Wait till Juan hears about this!* He searched in recent calls for the number to Kingston. He had to keep scrolling up and down; after all, thirteen digits is a lot to remember, and it was under a code name. He finally found it, and tapped the contact. After a *beep beep beep,* the call connected.

"Yeah."

"Number Two here. Confirm transmission."

"Go ahead, Number Two."

"I told him, but he's not reacting positively. He hung up on me."

"Fucker. Okay, we'll show him. Go to Phase Two."

"I can try again. I mean, Phase Two is pretty heavy, isn't it? Maybe he doesn't—"

"Just go to Phase Two. That's an order!"

"Okay, done. I'll check in tomorrow at 0700 hours, Eastern time zone."

"Good. And make sure everything runs smoothly."

"Will do."

Steve Suardino's specialty was true undercover work.

After he ended the call with Juan, Suardino continued to stake out Tom's apartment and continually monitor

Brad's movements. The next operation would put The Edge of Darkness above the rest. And it would all be Suardino's doing. He had to make sure events ran smoothly. He had to make sure the time was right. No matter what the cost.

Truth be told, Suardino was tired of waiting on the telephone. It seemed as if that was all he was doing lately. He made the necessary phone call to set up Phase Two.

A guy answered the phone after ten rings and the sleepy voice said, "Hello, Number Three! Well, how are you, this bright morning?"

Numbers One, Two and Three were code names used by all the members of The Edge of Darkness, untraceable to anyone listening. And people were trying to listen; that was one big reason for being in upstate New York. The National Intelligence Committee, or NIC, was especially weak there. They sent the bumblers and the careless, the fools, to Kingston. Every agent feared being sent there. So when The Edge of Darkness communicated in Kingston, they didn't have much to worry about.

"Yeah. Ready for Phase Two. I want it to happen tomorrow morning at nine-oh-two. I don't want people around. We'll have to handle the obstacle first, so I'll get that done in the middle of the night tonight."

"Okay, gotcha. Text me directions to the place, and I'll be there to help you."

"It's on Fourth Street, across from a little restaurant with a mom and pop shop on the corner. Do it, then get the same team together and we'll meet up there at 0800 hours."

"Hey, listen. What about the—?"

"The pay?"

"Yeah."

"Same as last time. Just do it."

"Count me in."

Suardino hung up the phone. Deep down inside he felt urgency, and fear. Things could soon become unraveled. *Is the end drawing near?*

~

A man snuck up to the door in front of Tom's apartment. He examined the lock, took out a long cylinder with a wire in the middle, stuck the cylinder in the lock and twisted the wire at the same time. Listening, he finally heard the unmistakable click of the lock giving way. The figure entered the apartment at two-twenty a.m. and there found what he was looking for: Brad O'Connor splayed on the pull-out sofa bed in Tom's living room, breathing deeply, lost in the dreams of the night. The man walked past Brad and into Tom's room. Tom, too, was out like a light.

The figure returned to the living room and picked up Brad's arm. No movement. The man smiled; he loved heavy sleepers. He took out a syringe and, in a quick, fluid motion, gently stuck the needle into Brad's upper arm. Needle in; plunger pressed; medicine deposited; needle back out.

Brad stirred during the process and turned over. The man hunched onto his hands and knees and backed out towards the door. Brad rolled back over. The door to the apartment closed quietly.

Half an hour later, a van drove up outside. Two men ran inside carrying a stretcher and returned soon after carrying a body. They slid it into the back of the van and drove away.

~

The next day, Dom Darrera stood staring at the body of an eighteen-year-old white girl named Darlene Capricorn who'd tried to escape from the clinic when shots were fired. He'd just knelt down on his haunches to examine her wallet and the contents of her purse, when John Paxton walked over.

"My God, Dom. What the hell are we dealing with here? This guy or these guys have no remorse. They really don't give a shit!"

"It's crazy," Dom said. "Two dead today, and six dead the other day. I don't know. We'll do whatever we have to do to get this son of a bitch. Did you take prints?"

"Yeah, but the guys didn't touch anything. They just came in and shot."

"We should've been protecting this place and all the abortion clinics in the city. From now on, I want coverage on each and every one!"

"There are tons of clinics. Who would've known that whoever did this would come way out here to massacre a few people in an abortion clinic! What point was he trying to prove?"

"Ya got me." Dom stood, turned around, and faced the other officers. "Let's stake out every clinic within the city limits!"

"But, Dom, that's a little too much, isn't it?" Paxton said. "I mean, we have nothing to go on here."

"That's why I'm doing it! We were negligent. The first one, well, okay! But the second clinic shouldn't have happened! The whole city is looking at us now! You do know that, right?"

"All right, all right! Don't worry. It's taken care of. I'm gonna go talk to these people. Apparently, there was a sale on over there at Dominique's. It must have been special because all these women were lined up waiting to get in. One of them might have seen him."

"All right. Go get 'em; what are we waiting for?" Dom continued to stare at the mangled body before breaking free and examining the other one.

The wounds in this kind of case were very similar: bullet holes flanked by torn flesh; tons of blood; insides coming out; outsides going in. These poor women were innocent victims in the wrong place at the wrong time.

~

Back at the station, Dom walked by the interrogation room as Detective Russ Hardwich questioned a young woman

"Yes, mister, I'm tellin' ya. I did see him."

Dom paused to listen.

"Can you say your name, please?" Hardwich asked.

"Monica Tambleau."

"Okay, and you're how old?"

"I'm twenty."

"Tell me what happened."

"Well, I got pregnant accidentally from Mr. Jarvis. He's, uh, a manager at ... where I work. On the day, I was outside the clinic, coming from across the street, when the thing happened. I'd gone for counseling but didn't make it inside. When the firing started, I backed up, retraced my footsteps, and ran to my car."

Damn, she's lucky to be alive! Dom thought.

"Can you tell us a little more?" Hardwich continued. "What did he look like? Exactly."

Dom planned to listen for a moment, but the moment turned into half an hour.

"He had this kind of big mark on his neck. I thought it was AIDS, but then a friend of mine told me it could be a birthmark."

"Really? What did this birthmark look like?"

44

"It was purple ... with little black spots on it. That's why I thought it was AIDS."

Dom peered in and stared at the girl as she spoke.

"And it was long and round on the sides. It kind of looked like a big fishhook."

Monica Tambleau continued to describe the birthmark in detail, confirming the authenticity of the photo from the first attack. Dom walked back to his office and got on the phone to the FBI. Contacting them meant, in most law officials' eyes, that it had become a very serious matter.

"FBI, Quantico headquarters," a young female voice said.

"Hi, this is Dom Darrera from Greensburg Police in Pennsylvania. Can I have Agent Mulberry, please?"

"Just a moment, please."

About twenty seconds later, Mulberry answered the call. "Hi, Dom, Mulberry here."

"Hi, Roger, I have some information on the guy who was seen at the massacre at the abortion clinic today."

"Really? I've been watching it from here ... two people dead?"

"Yes, that's right."

"What did the perp look like?"

"He had a big fishhook-shaped birthmark on his neck. Apparently, it's pretty big."

"Thanks for the info. I'll get a couple of profilers over there tomorrow. That soon enough?"

"Yes, all right. Thanks."

"Anything else?"

"Nothing more than that here. Thanks, Roger. Bye now."

After the call, Dom turned to Paxton, who'd joined him, along with Stone, while he'd been speaking to Mulberry. "I want you to contact all the hospitals here and get a list of dermatologists. Also, look for psychologists and pharmacists, anybody who might have treated a guy with a huge, purple birthmark on his face."

"Okay. Will do." John nodded.

"Stone. Did we get anything else on this thing?" Dom yelled impatiently.

"No. Hardwich has another lead, though. A woman came forth an hour ago. She was outside the shop across the street and saw the whole thing. She says she knows him. He lives in her apartment building. They chatted the other day on the stairs. Russ called her in, and she's going into his office now."

"What? Are you sure?"

"I'm sure."

"Hot damn. This could be a connection." Dom slapped his thigh and dismissed his colleagues, then he searched the Internet for relevant information. After that, he made a mind map of the whole thing on his white board.

An hour later, he heard someone call his name. He turned around.

Stone stood in the doorway. "Russ is done with the witness. She says he lives in the same apartment building, in 2C."

"Oh yeah? What's his name?"

Greg Stone yelled over to Russ in the witness room. "Do we have a name on the guy, Russ?"

After a brief pause, Russ shouted back: "Yes. His name is Brad P. O'Connor."

Dom stopped drinking his coffee and mouthed the name several times: 'Brad O'Connor.' He put down his coffee cup, picked up a pen and paper, and jotted it down. "All right," Dom said, "let's get a car over to his apartment. Where is it?"

"It's on Sheffield," Greg replied.

"Okay. We need to dig up anything we can on the guy. Hopefully we'll find him. Maybe he'll give up voluntarily."

"Right on, *señor.*"

Spanish, Spanish, Spanish ... all the time. I hope he gets tired of that soon.

"What else did the woman say, Stone?"

"She said he was a nice guy. He told her he had a job interview with some PR firm."

"They're always nice guys, right? I'll get someone to get in touch with all the job search firms in town. And you two, over to that apartment. Both of you. I'll follow in my car."

Dom watched Stone walk over and talk to Paxton in a hurried manner filled with gestures, then they both grabbed their coats and ran out the door. Dom set an assistant on the task of calling the employment agencies, then followed.

Once at the apartment, they wasted no time searching, but they found no Brad O'Connor. That didn't prove anything, of course. *He's probably hiding from us somewhere.*

"Not much here," Dom said. "Looks like the place hasn't been used in a few days."

"Yeah, he's not here," Paxton said. "He may be nice, but he's not stupid. We should have some cars scan this entire block."

"Yeah. Check every house. Check everything."

"Let's finish searching the apartment," Dom said.

"Okay, *compadre,*" Greg replied.

After a detailed search, which found no incriminating evidence, they waited for a while, hoping he might return. Three hours later, Brad O'Connor still hadn't shown, and Dom realized they were wasting their time, so they returned to the station.

Back in his office, Dom followed up on a note left on his desk by one of the assistants. He picked up the phone, dialed, then moved to the window, and stared down at the parking lot.

"Hello, Arrow Employment, this is Betty Smith. How may I help you?" Betty Smith appeared to be working on the night of Saturday, October seventh, too.

"This is Lieutenant Darrera from Greensburg P.D. I have a couple of questions regarding a Mr. Bradley O'Connor."

"Okay, sure. He missed an interview the other day, I can tell you that. What else did you want to know about Brad?"

"Just a few other character questions about Mr. O'Connor. Can I take about fifteen minutes of your time?"

"Yes. Okay." She sounded helpf ul—probably always looking for work for her clients.

"You were hired by Brad—is that correct?"

"Well, yes, I guess you could say that. Why do you want to know? Is he in some kind of trouble?"

"Let's just say we have a reason to believe he was involved in the abortion clinic shootings."

"What? Brad? No way!" It sounded like she liked this guy O'Connor.

"A witness identified his birthmark and knew where he lived."

"Oh, yeah, that thing. It's not like he can do anything about it, but a shooting doesn't seem like him."

"Has he ever had any problems on the job or anything? Violence? Tardiness? Unexplained absences?"

"Well, to be honest, we haven't got him any work yet. But ... on that day, the day of the first clinic shooting, he missed an interview we'd arranged for him. He said he lost his memory or something. Couldn't remember a thing. Sounded real serious."

"Lost his memory? That's interesting. What else did he say?"

"He said he woke up and thought it was the interview day, but it was actually the day after."

"Did he ever drink on the job that you know of?" Dom asked after a long pause.

"No. Not that I know of. His last job gave him a little bad luck. They closed down services. Had to let Brad go."

"Really? And what job was that?"

"He was media director at Weston College, and they didn't have any money left in the budget, so they started using Geneva's media department. And they didn't take Brad. He was so ... hurt."

"Did he ever go hunting or play any contact sports?"

"Brad? Not recently. He did take this survival training course thing when he was young, but that's it. Does moderate exercise. A bit chubby, but not overweight. Generally, he's a mellow guy, likable, thought of everyone's feelings first. I don't know how he could have done this. He seemed very peaceful."

"Could he have been doing drugs if he was so peaceful? Did he ever seem ... spaced?"

"Gosh. Forgetful, maybe, but never spaced. He was pretty together. And no drugs, not that I know of. I think he drank a bit, but not to excess, after he and his wife split up."

"When was that?"

"A few years ago, I think. His wife got the house."

"Well, thanks for your time. We'll be in touch."

"Sure, my pleasure."

Darrera put down the phone and rubbed his eyes. Things didn't add up in this case. Of course, anyone could be capable of flipping out, going on a rampage. Maybe he was a very good actor. Something set him off. Maybe he had two personalities. Anything was possible.

Though Dom, Paxton, and Stone had found no Brad O'Connor at Brad's apartment, they did find an iPad, some flash-drives, and a laptop that would be watched and analyzed. They also found notebooks full of notes about various subjects but no weapons of any kind, drugs, or abortion paraphernalia. Nothing. Not even any prescription medication. Dom went to the coffee machine, then took his cup of coffee over to the two desks occupied by Stone and Paxton.

"Jeez, this is a real boring guy," Stone remarked.

"Yeah," Dom said. "How old is he?"

"Forty-two," Paxton chimed in. "Married with a house."

"He got divorced, and the wife's got it now, according to the Arrow woman," Dom replied.

"Okay. Should we check it out?"

"Let's wait on that. Stats show that once divorced, many people don't stay in touch. We can do it later if we need to." Dom walked back to his office.

CHAPTER 6

Sunday, October eighth.

Brad awoke completely disoriented. Clawing, groping, he finally found his way into the world once again and realized he was back in his old apartment. *What? What's going on? I thought I was at Tom's ...*

He sat up with a start and rubbed his unshaven beard, feeling the same groggy, far-away feeling as four days before. He didn't know why, but once again he felt something was wrong, out of sync. The last day he remembered was the sixth, when he was still at Tom's. He checked the clock: the eighth. The same thing had happened! He suddenly remembered the call from the EOD, The Edge of Darkness, the explanation of the make-up they'd used, and the request for plutonium.

Brad dressed quickly and raced to a small deli on Smith Street, hopefully to find a newspaper article saying, "O'Connor Beats Terrorist Group at Their Own Game," or at least to confirm that he was fine, that it was the seventh, and that this was all a nightmare. His heart beat rapidly. In a state of mental confusion and exhaustion, he couldn't think clearly. Brad ran around the corner and nearly collided with an elderly lady pushing a wheel cart.

"Oh! I'm sorry!"

"Really! Young people these days! Watch where you're going!"

Brad turned and ran into the deli. He looked around at the faces who turned to stare at him and realized that with messy hair and without coffee, he must look like a madman.

He spotted the stack of morning papers, and, looking for the story that would exonerate him, raced over to read them. He stopped and stared at the top paper in horror and disbelief, then snatched up the copy and scanned, first the photo, then the headlines:

ANOTHER ABORTION CLINIC SLAYING.

All activity around him phased out. He shook, and then screamed, quietly at first, and then louder. "No! My God! Oh, my God, noooo!"

An elderly gentleman who stood nearby said, "Excuse me, sir. Is everything all right?"

His comment shook Brad out of his immediate funk, and he managed, barely, to respond. He breathed deeply and felt his eyes widen. His mouth was dry. "AAhhh, Yes. I'm ... I'm okay."

"If you need an ambulance or something, or anything, just let me know. I could—"

"No, I'm all right. I'm okay." Saying this calmed Brad down, and he gathered enough composure to pay for the paper, after which he raced back to his apartment and ran upstairs. *Gotta get outta here!* It would just be a matter of time before the authorities came looking for him.

He packed a bag with a change of clothes, threw in his phone charger, then—just in case—added a rope, a knife, two screwdrivers (one flathead, one Phillips), a flashlight, a camera, the press pass that had allowed him access to the facility when he'd written his news story, and a Nuclear Workers' of America union card that he'd received as a souvenir from a disgruntled maintenance man there. He'd held onto the card for all these years and was now glad he did. It might come in handy.

After a last glance around the apartment, Brad grabbed the bag and his jacket and ran out the door. Once on the first floor, he took off down the back alley next to the building, then took back alleys all the way to Tom's, where he let himself in and shut the door, panting. *Made it.*

Brad paced around Tom's apartment, running his hands through his hair, trying to decide what to do. He felt the unmistakable buzz of the phone in his left front pocket and yanked out the phone. Number 322-555-0055. Unknown. Should he answer it?

He swiped the oblong rectangle from left to right. "Hello?"

"Oh good, you answered us, Mr. O'Connor. Now you know that we're not playing games. We know you've seen the recent newspaper. You may not know that two people were killed in that attack."

"Two ... what! You ... bast—"

"Ha ha. Good to see that the cat hasn't got your tongue. Yes, *two people.* Mark my words, Mr. O'Connor, that if you do not get that plutonium, more people will die. Innocent people. Including your lover, Sally. And best friend, Tom."

"You'd better not touch them!"

"You know what to do. Do I have your word?"

"Fuck off. I'm going to the police!"

"You still haven't learned? Wait till the end of the week when we blow up another clinic!"

Brad paused. His heart raced as he considered the options. "Okay, all right. All right. Jesus. I'll do it. And then that's it! You leave me alone!"

The voice at the other end responded calmly. "Yes, we will."

"Say it! Say it will be over."

"We'll leave you alone if you have a good attitude, friend."

Brad pushed the red hang-up button. *Don't call me your fucking friend.* Brad couldn't believe that it had actually come down to his making this decision in a crime he would rather have not been involved in at all. *Goddamn it, why does this kinda shit happen to me? I need to call the police.*

He picked up the cellphone and dialed 911. A female voice asked, "What's the nature of your emergency?"

"Well, it's not really an emergency now, but I was set up by this crazy terrorist group who want me to ..." *I sound like a fool. They're never going to believe me. Maybe I'm digging myself into a hole.* He hung up the phone.

Brad realized he was caught in the middle of a dangerous game, and it wasn't of his own choosing. Now he had to fight, and that was an unusual thing for Brad. He didn't want to aid these people, but he also didn't want to go down so quickly, so innocently. If he did what they wanted, it would give him some more time, hopefully. Brad knew about nuclear reactors. Presumably that's why they'd picked him. *But why would they want plutonium? What are they planning?*

Angered, Brad grabbed a pencil and paper and tried to remember the directions to Chimerton Nuclear facility. He scratched out a quick map to the place.

He remembered he had the news report on DVD at his apartment. It showed almost every aspect of Chimerton: storage, procedure, security and other things. In order to know his route and carve out a plan, he'd have to see his data and notes. But was he able, desperate, and strong enough to go back there? Did the police have his name? He'd checked the news bulletins and knew they had several witnesses in for questioning. He could be identified already and not even know it.

The only way out of it was to change his identity even more. He'd play a game of his own! He'd keep one step away from The Edge of Darkness.

Brad went to the bathroom and looked around to see what Tom had kept over the years. He found other people's bathrooms so interesting; the things they decided to keep in their medicine cabinets were so odd, so different from his.

Maybe Tom has some hair dye or Halloween make-up.

In the cabinet, he found some Vitamin C, an old rusty razor, a bottle of cough medicine, cologne, a toothbrush, and some outdated prescription medication. In the cupboard under the sink, he found some bathroom cleanser, and some shampoo and conditioner. In the hall closet, next to the bathroom, he found more cleanser, some towels, and some vitamins, but none of it was useful in changing his appearance. What was he expecting? That he'd find makeup or hair color in a grown man's apartment? He hated his birthmark. Those fucking kids in elementary school never let him forget it.

Brad finally committed to the inevitable. He couldn't change his looks. He had to surrender and steal the plutonium. He remembered that during the documentary some employees were caught playing video games, napping, and watching movies. He just might be able to get away with it.

That night he and Tom didn't talk much. Tom seemed too busy on the computer in his office. Brad spent the better part of the night looking out the window and listening for strange noises.

What if they're out there right now?

He checked that he had everything he needed in his backpack and sat down to finish sketching out Chimerton from memory. Tom walked up, startling Brad.

"Hey, whatcha drawing there, Brad?"

"Oh, nothing." Brad slammed the sketchbook shut.

Tom stood in the doorway, peering over at him. "I'll keep my ears and eyes open. Right now, you're safe. I don't want you to get caught up in this. They need you to help them, so one good thing is, they won't let anything happen to you. If what you're saying is true ..."

"I know, right? I'm not sure what to do. Go to the police? Stay low and keep out of sight?"

"I think the latter is your best bet for now. If you go to the police, you're admitting something, and then they'll put a tail on you, and you're done."

"Yep, I'll just see what transpires."

"All right. I'm hitting the hay. G'night."

"Night."

Tom retired to his room. Brad waited until Tom's snoring filled the air, then he dressed quietly and grabbed his backpack. Before sneaking out, he went to Tom's room and listened at the door; Tom's snores could still be heard. Stealing, borrowing actually, Tom's car was easy. Tom had a habit of leaving the keys on the telephone table. Brad grabbed his tattered brown-suede jacket and left the apartment.

He got into the car and slowly turned the ignition, looking around for any observers. Seeing no one and trying not to think, he pulled out and drove in the direction of Chimerton Nuclear Facility. The radio played WKKD, Country and Western, which kept him awake, but mentally tuned out. He had a choice between committing a crime and possibly being killed by these terrorists, but he could play their little game.

Once at Chimerton, Brad remembered that the huge parking lot veered off to the left and extended for about a quarter mile. The ground directly around the facility was as barren as a desert, and further away, trees thickened until they became a vast expanse of woods.

On the approach, he slowed the car, turned off the lights, and eased to a stop at the far end of the lot on the other side of a small stand of trees on the edge of a park. He looked over at the sleeping giant. Only the front-entrance light was on. The area was pitch black except for that light.

He opened the car door slowly and got out. The facility was huge, but mostly hidden in the darkness.

Brad tried to recall the details of the plant: the security team guarded the premises for twenty-four hours, and they had an overnight team in the control room as well; the storage facilities were on the ground level on either side of the core unit, and the facility had exit doors around the ground floor. He could gain entry through one of these doors. He walked over to the reactor building. A notion suddenly dawned on him: *In a couple of minutes, I'm actually going to break into a fucking nuclear reactor. Jesus, I must be out of my mind!*

Brad stopped, his heart beating rapidly. He let the notion subside. And then he ran to the rear emergency exit door of Chimerton Nuclear Facility.

CHAPTER 7

Brad reached the emergency exit doors of Chimerton Nuclear Plant and looked around. He remembered that sometimes the doors were kept unlocked; however, the doors on this facility had no handle on the outside. Even if unlocked, Brad would have a difficult time getting them open. And once open, he'd still have to make it to the storage facilities and get away with plutonium. He couldn't help wondering again why they needed the plutonium. What were they planning?

Jesus, what am I getting involved in?

If he didn't do it, they might kill more people, including Sally and Tom, and if he did do it, he could be arrested and locked up for the rest of his life. Not a great choice! He sighed in resignation.

He felt around the circumference of the door, looking for some kind of lip or protrusion that he could grab onto to open the door. Finding none, he reached into his knapsack and took out the large flathead screwdriver. He pushed it in and tried to pry open the heavy steel door, but to no avail. The door was locked.

He stepped back and looked at the side of the building, then walked to the right, along the perimeter. After about twenty feet, he looked up and noticed a small grating that looked like some kind of air duct. About a foot under that and off to the side he noticed a rounded device under black glass—probably a security camera! *Shit.* Remembering from his days as a weekend warrior that many of those cameras were sensory operated, he got down on his hands and knees and stayed completely still.

A razor-wire fence circumnavigated the entrance to Chimerton, and it wasn't too far away from the security camera. He grabbed the hat off his head, bent down and ripped out his shoelaces as fast as he could. He tied them together in a long string, tied his hat to the end, then raced over to the razor-wire fence and flung the hat over the end rail nearest the security camera. As his hat flailed in the wind, the camera whirred around, trying to capture the scene. There it stayed, trying to focus on the swaying hat. The hat came down and so did the camera. Brad took the hat and flung it up, attempting to land it on top of the security camera. It took about six tries, but eventually the hat landed on the camera.

That problem solved, he took out the knife and tied it to the end of the rope with an old sailor knot, then he flung it up to the grating, hoping it would catch among the slats. Lucky it stuck on the first try. He pulled himself up the rope, surprised at how difficult he found this maneuver. He hadn't done pull-ups or shimmied up a rope in about fifteen years. Push-ups were part of his exercise routine, as were sit-ups, and he ran on the treadmill as well. Although running occasionally had filtered down to once a month, he felt he could be active enough if necessary. He was about to find out just how athletic he really was.

He grunted as he made his way up the rope to the top and grabbed onto the slats of the large air duct. As he neared, he saw that he would easily fit inside. The only problem would be getting the duct cover off or sliding between the slats which pointed downward, and were about six inches wide and six inches apart. He grabbed hold of a slat towards the middle of the duct and hoisted himself up further. He managed to get one foot stuck between the bottom slat and the edge of the air duct, helping him keep his balance. He then grabbed the screwdriver, slammed it into the join between the edge of the slat and the edge of the air duct and pried as hard as he could. The slat didn't move. He slipped the screwdriver into his pants and grabbed the slat, letting his body weight hang on it, but it still didn't budge. Again, he pulled, harder, and the weight of his body bent the slat. All of a sudden, the slat snapped, popping out of the air duct with a loud crack and sending Brad flying off the air duct and back onto the ground. He landed with a thud, the wind knocked out of him. For several minutes, he felt too stunned to move and just lay on the ground, trying to return to normal.

After a rest, Brad felt ready to try again. Once again, he flung the rope and screwdriver up to the air duct, but this time it took about five tries before the screwdriver stuck in the duct. Again, Brad yanked himself up, his arms almost bursting with pain.

I'm too old for this.

Eventually, he made it to the top and managed to fling his left arm through the new opening in the slats, then he wriggled his right arm in, followed by his head. The next step required him to squeeze his torso through the opening. He got stuck at the waist but continued to wriggle until he'd moved all the way through the opening. He shone his flashlight around but saw nothing other than the inside of the aluminum air duct, which turned to the right about five hundred feet ahead.

For a moment, Brad felt dismayed. Had he made a mistake? Was there no access to the plant? What if he were caught up here? What if someone heard him? Fear set his heart beating rapidly. He waited for several minutes, letting his fear subside before making the decision to continue onward into the long, dark tunnel.

Slowly, he shuffled along on his hands and knees, using his hands as eyes rather than use his flashlight in case someone saw it. He made it to the first turn and went around. A series of air vents lay ahead with a little light filtering through each one. He crept along to the first one and looked down into some kind of an office. Judging from his position in the building, he felt confident that the office was down the corridor from the control room. That was a relief. All he needed to do then was to somehow open the air vent and drop to the floor. Could breaking into a nuclear facility be that easy?

He pulled the air duct up and discovered that screws secured it, but the Phillips' head screwdriver soon had them undone. As he moved the duct, the screwdriver caught his elbow and dropped down into the office. It ricocheted off the metal desk with a clang and then onto the floor.

"Shit," Brad said in a loud whisper. He put the grill back into place and waited to see if it'd drawn any attention. Five minutes seemed like an eternity, but at last he felt it safe to continue. He pulled away the air vent, shimmied through the slight opening, and dropped onto the floor. The quietness with which he managed to do this surprised him.

~

Thirty-eight-year-old Sally Harris yanked back her long brown hair and pulled it in a bun, then put her hands on her hips and let out a huge, "Whew." She'd just finished tucking her two children into bed. Her phone buzzed. She pulled it out and looked at the screen; the call came from an unregistered landline number.

"Hello?" she asked cautiously.

"Hello. Is this Sally Harris?"

"Yes, it is."

"This is Lieutenant Dom Darrera from the Greensburg P.D. I'm inquiring about the whereabouts of a Mr. Brad O'Connor."

"Oh. Okay. I was about to call the police. Where is he? I haven't seen Brad in, I don't know, a whole week!"

"Isn't he your boyfriend? I mean, don't you two keep in touch?"

"I tried calling him about a dozen times, but no answer, and I went to his place twice, but he was nowhere to be found. It's as if he's dropped off the face of the earth! Is he okay? I wish I knew where he was. Is he in some kind of trouble or something?"

"We have reason to think he was involved in the abortion clinic shootings yesterday and last week."

Her heart skipped a beat. "What? Brad? Why would you say that?"

"He has a birthmark, right? On his neck?"

"Yes, he does. He hates that thing. He's tried to cover it up with make-up, but it just doesn't work well. Why?"

"Because a witness identified a man with a birthmark like his at the crime scene."

"Oh my God. Brad? I can't believe it."

"Okay, I've taken up your time, Ms. Harris. If you hear anything, please let us know."

"Okay; I sure will. I miss Brad. Could you let me know, too? I mean, if you hear anything?" She coughed, holding back tears. "I hope he's okay."

After the call, Sally went to the kitchen to wash the dishes, but, unable to settle to the task, she yanked the phone out of her back pocket and tried Brad again. It rang and rang, and then voicemail came on. She left a short message: "Brad, the police just called me, and they said you might have something to do with those abortion clinic shootings. I haven't heard from you ... Please get in touch with me! I'm worried about you. What's going on? Call me!"

She hung up and slipped the phone back into her pocket.

~

Brad felt surprised, shocked, and relieved to discover that he'd made it into the facility without real incident, but he again reminded himself of the consequences if he got caught. He pulled the flashlight out of his small waist bag, clicked it on, and scanned the room with its long beam. The screwdriver that had so rudely fallen and clanged off the desk, wasn't hard to find. He picked it up then waited, motionless, for another few seconds, listening for sounds in the night. He should hear some, since a crew worked in the control room down the hall. But there were no sounds now. He took a few deep breaths, wringing his hands. It was time.

According to his memory, the plutonium storage facility was on the ground floor on the other side of the fission dome. Getting there would be dangerous—deadly, in fact, because he'd need to go through the fission dome to get to the storage facility, and for that he needed a radioactive suit. The in-depth knowledge he'd once had of the facility had long since been lost, but he remembered the suits being kept in the lockers in one of the offices next to the entrance to the fission dome, across from the control room door. The next major task would be finding the right office with the lockers and then locating the suit.

He creaked open the door and peeked out. It all looked safe; there was no sign of any movement. He doubted there would be at two in the morning. The crew was probably for monitoring purposes only, and they might be playing video games. With the hallway scanned, he stepped out and walked down the hallway. A funny metallic taste formed in his mouth. Did that taste have something to do with being inside a nuclear reactor? Not really wanting to find out, he dropped the question and snuck down the hallway. On the left side of the hall he saw what he thought was the control room and emergency washing room, and on the right side, more offices. Brad hoped none of them would be used at two in the morning. He reached the first door and turned the handle, ever so slowly—he didn't need to be drawing attention now. The door clicked open. Brad swung the door wide, slipped in, and shut the door again in one fluid movement. He thought himself a good cat burglar with all the sneaking around lately. Maybe it would come in handy. He looked around. No lockers. He backed out again and went to the next office. Voices came from the control room, arguing over who would get the next drink.

A man yanked open the door to the control room just as Brad slipped inside the empty office. "All right, all right, I'll get it," he said.

Brad froze, his back to the wall, too afraid to move a muscle. The door to the control room slammed shut. The man shuffled on down the hallway towards the employee lunchroom, where the drink vending machines were kept.

Brad heard the door slide open and then nothing for a moment, then the man mumbled, "Shit, what to get ... Coke ... nah. Ah, 7-up!"

Coins rang down the slot. A can clunked into the tray. More coins, another can. He listened as the man opened the door, stepped out into the hallway, and shuffled back down the hall.

Brad remained still, not wanting to let even a fly know he was there. While he waited, he looked around the room. No lockers. Out again, and to the next office he went, sneaking quickly inside.

Again, no lockers. He opened the door and peeked out. *No one. Good.* He slipped out of the room and trailed the wall down the hall, past the control room. Inside he heard the beeps and squeaks of the computer and two muffled voices talking about something, keeping the boredom away.

He crept further down the hall. On his left, he found two more offices. He tried one of the doors. At first, he thought it was locked, but then, click, the knob gave way. He opened it and stepped inside.

His flashlight beam landed on a large cardboard box labelled Detrox, Inc. 24 Sterilized Rubber Gloves. Good. At least he had rubber gloves.

On the left of the office, he discovered the uniform lockers. He opened a locker and found a white protective suit hanging inside. Perfect. He changed into the suit, wanting to get this business done and over with as soon as possible. The suit felt hot and uncomfortable; the eye mask and ventilator restricted his vision a little, but it was unthinkable not to wear it. Any breach that allowed entry of even the smallest radioactive particle could be disastrous, so he took the time to put the suit on properly.

He didn't like being in the middle of a nuclear reactor in the middle of the night. The thought that he wasn't far from a radioactive substance deadly to humans sent shivers down his spine.

These mo-fo's are friggin' making a friggin' nuclear bomb! The fuckwits have to be stopped. No way am I gonna be caught up in that crap! Oh my God, Sally, where are you? He continued on, more careful than ever. *Jesus, if anyone catches me, cops or EOD, I'm out. It's all over.*

The narrow room continued for about ten yards and toward the right. At the end stood an air lock, the entrance to the 433 Reactor fission dome and beyond that the storage units. Also in the area were the extraction chambers, where workers slipped their hands into rubber gloves dangling on the inside of a large glass box to work with radioactive material. Even with the rubber gloves, all workers had to wear radioactive-proof suits and respirators in case of a leak. His report on this aspect of the facility had shaken Brad: one little leak in a suit could mean death; first cancer, then suffering, and finally death. He remembered with cruel clarity the specifics involved with putting on the suit properly, and made sure he followed them precisely: put on the suit; tape around the cuffs; add rubber gloves, boots, and the hood with the respirator; then double-check to make sure there were no holes in the suit.

Brad took a deep breath, built the right mindset—he could do this—and then was ready to go. But is anyone really ready to go face to face with radioactivity?

He walked to the airlock to the fission dome, knowing the airlock had no lock on it for safety reasons. If someone needed to enter or escape in a hurry, fumbling with a lock was the last thing they wanted to do.

He opened the suction door and felt the air *whoosh* in on all sides of him. Once inside, he caught his breath, and went for the doorknob to the inner door. He pulled it open, feeling a little woozy—again he couldn't believe that he was actually breaking into a nuclear reactor. When he pulled, however, he realized he'd forgotten one small detail: the inner door had an alarm.

Waaaaaaaa! Waaaaaaaa!

The mind-numbing sound almost made his heart stop. How could he have been so brash and not take this into account? He knew it'd seemed too easy to break into this place. Caught in a tight position and not sure what to do, Brad jumped back from the airlock and flicked off his flashlight. *Which way? Shit; what do I do?*

"What the hell is that?" a voice yelled from the direction of the control room.

Brad froze at the entrance to the dome. He heard footsteps running over to the alarm-control board. The alarm board displayed blinking lights at every point on a map of the facility to let the control room know if and where a door or airlock was open. An airlock being open could mean something deadly serious was happening.

"Where is it?" another voice asked.

"Just down the hall! In the airlock to the fission dome!" the first voice replied.

"Shit! Let's get the hell over there!"

Footsteps and voices sounded in the hall. Still unsure what to do, Brad listened. Perhaps he'd hear their plan. If they had one.

"I don't think it's an intruder; we should have noticed by now. Maybe it's a rat or something," voice number one yelled.

I'm a pretty big rat.

"I don't know. We've never had problems with rats or anything before," voice number two said. "What about a malfunction?"

"The alarm board's usually pretty accurate. It'd take some kind of freak thing for that to happen."

"Well, we'd better check it out."

"Yep. Time to suit up."

Brad's pulse shot up. *Fuck, they're coming in.*

The door to the unit opened and a light came on. Brad leapt through the airlock, closed the door behind him—an open door would indicate an intruder—and jumped on the steel stairs leading down inside the dome. It would take the men a while to put on their suits.

Brad slid his flashlight back into his waist bag. In facilities such as this, some kind of lights are always on, mostly to illuminate the areas for the security cameras. In this one, rows of small lights sat overhead, not illuminating things brightly, but giving just enough light to be able to see without trouble.

He edged down the inner staircase, looking around, searching for a hiding place. Nothing obvious presented itself, and all too soon he heard air being whisked through the airlock at the top of the stairs of the fission dome. He raced to a dimly lit hall and hid just around the corner, hearing the inner door of the dome open behind him. A powerful beam of light swept around the space.

"Well, I don't see much," one of the control personnel said. "Maybe there was a malfunction. Let's go down."

At these words, Brad's heart raced faster. He couldn't see the men, but the squishing sound of their rubber boots as they came down the stairs told him they were right on his ass and reminded him that his life was on the line.

Brad remembered that the fission dome lay underground at a distance of about twenty feet. The stairs came down onto the floor surrounding the actual fission dome and extended around its outside circumference.

That was where he'd done most of the interviewing for the report. Airlocks flanked the floor, leading into storage rooms, extraction facilities, and out into the air stacks that looked like some kind of huge drinking glasses. Above the fission dome, the stairs led to access points for rod manipulation and three triple-locked emergency exits above at ground level. He had to go through the fission dome to get anywhere.

The rooms Brad wanted were, if he remembered correctly, through the right-hand airlocks on the first floor of the dome next to the extraction facility where the glove-boxes were kept.

The two men's footsteps stopped at the bottom of the stairs.

"We should split up and search the hallways and airlocks," voice number one said.

"Okay," voice number two said, "I'll go straight and around to the other side."

"Okay, I'll go back around and check behind all the stairs."

"Right. Keep your eyes open. Holler if you get into a jam."

"Okay. No problem."

Brad watched a figure walk past the stairs and continue around for about fifty yards, one quarter of the length of the building. The man didn't search much. Brad remembered that the hallway in which he hid ended and then joined another one that led to the airlock around the north end of the building. This hallway was under a separate sealing system because workers transported many things into the building on that side.

The end of the hallway was kept dark—nothing much there to light. Up above, on the south wall, was a catwalk used to survey the surrounding areas and the window locks. It served as a separate, second-level entrance to the fission dome.

Ah ha! Hiding place.

Brad raced to the end of the hallway and hid, perched between a steam pipe on the wall and the underside of the staircase.

The man walked down the hall.

Don't look up; don't look up.

Brad stuck there, motionless, hanging like a spider waiting for its prey. His arms burned with exertion. But he wasn't a spider; he was very much the prey, and that prompted him, more than anything, to remain calm, silent, and alive. He hung, limbs on fire, motionless, breathless, waiting for the man to pass. It seemed to take not a few moments but an eternity. The man went to the end of the hallway, looked, found nothing, and turned, revealing a sour expression and a look of fear in his eyes; then he walked back towards the stairs. Brad prayed the man wouldn't look up. He didn't. He just walked by and caught up with the other man.

"I didn't see anything," he heard voice number one say. "The hallway was empty."

"Nothing over here, either. Let's head back to the control room and check the system board," voice number two suggested, and they walked away, their footsteps squeaking on the floor.

Relief washed over Brad, but the night was far from over. Their footsteps slowly ascended the stairs, and Brad cringed as they passed directly overhead on the catwalk.

Near the door, voice number one said, "We've got to reset the alarm. Don't let me forget."

"Right. Good thinking."

Brad's heart sank. He regretted overlooking such a small but important detail, He couldn't get out the same way without setting off the alarm again.

He dropped to the ground, bending his knees to land as quietly as possible, then he stood, motionless, under the stairs, sweating from the heat and claustrophobic enclosure of the suit. An old and presently appropriate saying came into his mind: sweating bullets. He leaned against the wall, then slowly let himself fall to a sitting position on the cold cement floor of the Chimerton nuclear facility. Clutching himself tightly, he closed his eyes and sighed.

When he heard no more commotion from the catwalk overhead, Brad assumed it was safe to move on. He looked at his watch—four thirty-five in the morning—and was surprised to see that he'd been sitting in the same position for over half an hour, easily plenty of time to get back to the control room and reset the alarms. He assumed it was already done.

He got up with a sigh and began to regroup. The storage facility was ahead, through the airlock, on the right. As he walked past the stairs, he glanced upwards to make sure no one loomed overhead. *Good. No one in sight.* Brad remembered that the airlocks into the storage facility were never kept locked, in case of emergencies. Nor did they have alarms. That made him feel a little easier. He opened the airlock with a whoosh and slipped into the storage room.

Piece of cake!

He walked into the room and turned on his flashlight. The plutonium, he remembered, was kept in lead containers on a large shelf inside an inner room sealed by an airtight door with a reverse airflow. Though glad to see the precautions he encountered while inside Chimerton, the immensity of them staggered Brad. He could barely fathom the problems that could arise from having radioactivity released into the atmosphere. For a moment, he hated man for being so curious, for discovering and knowing too much.

The inner security room looked clean, pristine, in the reflection of the flashlight. It almost resembled some kind of space-age burial chamber, untouched by human hands for centuries.

He recalled that lead lined the foot-long, six-inch-high steel plutonium cases, which made them extremely heavy. The vials of plutonium, already extracted and formed, lay inside in small, square holding compartments. Lead also lined the vials as a further safety precaution. The vials had a small flip lid on their tops with a catch on the side that was released by pushing a button. A ring resembling a large alien-like wedding band held the plutonium itself. Fortunately, as he also remembered, the plutonium in the lead containers was safe for anyone carrying the material. This allowed for easy transportation without the need for everyone to wear safety clothing.

The inner seal of the door sucked apart as Brad opened the door. He slipped in with the inward-pulling air and spotted the boxes sitting on storage shelves. *This hell ride is just about over,* he thought with a sense of relief as he walked over.

He found a loaded box but was dismayed to discover that the box had a lock. He'd have to take the whole box despite its weight. He lifted it up gently, in order not to shake the contents, and almost dropped it while trying to find the right carrying position. Just when he had it in a satisfactory place, he felt a bump on his left leg.

"Whaa ..." His heart skipped a beat, and he whirled around, still juggling the box, expecting to see the control-room crew with a machine gun in his back, but there, on the floor, lay a cylindrical AI search apparatus. The thing had a flat top with what looked like a periscope coming out of it. The periscope spun around as if searching for something it couldn't find. The lens at the end looked like a video camera's, one with an automatic focusing adjustment. The focuser was busily spinning around and back, attempting to focus in on its target.

Fascinating!

Brad stared down in amazement.

Wait, is that what I think it is? I didn't think such a thing existed yet.

He shone the flashlight on the silver, streamlined body of the robot. The label confirmed his suspicions:

ZARIS XB-807
PROTOTYPE SECURITY DROID
MODEL T120.

A security robot, an android. Brad had read that these would be developed in the future, and here it was. He guessed that this particular one watched for any unusual activity. Would the pictures from the android be picked up in the control room? Worse, could they be transmitted to some security company somewhere? Logically, that would be a key reason for having an android, but he doubted it would be monitored at five in the morning. Even so, he couldn't take any chances. He had to get out of there ASAP!

In his mind, Brad quickly traced his exit. If he went back the way he came, up and along the air-duct, he'd risk setting off the alarm again and possibly meeting someone on the way out. What to do?

He looked down at the robot; the lens stared directly at him with the focus still spinning madly. The thing made him nervous, and the signal had to be being transmitted somewhere. He yanked up the box, rested it on his thigh and started towards the door, limping along as fast as he could manage. He looked back; the robot was following him! Silently. To get it off his tail, he needed to cover the lens. He scanned the room and spied a roll of gaffer tape sitting on the shelf. After setting the box on the floor, he grabbed the tape, tore off a piece, and stuck it directly on the AI's lens. The thing whirred and spun, started forward, went back again, moved from side to side, and then it stopped.

~

In the control room, Phil Malterese and Sam Jordon had reset the alarm to the airlock, and they'd nearly finished resetting the system and checking the instrumentation on the control board to make sure there were no leaks or any contamination when suddenly the "Red Line" began beeping out of control.

"Holy shit," Phil said as he jumped towards it. "This is the fucking security line." He snapped up the receiver. "Hello. Yes. This is Chimerton."

"Hi, Dave Horton here. From National Security Force. We know you guys don't want to hear this, but there's some kind of intruder in the storage units."

"Are you sure about that? We just went down there. There was nothing there."

"We're sure. I was trying to adjust the manual override function on the robot so I can focus in on whatever is over there, and everything suddenly went black. You didn't see it? The action's as plain as day on the monitor. Don't tell me you haven't been checking the monitor!"

"Who woulda' thought we'd have to at five in the morning?"

"I can send the video to your smartphone, but we know it's a tall guy, and it looks as if he's got a box of something."

"Shit. An intruder! We never have any intru—"

"I suggest you guys go down there as soon as possible. You can activate the EX button if you need assistance."

"Yeah. Right." Phil turned to Sam. "Let's get the hell down there. NSF says we have an intruder. He says he was in storage and he had a box." They looked at each other and ran out the door.

~

Brad struggled to hoist the box and slip out the door at the same time. He looked from side to side, wondering which way to go. How could he get back up to the ceiling to go out the air duct with the box? He ran his mind back over the tour of the facility he'd taken a decade ago and remembered what could well be his lifeline: an emergency exit between the control rooms and the bathrooms on this level.

He hurried down the hall towards the emergency outside airlock, trying not to make a sound. When not far from his destination, the inevitable happened: he heard the familiar *whoosh* of the airlock door upstairs. Someone was coming.

He cleared the rest of the distance to the emergency airlock to the sound of rubber boots clunking quickly down the stairs. One turn of the handle and, fortunately, it opened with a loud click. He ducked in, closing the door behind him, and then opened the outside door, not caring what obstacles stood in his way.

I'm outta here.

A loud *beee beee* filled his ears, but the alarm didn't put him off because he'd been expecting it.

"Shit! There he goes!" Brad heard one of the men say as they followed him out the emergency exit, but Brad had disappeared into the night.

As he rounded the corner of the building, Brad heard voice number one say in exasperation, "Ah, fuck. Let's go after him!"

"Yeah, which way?" the other man said.

Panting from lugging the heavy box, Brad rested for a moment in front of the huge Chimerton sign on the edge of the front lawn.

"He's over there!"

Brad looked back; the two men raced towards him, almost stumbling down the lawn. Brad took off again, lugging the box, and ran through the gravel garden to the parking lot. Their footsteps grew closer, gaining on him.

"Oooouuuuch! Fuck!" one voice screamed.

"Phil. What happened?" voice number two yelled.

Ah, dude's name is Phil.

"I tripped. Sprained something, I think."

"I'm coming over. Stay put." Voice number two.

"No! Go after him, Sam! I'll call NSF and tell 'em what we know. Let them handle it from here. I mean, the guy's getting away. Keep going!"

And that one's Sam.

"Okay." Sam turned and continued after Brad, who realized his opportunity to take a rest was over.

I'll take him out with a little detour.

The outer portion of the large Chimerton parking lot butted up against the woods. Brad had parked his car off to the right in the portion only used on busy days, like when there were school tours. A small rectangular park with a tree in the middle sat on the left side of the parking lot. Brad ran towards it, swerved around the tree, and headed for the woods. There, he cracked branches, the sound loud in the stillness of the night. Sam followed, but stopped at Brad's car, not going directly to the woods as Brad hoped.

"Hey, you! I know you're in there. Come out and let's end this thing," Phil yelled.

Fuck, bad call.

Brad broke more branches as he backed through the woods towards the lower end of the parking lot. He waited. A long pause ensued with no sound from Phil. In line with a training exercise he'd done at Wildlands on dealing with a stalker, Brad enticed him over by crushing leaves and breaking sticks. When close enough, he'd bash him in the head.

C'mon over, little deer.

Another long pause. No movement. Then he heard cracking in the branches at the other end of the woods.

Shit, there he is.

Brad moved as silently as possible towards the upper end and the parking lot. He paused and for a second heard no sound. He felt around on the ground, found a melon-sized rock, and tossed it as far as he could into the woods. It landed with a heavy thud. Again, no movement. Brad stayed as still as possible. Suddenly, footsteps raced towards him.

Brad took off out of the woods, balancing the box on his right thigh, lumbered down the small hill, and huffed it as fast as he could towards the car. He made it just in time to hear branches and see the guy pop his head out of the woods. Brad yanked open the car door and jumped in, throwing the box on the passenger seat. He turned the car over and at the same time flipped on his high beams with the dexterity of someone who'd done it a thousand times. The high beam caught Sam directly in his eyes, blinding him. He put his hands up in front of his face, and Brad knew he had time to escape.

Haha! Catch me now!

Brad jammed the car into drive and sped off down the parking lot, out of the entrance to Chimerton, onto the main road, and off into the night. His plan: *make it to a motel and lay low. Maybe Starlight Motel will do ...*

CHAPTER 8

The next morning, Monday, October ninth, Dom was sitting in his office shuffling through some of the paperwork piling up on his desk when Police Commissioner Davis came through the door, slamming it closed as he passed. Dom looked up, pencil still in his hand. The commissioner tossed a notebook on the desk, along with that day's newspaper. The Herald landed squarely in the middle of Dom's papers.

"Good morning, Commissioner. Nice to see you, too." Dom peered over the top of the glasses balanced on the end of his nose.

"Chimerton nuclear facility was broken into last night," the Commissioner said. "They caught the intruder on the security android over at NSF. Guess what?"

"Holy shit. What?"

"The guy was the same one: the guy at the shootouts at the abortion clinics."

"No way. Are you sure?"

"Almost positive. We were able to get some shots of the guy's face and his birthmark. Wasn't that in the report?"

"Yeah. He does have a birthmark."

"We tied him to the witness's description, the paper photo, and the android video. It all appeared to be him.

And he took something, too. Apparently, he stole a plutonium storage box. Which means he's out there, goddam it, with enough fucking plutonium presumably to build a bomb. I want you to find him!"

"All right. We're working on it. Just give me ..." But Commissioner Davis was already backing up and getting ready to split. "Wait a minute, sir."

The commissioner waited, reluctantly.

Dom picked up the phone and dialed Greg Stone's desk.

Stone picked up on the first ring. "Yeah, Stone."

"Greg, Dom here. We've got a problem. That guy, what's his name, O'Connor? The guy who did the shootouts. Looks like he broke into Chimerton last night. Might have stolen some plutonium."

"Are you serious?"

"Yeah! I need you and everyone else on this case! I want you to find this guy, now; whatever it takes. The commissioner's pissed off in a big way. He wants it done, so let's do it. Go bring him in."

"All right, we will! That's what we've been trying to do! I mean we—"

"I don't want to hear about it. I want to see it."

"Okay, Dom," Stone said, slowly, pointedly. "We'll bring him in."

Dom dropped the receiver back on the hook, staring at the commissioner to make sure he heard. "Sorry, Commissioner. Sometimes Stone has to be pushed. I'm sure he'll get on it right away."

"He'd better, Darrera, and you, too. For you and for me, and for the people of this town."

Dom bit his lower lip. The commissioner turned and walked out the door.

Dom shook his head. He couldn't believe his ears—first the abortion clinics, and now this. The guy, whoever he was, was a bad apple, and also smart in avoiding capture. But why had the same guy broken into a nuclear facility? It just didn't make sense. Something was odd about this case. He just couldn't put his finger on it. He would, though, eventually. He'd nail it down. Somewhere, there was a connection. Someone would slip up, and he'd work it out. It was only a matter of time.

He turned and stared out the window. Stone, with trench coat over shoulder, left the building, got into his car, and drove out of the parking lot, clearly heading out in search of O'Connor on his own.

Darrera called Mark Daniels, the commander of a SWAT team and noteworthy not only because of his stocky five-foot-eleven frame but also because he wore medals all the time on his green uniform jacket.

"Mark. Dom Darrera here. I need you guys on this abortion case; can you do it?"

"I'd like to be able to help you, sir," Daniels replied in a brutish voice that Dom didn't like—it sounded as if he were responding to a cruel sergeant. "But we're on a drug stakeout case in four different places at the moment. We need at least two days. Then we can talk. Fine with you, sir?"

"I haven't got two days; I've got today. We need someone out there. I gotta bust this asshole."

"Sir, excuse me, I'm trying my best here. What's it now, nine thirty? I can get a couple of guys, say three, for seventeen hundred hours. That's the best I can do. How does that work?"

"All right, if that's all I can get. Just get them out to one hundred and twelve Sheffield. Paxton will give you the details. And thanks."

"Yes, sir. My pleasure, Lieutenant, sir."

Dom wondered why the man spoke so formally, but he hung up the phone feeling at least partially fulfilled, like he was on the route to accomplishing something. He had a positive feeling that it would all be over soon.

~

Brad didn't sleep after he made it to Starlight Motel; he had to get rid of that plutonium. He had to make the call, do the deed, give up, and give in. He hated to aid the group, but it was necessary to save his own skin. Then he'd sort out his life and get back on track. He'd give them what they wanted, and surely that would be enough. No more running and sneaking. It would all be over. Wouldn't it?

At ten fifteen, he noticed that he'd been out of the reactor since four fifty. It didn't feel that long. He yanked the cell out of his pocket and dialed the number the EOD guy had given him. He hoped they'd wait until he delivered the goods. No more set-ups. He'd soon find out.

"Hello," a pleasant female voice said. "How may we help you?"

What better way to divert attention than to sound like a doctor's office?

"I'd like Number Two, please." Brad followed the EOD guy's instruction to use the number code.

"Just a moment."

Brad heard a whir in the background, and then a series of clicks and two beeps. Finally, a low husky voice filled the receiver, obviously transformed by some vocal effect—the voice that sounded like it came from a mouth full of marbles.

"Yeah. This is Number Two."

"This is Brad O'Connor. I hope you remember me."

"Of course, Mr. O'Connor. As I told you before, you are extremely important to our mission."

"Yeah, well, I have your stuff. Let's meet, and I'll give it to you. Let's get this over with."

The EOD guy chuckled at the other end of the phone.

Bastard's laughing!

"Okay, fine idea," the EOD guy said. "Now, listen carefully; go to the Mobil gas station at Shady Avenue. In the bathroom, you'll find a small piece of paper taped to the side of the mirror. If the paper's there, it will instruct you where to find the remaining details of our meeting. I know you won't have the police with you since you're on the wanted list for shootings at two abortion clinics, but do make sure you follow through, because if you don't, we have another abortion massacre just waiting to be set into motion."

"Whaa ...! Wait a minute! I'll be there. I'll be there! Then that's it! You understand me? That's it. I don't ever want to hear from you again!" Brad didn't bother to conceal his anger—he was downright livid—but by the time he regained his composure, the phone line was dead.

He put the box of plutonium in his large blue duffle bag with Weston College in gold and purple on the side, then he shoved it under his bed. He clicked off the light and tried to get some shut-eye. At last, he felt a little safer and able to relax a bit. His decision to stay in a motel that morning had been a good one. In the space of several days, he'd drawn the attention of a long list of people, and they were all after him: the EOD, the police, and perhaps the FBI. It seemed he was getting in deeper and deeper.

Good thing the employees of the Starlight Motel have no idea a wanted man is staying in one of their rooms! And that a very volatile substance is right under one of their beds.

~

Greg Stone drove by Brad's apartment but felt it fruitless to stop. Brad would surely not be stupid enough to come back—it'd be walking right into a trap. Since he'd avoided capture for this long, he must be becoming more and more adept at keeping himself hidden, which would make him that much harder to find.

Darrera would send out a team to the apartment, but he found no logic in this reasoning, because he and Paxton had already checked the place out. He felt as if Darrera had overstepped him, like he didn't trust him or his judgment. Darrera had probably decided to call in SWAT and also send someone out to the facility to question as many people as possible. He was predictable, playing by too many rules—not too good for a police lieutenant. Stone could beat him to the punch. Not that he wanted to show up his boss, but he felt he could make sense out of things.

Greg Stone's first stop was Arrow, Brad's employment agency. He wanted to gather as much information as possible about the culprit and figured an employment agency would know something about their clients' lives.

Betty Smith gave him all of the long and meandering aspects of Brad O'Connor's life that she knew. This included college, his marriage, the divorce, friends, and home life. Betty also had digital copies of several reports Brad had done as an investigative reporter in his early days.

"He did a story on Chimerton Nuclear Facility," Betty said. "You know, the one south of Bedford?"

Greg's face lit up. He almost couldn't believe his ears.

"It was an in-depth report, right around the time of nuclear awareness. It turned out to be pretty good. He even got a little famous from it. I think it was—"

"Wait, you mean he did a whole story on the place? He's been there?"

"Of course! He had to go to get the video and interview. I have it here. Want to see it?"

"Yeah, sure. If it's not too much trouble."

They watched the tape in silence, Greg absorbing every word. The report was serious and detailed, and by the end, Greg Stone was convinced that Brad O'Connor had broken into Chimerton and, therefore, had done the abortion clinic crimes as well. The question was: why?

"I need to know about Brad's close friends," Greg said. "I mean, we're looking for him and he's nowhere to be found."

"Well, there's this one guy, Brad's best friend. His name is ... uh ... oh yeah, Tom. Tom Ratner. That's it. He owns some small construction company on the north end. He acted as a reference for Brad when he came over here." She searched through her desk, pulled out a business card, and handed it to Greg. "Here's his card. But I have to tell you that Brad didn't do anything. I know that. He's a very, very upstanding guy. Like I told the other guy who called on Saturday night. Brad is one of the nicest guys I know."

"Well, everybody has two faces; everyone has two sides. Some people keep that other half hidden very well. Look at the infamous serial killer Ted Bundy who killed young girls in the 1970's; he was a nice guy, too. If it later comes down to O'Connor being falsely accused, well, then, my apologies." Greg stood ready to leave. "Thank you for the information. We'll be in touch."

~

Sally Harris had just finished teaching her last class at Madison Junior High School and was walking back to her homeroom when she heard the announcement over the loudspeaker.

"Ms. Harris, Ms. Harris, please come to the main office. Sally Harris, come to the main office, please."

Sally grimaced. *Shit.* She turned around, juggling her two American History books and a stack of turned-in essays, and made her way to the main office. She hated the main office, because it reminded her of her school days visiting the guidance counselor for endless meetings on choosing a career and a college to go with it.

She wriggled her way through the large automatic door, past several teachers and a great number of meandering students, all with their own agendas.

She finally made it to the front desk and to Mrs. Wiegers, the clerk. "Hi, Mrs. Wiegers."

"Oh, hi, Ms. Harris. You got a package from Prentice Hall. Here you go. Must be new textbooks?"

"Thank you. Glad they came so quickly."

"And there was a phone call for you from a man, a Mr. Boggs," Mrs. Wiegers said with a glint in her eye.

Why is she always trying to make me the fool?

"His number is on your desk." Mrs. Wiegers handed her the package and Sally took it.

She wanted to get to her office to see the number from this man. At first, she had no idea who Mr. Boggs was, but as she placed the package in her bag, it hit home, leaving her feeling slightly dazed. Boggs was Brad. She'd given him the name a few years ago, when they first dated after their divorces. Brad used to get down in the dumps from time to time, usually when he was trying to write something or put a story together, and she used to tell him that she thought he looked like he was trotting through the bog. The name stuck.

She hurried to her office, almost flattening Principal Kelis Fench as she went. "Oh, hi, Mr. Fench. Sorry." She gave a small smile and pulled the books closer to her chest.

"Hello, Ms. Harris! Don't knock over the football team on your way out!" Fench was a big man with a roly-poly belly, like a bowl full of jelly. He had the look of an oversized elf, and was always in a happy, content mood, complete with shiny red nose and round glasses that were always perched on the end of it.

She walked out quickly and then increased her speed almost to a run. Once at her office, a large room shared by five other teachers, she dropped the books on her desk with a thump. Fortunately, all the other teachers were in homeroom now, so she had a bit of quiet time. She was desperate to make this call, and her fingers couldn't punch in the number on her phone fast enough.

"Starlight," a voice said.

Fortunately for Brad, Sally Harris was a smart woman. She knew a phone call could be dangerous for a fugitive. She tried to see into Brad. Catch the plan. From now on, Sally guessed, he was to be Mr. Boggs.

"Mr. Boggs' room, please."

"Boggs? Let's see; oh yes, here we are. One minute."

The phone rang three times. Five times. An eternity! And then someone answered in a deep gravelly voice unlike Brad's.

"Hello."

"Boggs? It's Ms. Harris. How the hell are you? What's going on? Where are you? I've called you hundreds of times! And the police called me, too."

"Oh, baby, you know I can't tell you a lot of details. I've got to get off quickly so they can't trace the call."

"The police said you might be involved in that shooting? Is that true?"

"Of course not. I have to see you. You remember our favorite stomping ground? Let's meet there. This afternoon at four thirty."

"Okay. Just promise me you'll be safe."

"Don't worry about me. You be safe, too. If you notice anything out of the ordinary, stop and call it off."

"All right. Will do. Love you."

"Love you, too. And see you very soon." They hung up.

They'd found their favorite stomping ground—a little inlet by a small stream on the south end of Elm Park— quite by accident. *What great times those were. Just walking through the park hand in hand, then we decided to go through the woods ...*

~

At three-thirty p.m., the SWAT team assembled itself outside Brad's apartment. Mark Daniels could only spare four members: Steve Drake, Bobby Hoswell, D.J. McInerney, and Collis Billings. Collis, the second in command under Mark Daniels, was a good leader in his own right. He'd spent eight years with the marines and had been to Afghanistan and spent a short time in Iraq. After his tour of duty, it was inevitable that he make his career in the police force.

Near the seventeen hundred hour strike time, Hoswell, McInerney, and Collis assembled around the corner from the building and gathered in a tight circle to discuss the plan of action.

Daniels overheard Hoswell say to the others: "This is fucking ridiculous. The guy isn't here. What does Daniels know?"

"If I don't know so much, then why am I in command?" Daniels pounded his helmet on his leg.

88

"Ah, sorry." Hoswell rolled his eyes at the others.

"No, that's sorry, *sir*!"

"Sorry, sir."

They walked around the corner of the building. "Here it is," Daniels said. "Hoswell, you and Drake go first. You flank us going up the stairs. When we get to his door, you guys take either side of the door. Then we'll come in the center and blast through. Got it?"

Everyone nodded, some with more conviction than others.

With a down-sweeping motion of his arm and a silent *one, two, three, now,* Daniels initiated the plan.

They raced up the stairs and slammed through the door, each covering one part of O'Connor's apartment, then they assumed the stance made famous by all SWAT teams and combed the apartment. They went through closets, cupboards, and the bathroom, but once again, no Brad O'Connor.

"Wait, what's this?" Hoswell said, pulling an old book from a bottom desk drawer. "The Ins and Outs of Nuclear Energy."

"Thanks, Hoswell, we'll follow that up," Daniels said. "Take that book with you. Let's blow."

They relaxed for a moment and looked at each other. Daniels gave the thumbs up. Hoswell looked around. McInerney said, "Good job, Hos; considering there could've been blood spattering and human lives being snuffed."

"I'll call Darrera," Daniels said. "Tell him his man's flown the coop, but we found this book." He yanked his phone out of his inner vest pocket.

~

Sally arrived at their meeting a couple of minutes early and stared out at the water, remembering the good times.

Footsteps through the opening to the inlet startled her. She turned around. "Hi! Oh, Brad, how are you? I've missed you so much. I'm confused."

"Hey there. Me too. Not sure how all this happened so suddenly. The authorities ... they think I did the abortion clinics thing. The bottom line is, this terrorist group called The Edge of Darkness is after me. One of their guys disguised himself to look like me and then did the shootings at the abortion clinics! And then they tell me to go to Chimerton and steal some plutonium or they'll attack another clinic or kill you and Tom. So I did it, and I just have to give it to them. Then it'll all be over. I hope."

"Oh, Jesus, Brad. If what you're telling me is true ... I mean ...!"

"Believe me, it is. I can't stay here much longer. Just do me a favor: stay low; stay out of sight; be strong. It's best you stay out of everyone's way."

"Okay. Is there anything you need me to do?"

"Not really. I need to get proof that these guys are after me. Try to remember any strange things or people you've seen around lately. And stay low."

"Okay, sure. I'll stay low. Just take care of yourself. The police did call me, by the way. They're looking for you in full force."

"I figured as much. Thanks. I appreciate it. That's why I can't stay at Starlight anymore. I'm outta there. I'll call you when I get another chance." He leaned over and put his hand on her thigh, then he lightly kissed her on the cheek and brushed a strand of hair out of her eyes.

"Okay, I just hope everything works out. Please keep in touch!" Her eyes filled with tears.

"Yeah, me too. It's no time to get sentimental, but I love you. And I hope I can get out of this alive and we can be together. Finally." The next second Brad was gone.

Sally put the cell in her purse, then rubbed her eyes, using both fists. After a moment, she went back to her car, got in, started the engine, and slowly drove down the street.

She didn't make it far before her cell buzzed again—a call from an unregistered number. She never answered those kinds of calls, but something about the situation made her feel as if she should. "Yes."

"Hello, Ms. Harris. You don't know me, but we asked a good friend of yours to help us. He needs to get us something very important."

Sally almost dropped the phone. "Who is this?" She had a slight inkling already. "Are you that fucking outfit that's setting Brad up? You'd better leave him alone!"

"Ha ha! Well, I'm happy to see you're up to date."

Fucking condescending ass. "Now you listen. I've spoken to the police, and I'll certainly talk to them about this call."

"Do you think that will do any good? We know how to evade the police. You just tell him to do what we say, or we'll come after you and Brad's best friend, Tom. Do not underestimate us."

"Now listen, you. I'll have you ... hello?" The cell was already dead. "Dammit!" She slammed her open palm on the steering wheel and stared off into the mass of trees beyond.

~

Greg Stone was too impatient to follow Darrera's orders on this one. He knew O'Connor wouldn't be stupid enough to show his face near his apartment. After speaking with Betty Smith and watching the video, he had a feeling he might be able to track O'Connor down through Tom.

He showed up at Ratner Construction just as Tom was finishing a meeting for a new project on the south side of town. Stone walked straight in as soon as the clients left, which gave Tom little time to guard himself against the surprising arrival and sudden questions.

"Hi." Stone stuck out his hand graciously. "I'm Greg Stone. Greensburg P.D." He gave an adept flip of his badge. "I'm a detective. Thought you might be able to help me with a friend of yours, Brad O'Connor." Stone noticed Tom's eye contact veer suddenly to the left, a sure sign of nervousness. *This guy knows something.*

"Yeah, sure."

Stone watched Tom shake his big hand. The man was clearly nervous.

"Uh, what do you need to know?"

"Well, I'm sure you've heard about the break-in at Chimerton and the shootings at the Greensburg Women's Clinic and another abortion clinic. We have reason to believe that Brad's in on it. Do you know anything about that? And especially about his whereabouts now?"

"Yeah, actually."

Stone's eyebrows rose, surprised at Tom being so forthright.

"Brad called me after seeing his ... uh ... that photo in the paper. He claimed up and down that it wasn't him, but he also said he couldn't remember the day before."

"That's funny. He said the same thing to Betty Smith at Arrow." Stone thought something was off kilter. *Either the guy is a good liar and has everybody believing and covering for him or he's telling the truth.* "Do you know where he is now?"

"I have no idea. I let him stay with me for a couple of nights."

Stone glared into Tom's eyes. *If he lies, I'll know.*

"But this morning, I woke up and he was gone. Took my car, too." Tom's eyes never moved.

Shit, he's telling the truth. "All right. We'll look into that. Thank you very much. Could someone be hiding him? Like his parents, or ex-wife, or girlfriend Sally?"

"Na, not his ex. They don't get along at all. Like oil and water, you know. Sally, uh, she's pretty mellow; I don't think she has it in her to hide him like a fugitive. Besides, he wouldn't want to involve her."

"Okay, thanks, Mr. Ratner for your time. If you hear anything, would you let me know?" He handed Tom his business card.

Ratner eyed the card from top to bottom as Stone put a few notes into the phone note app. Stone picked up a Ratner Construction card from Tom's desk and stuck it in his wallet. Then he spun around and walked down the hall. He stopped at the front door, turned, and said, "If you see him again, you'd better get in touch, or I'll have a tail on you faster than you can say Jack Spratt."

~

After Stone left, Tom paced around the office, wondering if Brad could actually have attacked the clinics and broken into a nuclear facility. He thought he knew Brad, but there could always be a deep dark secret hidden somewhere. People do live double lives, having secrets that not even their children know about.

He took the card and flicked it over his fingers, making a dull *shick, shick, shick* sound. Then he took out his wallet, put the card in, plopped down on his chair, and rubbed the newly formed stubble on his face.

He got back to work with a sigh, going over a measurement diagram and blueprints for a warehouse space to be utilized by his new clients, Burhart and Co., on Sayville road. Finally, after long negotiations, the job was his. He was figuring the measurement for the basement level storage facilities but had to cut his work short when Sally Harris rang.

"Hey, Sal. What's up?"

"Tom! I just met Brad!"

"Really? How is he?"

"Sounded and looked nervous after being set up by this terrorist group and all."

"He told me the same thing—that someone was watching him, and that they'd called saying they'd set him up."

"Yeah, well, they called me, too," Sally said.

"You're kidding." *I should've stuck up for Brad more with that cop.*

"No. They said they wanted him to steal plutonium or they'd attack another clinic or kill you or me."

"Holy shit! Now we're in this, too! He needs us to stand by him, but we need to watch our own butts, too."

"Yeah, he said he did it. Last night. He just has to give it to them."

"Oh my God. That means the cops are going to be everywhere. Did you tell them he did it?"

"Was about to, and they hung up on me. I think he's telling the truth about the shootings at the clinics. He's too—"

"I know, we're talking about Brad here ... He's so mellow. Likeable."

"Yes, he's an honest guy, and that's what he said, that they forced him to do it. Brad's one who'd give them the time of day and actually do it to try to make things right. You know what I mean? So I think he did."

"That's it! You're right," Tom said. "We've got to save him. He's gotten in way over his head!"

"Yeah, he called me from Starlight Motel. But he said he was leaving there, and ..." Tom could hear Sally holding back the tears. "I love him. He's everything ... he's ... please, Tom. You have to ... try to—"

"Don't worry, Sal. I'll do my best. I'll try to ... to find him." But he had no idea where Brad might go.

"Okay, thank you."

"Bye. I'll be in touch."

Tom hung up, then stood over the blueprints staring at the mass of horizontal lines on the paper. Suddenly he grabbed his coat, ran out the door, jumped into the Jeep, and sped down to Brad's apartment.

When he reached the apartment, he sat in his car beside the large steel trash receptacle and surveyed the situation. Not time to get spotted or questioned by anyone, including the police.

Shit, feel like Starsky.

He waited for fifteen minutes, scanning everywhere around the apartment, hoping he might see Brad, but he saw no sign of him. He studied the front door, the parking lot, and the right side of the building where it converged with the woods. Nothing. *All right, screw it. Might as well get going.* He drove slowly down the street. Still nothing.

In need of gas, Tom stopped at a Shell station next to Elm Park on the way home. He popped open the gas cover, put his credit card in the machine, and started pumping while staring off into the distance.

Something caught his eye: a man carrying a box walking through the woods, down the path to Route Four. Tom squinted to get a better view. He recognized the cap and the green jacket. It was Brad. He dropped the gas nozzle. *Holy Jesus.*

Tom stuck the nozzle back in the pump and ran down towards the woods, searching for Brad, but he'd already gone. Tom climbed back up the rise and got back into the car, then he grabbed his phone and punched Brad's cell number. It rang seven times and then went to voice mail: 'Hey, this is Brad, leave a message if you want!'

"Hey, Brad, where are you now? I could've sworn I just saw you by Elm Park near the Shell station! Would you tell me what the fuck is going on, please?" Tom hung up the phone, finished filling his car, then paid for the gas and drove off.

CHAPTER 9

Juan instructed Dave Patina, chief maintenance mechanic, on how he wanted the missiles faced and where to place the bombs.

"The Edge of Darkness is busier than ever, placing itself in line for the most abrupt and serious action it has ever taken. Mark my words, Patina. It's preparing itself to be a powerful force in the world. There will be events yet to come."

"Yeah, I believe you." Patina responded, flipping a crescent wrench on the palm of his left hand. He scratched his graying goatee and patted his protruding stomach.

"Don't forget we have to get the missiles in place. And soon."

"But, Juan, the surface-to ground missiles are frequently duds, unless they're checked, and sometimes they go off accidentally. That could be disastrous. It could absolutely ruin all we've spent so long trying to create." Dave Patina went over the electrical plans as he spoke.

"Jesus, how long'll that take?"

"For the surface-to-ground from here? About two weeks."

"Two weeks! Goddamn it! That puts us way past the window. I want those things checked in no more than a week. We already have the detonator configured."

"But, Juan, you're pushing us against the wall! I don't—"

"Just do it! I don't like back-talkers! What about the mole?"

"It's almost ready."

"Jesus Christ, at least something is ready to go! Hey! Someone's not such a fuck-up after all!" Juan punched Patina on his upper arm.

Patina stepped back and pulled his hand through his hair. "Cut it out, Juan. I can't take any more of that kind of shit from you!"

Juan snorted. "Just make sure everything's all ready to go. Or it's gonna cost ya." He jammed his index finger into Patina's chest, then walked out.

Patina's thoughts went back to explaining the mole to Carmine Brant after Brant had been recruited to be a strongman. "The mole is an underground boring machine based on an idea from Project Camelot where the US Army bored huge tunnels under Area 51. This one, though, was actually quite revolutionary as it was designed to create its own power by nuclear fission and move quickly through topsoil, rock, and bedrock."

"Uh huh," Brant said.

"In theory, it could break records, win science awards, possibly even win the Nobel Prize, make someone a millionaire, but at the same time, it would create more damage than the world has ever seen. Now the EOD is developing it!"

"Wow. This ain't chicken shit."

"It certainly is not." Patina continued, "In a sense, the mole was a nuclear-powered, under-earth combination boring and missile system, enabling the missile to dig its way through the ground, under cities, towns, and villages, and then come up at a specific location and blow from the bottom up, causing the base to crumble and everything to cave in on itself. Cities and their entire infrastructures would be completely devastated at the touch of a button. And the EOD is planning to test its grand invention on Washington D.C. to get the president!"

~

In order to make progress on the mole, Catorso, Juan's right-hand man, would have to get his butt up to the storage facility in Pennsylvania and get to work. He needed time. And privacy. And help. He swiped the phone to the main screen and pushed the phone icon. After scrolling through the received-call list, he found Juan's number, and tapped 'Call'.

A second later Juan answered: "Number One here."

"I'm gonna have to come up there and get the mole finished. I need some money to do some reworking, and I need some helpers that have tight lips."

"Ah, right. Okay, get up here and show me your needs list. And keep your mouth shut about it. I'll try to get some people together. And get it finished, will ya!"

"I know, we'll get it here as soon as we can."

"I don't want as soon as you can, I want it done! Now! Jesus ..."

~

After leaving Elm Park, on the evening of Monday, October ninth, Brad slunk along Route Four on the outskirts of the road, dragging his newly found companion with him: a lead box of plutonium inside a college duffel bag.

Shit, this thing is heavy. Can't wait to drop it off.

He walked on, finally spotting Shady Avenue ahead. He located the Mobil station, slipped into the bathroom, locked the door, and clicked on the light. Following his instructions, he searched around the mirror, slipping his hand around the bottom, up the side, on the top, and there it was: a small slip of paper about the size of a business card, folded three times with his name written on the outside. Brad unfolded the paper, and read the contents: ALVAR PLATE GLASS Awning B12 Beware of Dog 2300 hours.

"What?" Brad couldn't make out the request. He folded the paper and stuck it into his right front pocket, then cracked open the door and looked from side to side, checking his exit. Good. No one.

He stepped out of the bathroom and inched his way along the wall, his goal the woods behind the station. He could hide there until he had to meet the EOD, and if everything went okay, he could get this thing over and done with for good. On his way, he spotted the phone that hung on the outside wall of the gas station. He crept to it, all the while scanning from side to side in search of anyone suspicious, and yanked up the receiver. He'd never been more focused, and a plan took shape as he dialed the number of Von Roberts at the Latrobe Press. Again he heard the antiquated ring and the rude receptionist, and as calmly as he could, he asked for Von.

"Von Roberts, please."

"Okay, wait a sec. Who's callin'?"

Brad wasn't sure what to say, and he found the muffled sound on the earpiece distracting. But the truth should be let out, and he was short on time. "Steve Simons."

"Okay." A pause.

Von picked up the phone. "Hey there, buddy! What are you trying to pull? Don Harold's a good friend of mine, and when I told him about you, he told me he'd never heard of you!"

"I know!" Brad said in little more than a whisper. "If you can just let me explain—"

"Why should I?" Von lowered her voice. "I don't have time for this shit!"

"Please, listen! I need to tell you something, and you need to believe me!" Brad waited.

A heavy pause filled the distance between them, then, finally, she said, "Oh crap. All right. I'm listening."

"First, my real name is Brad O'Connor, and I—"

"Brad O'Connor? The guy who did the clinics? And then the plutonium? Man, it's all over social media!"

Brad felt shocked at how quickly the news had spread, but of course, she was in the media business. "No! Listen. I didn't do the crimes. I didn't do anything! There's this group following me; they're terrorists or something. They're doing these things and then blaming them on me! I need you to check some things out for me. Really, please, you're my only hope."

Another long, uncomfortable pause followed; Brad figured Von was thinking it over. *Please believe me.*

"What are you talking about?" she said suddenly. "This is some crazy game; I mean—"

"I don't expect you to believe me. Just listen, and just check it out. Please. These people will do anything it takes to get what they want. Their name is The Edge of Darkness. That's all I know. They made me break into the nuclear plant. Steal the plutonium. They set me up, said they'd do more massacres if I didn't do what they wanted. Once you start digging, you'll find out I'm not lying."

"It's so far-fetched! But these days, one never knows." Another pause. "All right, I'll give you the benefit of the doubt. You sound convincing. For now. I'll do some digging. But if you're lying to me, I'll—"

"You won't regret it, I promise. Please hurry! These guys are crazy. I don't know what they'll do next."

"Get in touch with me in a couple of hours. I'll see what I can do."

"Thank you so much."

Brad hung up the phone, nervously looking from side to side, and inched along the wall to the edge of the woods. He'd been checking the media for any mention of him or photo of his face, figuring that as soon as the police had something, the media probably had it, too. Sure enough, he'd seen several reports on the clinics and the break-in at Chimerton and discovered he was a wanted subject for both. *One, yes; I admit, I did that one. Had to.* The others, though, were a frame. How would he ever get out of those? How could he ever explain it?

He slipped behind the building and went into the thick woods. A hill led down into a small ravine, and he noticed a pile of trash there: an old refrigerator, a burned-out TV, some cans, a broken chair, a pile of dirty bottles, and an old, wet, sagging sofa.

He trudged down, slipping on the wet leaves and muddy embankment. Once there, he noticed one other thing: a pile of old grocery carts that had a lot of wood, leaves, and other debris piled on top of them; the perfect cave. He was in luck, for a little while anyway.

Until nine fifteen that evening, Brad sat in that little makeshift shack behind the Mobil station going over the battle plans in his head.

I'll go, I'll give them the stuff, and then that'll be it.

He ate a McDonald's Filet-O-Fish and French fries that he'd paid a young boy on the street to get for him. The boy had stared him down like he'd flown in from another planet and asked too many questions, but he'd come through with the food.

"That's it. I'm gonna end this. Who does The Edge of frigging Darkness think they are?" Brad said as he tossed the napkin across the shack. He stood and wiped his hands on his pants, wishing he could take a shower.

At ten p.m. Brad began pacing in the tiny house, getting very nervous. Questions flooded his mind:

What if they kidnap me? What if they kill me? What if ...?

He measured out both of those, though. The EOD would surely want to continue having him as their scapegoat, which meant that they'd want him alive and free, yet, possibly, still under very tight control. This worried him.

I might not ever be free again.

He looked at his grimy Citizen's Reguno—ten forty— took two deep breaths, and swiped open the makeshift door. From there, he walked along the woods to a small alley, walked two blocks and made a left. There it was:

ALVAR PLATE GLASS.

One solitary light shone under the sign, but no others.

He walked to the sign. The next direction on the card said: AWNING B12. He looked around, but saw no awning on that side, nor down the left side of the building, and nothing to the right. After walking around the building and still finding no awning, he felt like giving up altogether, but as he rounded the corner back to the front of the building, he saw an awning across the street.

He raced over and looked up. Sure enough, the awning displayed the letter and number B12 in small print. Now he was onto the game, he looked around, scanning everything in sight, and there, to the left, he saw a chain link fence with a *Beware of the Dog* sign.

"That's it." He walked over to the sign. A small opening to a very dark passage sat right next to it. Brad couldn't tell where it went and felt very unsure of going in, but it had to be the right place.

Before entering, he stared into the darkness, trying to make his eyes accustomed to the dark, but it was no good. It was just too dark in there, pitch black.

He looked at his watch: ten fifty-six. *Good.* He thought back to the time he'd had that same feeling when he'd looked at his watch: at his job interview. He remembered feeling reassured that he'd made it just in the nick of time, and here he was again, looking at his watch and having the same feeling.

Not late yet. Thank God.

He took two deep breaths, hoisted the bag over his right shoulder, and walked into the alleyway. After fifteen slow, even paces, he got scared and stopped. He turned and, wanting to flee the dark place, dropped the bag and headed back towards the light.

"Stop! Mr. O'Connor. Stop, please," a mechanical-sounding voice said out of the darkness, the same voice he'd spoken to before.

Brad froze. Whoever was back there could have a gun at his back. Or worse yet, there could be five of them, all with guns at his back.

"You did well, Mr. O'Connor. But don't leave so fast! Bring that bag over here and then turn around. We'll have to frisk you."

He picked up the bag and took it further into the black.

"That's fine; right there. Drop the bag. Turn around."

Brad did as the voice asked and felt two hands pat him on either side of his body.

"All right. Go back out of the alley, under the light, and wait."

Relieved to get out of the darkness, Brad walked quickly to the entrance. He heard the bag being picked up and taken somewhere at the end of the alley, then he thought he heard sounds moving to the left.

Soon the voice returned. "Good job, Mr. O'Connor. We asked you for a task, and you followed through. Now we're going to need a few more things."

Brad couldn't believe it; they wanted more. "No!" instinctively came out. "I told you that was it!"

"You told us? Hmmm. That's interesting. You seem to have forgotten that you don't tell us anything. We tell *you* everything!"

"But I don't know anything! I don't want to be involved."

"Too bad!"

Brad couldn't stand anymore. He backed up.

"Mr. O'Connor, unless you want this thing to start all over again, you better agree to what we want to do! Now Mr. O'Connor, come ..."

Brad had heard enough. He turned and ran.

"Mr. O'Connor! That's it!" the voice said in the distance behind him.

Brad didn't listen. He couldn't. He just ran and ran and ran. It might be a mistake, but he did it anyway. He ran all the way back to his hideaway down by the creek behind the Mobil station and made himself disappear into the surroundings.

~

Von Roberts had just closed the desk drawer and was busy contemplating the nervous phone call she'd received from Brad O'Connor the previous day. He'd said he was in trouble, a fact Roberts had already known well; Brad's picture and the story of the abortion massacres had been shown all over the country on television, been in all the newspapers, and had probably even been on CNN. Von had been surprised to find out that Brad had lied about being the reporter at channel 37 out of Holyoke. Von had just happened to ask Don Harold how that guy was doing, and Harold had promptly explained that he had no idea who Brad was or what he was talking about, and that had got Von wondering. She'd wondered all the way up until she got the hysterical call from him.

After watching the news and hearing some strange things, Von began to take Brad's claim a bit more seriously. The whole situation kept eating at her brain. What if it was true? Why would the guy lie? To get out of trouble, of course. But his story had her intrigued. She wanted to find out the truth.

~

Knowing how impatient Juan was, Catorso hoped this plan would work out. It was a crazy plan, but it was the only way Juan could get everything he wanted and then some. And they needed that bastard O'Connor to do it!

Catorso looked down at the paper with notes scribbled in red ink. What he read meant that, no matter how unbelievable it seemed, it was gonna happen no matter what anyone had to say about it.

Catorso, along with chief designer Lorel Hudson, stared at the detailed plans for the mole. The beast was a huge machine that could chew through mega tons of rock, magma, and soil in order to move around under the earth. Many years ago, the mining industry had developed an underground dozer and then, later, this new nuclear boring machine. Catorso remembered reading about it in Popular Science, probably six years ago:

NEW NUCLEAR TUNNEL BORING MACHINE DEVELOPED
Report by Jim Marshall

The mining industry is developing the world's first nuclear tunnel-boring machine and have filed a patent. The machine is capable of boring a thirty-mile tunnel in two weeks, cutting the usual boring time in half. The machine will be based on technology used in Project Camelot for drilling tunnels under Area 51 in Nevada as well as other test sites like Antelope Valley, California.

The new machine is still large but sleeker, small and powerful enough to move quickly and efficiently through tons of rock and soil. It does this by combining traditional tunneling and nuclear powered boring with a rotating cylindrical steel tube, capable of relentless digging. This amazing device melts solid rock, turning it into glass walls as it tunnels into the earth. Several underground bases have already been constructed and connected using the device, and more military installations are being planned.
The only one like it in the world.

The Edge of Darkness's machine was an offshoot of that, although much bigger.
Juan just has to have it that complicated!
Lorel Hudson had designed it, and now Catorso was in charge of finishing it off. The problem was that the thing was in the transition stages from a simple ground-dozer into the mole. This meant it had to go through numerous changes to get it the way demanding Juan wanted it.

Juan had said that the engine had to be changed and bored out, the sides had to be cut and widened, the body lengthened, and all the interior elements added, not to mention the barracks and kitchen. They had to model the mole on the tunnel boring machine, TBM, and nuclear boring machine technology where the tube tip virtually melts away rock and turns it into solid glass.

The way Juan talked, it looked as if he was thinking of having people stay down there for weeks, and with that, the thing had to have plenty of water, food, and human waste disposal, not to mention oxygen.

"Guess who I think has to go down there?" Catorso grumbled. "Probably Patina and me!"

"You'll get a pretty penny in your bank account, though," Hudson said.

There was that. But even so, Catorso wasn't sure if he could handle it all the way through to the end. He called the crew: just one electrical engineer, Dave Patina.

"Hey there, Patina," Catorso said into the phone. "Can you get your ass up here tomorrow? We need to work on the project. We gotta get it done as soon as possible."

"Yeah, I'll get up there ASAP." The phone went dead.

~

Brad awoke with the birds and immediately the impact of what he'd done hit him. He'd always been an even-keeled person, except for when a slight temper had him flying into fits of anger at a whim, leaving him to wipe up the mess later. He hoped he wouldn't have to wipe up one here—it was conceivable that the EOD could do anything.

He picked himself up and brushed off the pine needles that had stuck to his coat the night before, but when he tried to stand up, he banged his head on the roof of the makeshift shack.

"Ouch! Shit!" He rubbed the top of his head, then collected his remaining articles and prepared to leave while it was still possible. He didn't know what he'd do or where he'd go, but it was time to flee. He stepped outside and immediately wished he hadn't.

A man stood directly in front of him with a rifle zeroed in on its target: Brad's head.

Shit.

Brad flinched and let out a little 'Yaa!' His heart rate increased two-fold. "What the hell!"

"Hello, Mr. O'Connor."

At once Brad knew who it was, knew from that distinctive voice with the marble quality. Finally, he could see what the man looked like up close and personal. Though larger than Brad, he had a small but stocky frame and looked physically fit, broad in the shoulders and chest. He wore sunglasses, but that didn't stop Brad noticing that this guy was the same guy he'd seen in front of the store and from Tom's apartment—the very same guy.

"I gave you the plutonium, so what are you doing? I mean, it's over, right?"

"Ha! It's over when I say it's over. Let's go. Up to the parking lot."

Brad wanted to run, but he also wanted to remain alive, so he complied.

The man jammed the gun into Brad's back, hard, and pushed him up the hill to a blue van parked in the lot of the Mobil station.

"Get in." The man opened the door with one hand while he clumsily grasped the rifle with the other, trying to keep it pointed at Brad.

Brad climbed through the door of the van and moved to the opposite wall, where he sat in disbelief, waiting for the next chain of events to unfold. At that point, Brad thought nothing would surprise him.

The man didn't utter another word. He slammed the door, walked around to the driver's side, got in, and started the engine. A cage behind the driver's seat separated the cockpit from the back area of the van, cutting off the driver from Brad, who could barely see out of the front window. They drove for what seemed like an eternity, eventually turning onto a small road through the woods. They'd just gone over a small bridge over a river, when the man spoke again:

"Have you learned yet?"

"Learned what?"

"That you're ours? We own you? You're our scapegoat?"

"Yeah," Brad said as he slumped down where he sat. "I guess I have."

After that Brad zoned out until, after about an hour, the van screeched as the driver slammed on the brakes.

"Fuckhead! Watch where the fuck you're going! Goddamn, Prius," the man with the gun yelled.

The van took a hard left, shook violently, and almost flipped over. Brad thought the man with the gun would get out and either reprimand or kill the driver. But the driver just paused, put the car back in drive, and continued on. After another hour of driving, they finally arrived at their destination: a stone house nestled in the woods. It looked like a weekend get-away place.

The van pulled into a dirt and gravel road that extended in the front for about two miles. Brad had grown accustomed to peering out of the front and rear windows of the van to see where he was, but he'd lost track because the woods all looked the same. It was unfathomable how, in such a short time, he'd gone from being a guy with a life seemingly on the right track, to a fugitive, a hunted man.

The van pulled into the parking area in front of the house and skidded to a stop. The man grabbed his gun, got out, and went around to the back of the van.

Two men came up from either side of the van and flung open the sliding doors.

"Hey, whatchya got here, Suardino?" one of them said, and they yanked Brad out by the arms.

Ah ha. The guy's name is Suardino.

Suardino held the gun on Brad, watching for the slightest flinch, the smallest move. But Brad wasn't that stupid. These men were ruthless. They attacked two abortion clinics, and who knows what the hell else. They'd stop at nothing.

They dragged Brad towards the house, which had ornate bay windows and large towers on all four corners of the building. It looked like a castle.

The next thing he knew, the men shoved him into a magnificent lobby. Why was this here? This stone building virtually in the middle of nowhere? And why was it so manicured, yet hidden from all to see?

They went down a dark hallway. One man flung open a door, and the other threw him down a set of stone stairs. He stumbled down into a dark, narrow hallway, with small openings on either side. They rounded a corner to the left, then down a flight of stairs, turned right, and walked about twenty paces down another long, dark hallway to an old, solid-looking, tall wooden door. The man knocked on the door with the butt of his rifle. It soon opened, and they shoved Brad in.

"Welcome to your new home." The man jammed his hand outward in a welcoming gesture.

Brad remained standing, staring around the room, stunned by what he saw—men sitting around the room on wooden benches. Brad counted six. They looked American, similar to Brad in appearance and mood.

One of the thugs gave Brad another shove, stuck a gun into his back, and motioned him over to a bench. Brad sat down, hard, and glanced around at the other men.

Suardino and the rest of the cohort left, but before he shut the door, Suardino gave a parting shot: "Well, O'Connor! Here ya go! You're ours now!"

Brad sighed. The door slammed and a lock clicked into place. He looked to the right. The man there looked to be about thirty-eight. He looked gaunt, as if he hadn't eaten in a while, and stubble covered his chin.

Looks like my fate.

The other men were also unshaved and silent. Their hair was matted and they smelled like age-old sweat socks. They stared into the distance, almost looking through him, eyes like stones.

"Hello." Brad waved in the air. "Uh, what is this place?" He didn't know if his attempt to communicate would be useful or futile, but he had to give it a shot.

No response. The others just stared into space. But all of a sudden one man, the one directly across from him, blurted out: "It's what you think it is."

"Huh?"

"This place. It's what you think it is. It's a prison."

"What? I don't underst—"

"Listen. You're the seventh. Us six have already talked about the whole situation. We're here for the same reason. We assume you are, too."

"What reason is that?"

"Because. These people. They used us. They did some things. Then they blamed them on us."

Brad stared at him, dumbfounded. These men were in exactly in the same situation. He said it; they made us do things. Here was the proof.

"Like what?"

The guy across from Brad with glasses spoke first: "Well, for me, they bombarded a jewelry store and killed the employees. Then they made me break into the computer, as I'm a computer technician by trade. Then they pinned the crime on me until I agreed to work with them."

"Holy shit!"

"Yeah!" another man said. He had dark eyes and long, stringy blond hair. "For me, I own a club. They gunned down a group of guys in a restaurant, and told me they'd pin it on me unless I worked for them. I had to get 'em some heroin. Of course, I had to comply. The thing was, the police, they had these composite photos of me in this restaurant, talking to the people who got killed. But I was never in that restaurant. I never even knew those people. Somebody did some kind of makeup job or something."

"Shit! I can't believe it!" Brad stood, rubbing his arms. The others watched him, becoming more animated. "What about you?" Brad pointed to a big, burly man sitting at the end of the bench. He wore a sullen expression and showed virtually no emotion. Brad tried again: "What did they make you do?" The man continued to stare. "Hey!" He rubbed his hands in front of the man's face. "Hey, buddy! What did they make you do?"

"Hey, leave him alone," the first man said. "They did the worst to him."

"Really? Like what?"

"They killed his family and pinned it on him until he funneled out seven million from his father-in-law's construction company."

"My God. Did he do it?"

"What the fuck do you think?"

"I'd say so."

"Listen, chump," the first man said, "you found out about us! Now what about you? What'd they make you do?"

"They massacred people at two abortion clinics and then made me break into a plutonium extraction facility and steal some plutonium."

The men laughed. The first man gestured, and the man sitting next to him sighed deeply, then said, "Goddamn. We're all up shit creek."

"Yeah, who knows what they'll make us do next," the first man said.

"Fuck. Here we are trapped in this dungeon with walls three feet thick. No windows. We're screwed," the blond guy said.

Brad's mind whirled. *Jesus, this is unbelievable.* Now that he'd found out he wasn't alone, he felt a little better, but no more in control. "How does this place operate? I mean, what do they do here? Do you get food? Showers? What?"

The man next to Brad spoke: "Yeah, we get food, if you could call it that. Usually chicken or some kind of mystery meat crap mixed together with some kind of gooey rice. Not great, but edible if you're hungry. We used to get bread for breakfast, but now ..."

"Used to? What? Wait, how long have you been here?"

"Me, I was the second. It's been, I don't know, it feels like ten fucking years. But I guess almost a year." He pointed to the wall, at a crude calendar they'd etched into the cement.

"A fucking year," the one with long hair growled. "It's going on about four months for me, I guess."

114

"Wow." Brad couldn't believe this whole situation, that there were actual prisoners here. And it seemed as if nothing could be done. "What's your name?" Brad asked the man next to him. He looked quite handsome, and Brad could see a likeness to Al Pacino, the actor, with a beard. Brad always liked Al Pacino, the hardest and cockiest of all actors.

"It's Donald Clemmons. But most people call me Clem." Clem turned to the other six. Motioning around the room, he called out the others' names. "This is Chuck Jackson, with the long hair. Just call him Longhair. Next with the glasses is Reamy. Don't know his first name, but he's pretty noisy. The sleeping guy is Frank Pedron. The skinny one is Ted; I call him Skin. And then there's that one. We don't know his name, so we all call him Rock, because he's so quiet. Doesn't do anything but sit still all day like a rock, and never says a word."

"Okay. I'm Brad O'Connor. Nice to meet you."

"Aaah. Is it time for formal introductions?" Longhair blurted out.

"Oh, no. Sorry. I didn't mean anything."

"Don't mind him, man!" Reamy said. "He's all pissed off because his boyfriend left him. Ain't that right, longhair fag-go?"

"Fuck off."

"I'm glad to see you guys all get along well!" Brad said under his breath.

Clem piped up: "So what do you think these people are trying to prove, my friend? You're the freshest mind, and have been out there the longest. What do you think?"

"From what you guys just told me, they have money, drugs, computer software, and plutonium. Sounds to me like they're getting ready for World War Three." Brad really didn't know what to make of it, but he also knew that there was a way out; he just had to hang onto that belief long and hard enough to find it.

~

Juan updated the files on the computer program he'd designed specifically for the purpose of the scapegoat operation. He sat in a bar in upstate New York at the same corner booth he'd used on many occasions. Pedro Catorso sat with him.

The last name and entry on the list was Brad O'Connor. The last entry read:

LEVEL 3	:	complete. Detain
SUBSEQUENT ACTION	:	terminate
TERMINATE STATUS	:	1 year

He pushed the 'Enter' button and the screen flashed. Then it went blank.

Juan closed the lid of the laptop, and then stood and walked to the phone, where he dialed Steve Suardino in Greensburg.

Pete Decatur answered: "Tohay Resort Complex."

Used to the routine, Juan said: "Suite 4B, please"

The call was transferred immediately. "4B."

"Yo, Number Two. It's Number One. I want to go to the West Coast. Facilitate activity. A-1. Go."

"We're on it."

"Ciao."

That was it. So far, the action had taken place in the eastern part of the States from Detroit to Miami. But all that was about to change.

The Edge of Darkness had the east covered, with several dirty front businesses and dealings on a list so long that it confused even the top dog, Juan. He kept a staff whose sole responsibility was to keep track of all the operations within the EOD umbrella. And those were numerous. They had a series of doctors' offices in effect only to pull insurance scams, a resort complex that thrived on gambling, and a limousine rental agency that had its hands in drug dealing, prostitution, and money extortion.

So now the EOD was bringing in money, lots of it, and they had their tendrils reaching far into the heart of modern society in the US. This made them very versatile, and very dangerous, because greed got the better of them. They were dirty. They had to be bigger, and they had to have more power. They wanted to go right to the top, the very top of the world, and Juan thought the timing to do so was impeccable. He wanted—no, needed—to rid the world of that lying, cheating president, Frederick Flood, a multi-millionaire with an egotistic, almost pathological personality. He'd been in the news for years during which time he'd built a real estate empire in New York, Chicago, and Miami. Flood became president after beating down several opponents and moving on to a surprising win to become the republican presidential nominee.

Juan remembered when The Edge of Darkness took shape, around eight years ago, when the idea rose in Juan's head. He hated the government, the police, the politicians.

"We need to start something, to get rid of this guy Flood, and this fucking, whaddayasay, political regime." Juan remembered saying to Catorso over drinks in that local upstate New York pub seven years prior. "It's really too important to sweep under the carpet, as Americans say."

"Cheers."

"We can change things here, Pedro. Or is it Pete?"

"Whichever."

"Ya know, I got a freaking brilliant idea. We force people, unknown and without-a-cause people, to ..."

"To what?

"To do what we want. Pure. Simple."

"Uh-huh, you think it's that simple?"

"Yeah, it is. You'll see." And Juan, staring Pedro directly in the eyes, had picked up his Jack on the rocks and held it up. "It's the fucking Edge of Darkness. Ya got it? A whole operation. We'll take control, *compadre*."

"I got it, yeah. All right." Pedro picked up his shot glass, clanked, and drank.

After letting his mind wander, Juan brought it back to real time. He stared at the front door of the bar, watching random people enter. They'd done a lot so far, had six prisoners, soon to be seven. He'd known they could make people see their way. Their first gig had been Vince Archer, the once proprietor of Thomas construction company, owned by Dan Thomas and Celia, Vince's wife, and Dan's daughter.

He remembered that Vince and Celia had two lovely daughters in their primes ready to tackle life. They were in college but home for the weekend when the EOD struck. Vince had been out of town on business, but when he got back, he'd been confronted with the terror. They'd given him an option: do it or else. He'd refused and tried to fight back. Shouldn't've tried that. The gruesomeness of it all would probably remain with the man the prisoners called Rock till his dying day.

~

Brad paced around the prison, running his hand through his hair. "The next move is to somehow get the hell out of this place," he said as he pinched his chin with his right finger and thumb.

"Yeah? How do you plan to do that, hotshot?" Reamy asked, not short with the questions.

"I don't know yet. But there's got to be a way."

"We've tried. The walls are concrete. You need a drill with a carbide tip just to get through 'em, but that would probably take a week. By the way, there are no openings, except for a little drain in the corner." Reamy again.

Fucking big mouth, Brad thought, and the reference stuck. "Where's that?"

"Over there. But it's too small—about the size of a softball. Nothing but a rat could squeeze through that thing." The big mouth pointed half-heartedly at the drain, but didn't move his eyes there.

The men all seemed hopeless, like these dank, depressing cement walls.

Brad got up and went over to look. He bent down and eyed the drain. Sure enough, it was tiny. Not even a fist could fit through it, and it would take over a year to dig it out. He remembered seeing *Escape From Alcatraz* with Clint Eastwood many years before and remembered how he dug around the vent and snuck out. The cement had seemed to be a different consistency than this: hard and dry. And the sheer work needed to dig it out had astonished him. He immediately put the thought out of his mind. He did notice the makeshift drain cover; it had little pieces of steel crossing each other and cut off in circles to fit in the drain. The edges were jagged and extremely sharp to the touch. Perhaps he could use this as a weapon somehow.

Brad didn't know how it would be possible to get out of there, but he knew he'd better find a way or these men would die. Others had died. And if the EOD got its way, hundreds, maybe thousands, of other lives might be at stake.

CHAPTER 10

The next day, October eleventh, dawned rainy and cold. Catorso sipped his black coffee and read the paper until a knock came on the steel door. He walked over and unlocked the huge door, sliding it open.

"Thanks for coming. Good to see you," Catorso mumbled, sticking out his hand for a shake as Dave Patina walked in.

"Yeah, you too."

Catorso got on the walkie talkie to Lorel. "Lorel, can you come over here to the meeting room?"

Lorel arrived and sat down with Patina. Catorso stood at the desk, hands on hips. He swung around to the white board and drew as he spoke. "As you both know, the plans call for the device to have the ground chewer at the front, a rocket launcher, a computer control room, a kitchen, and lodging for ten people. Not to mention nuclear capabilities. It's a huge undertaking, and we're getting it done slowly, but ... it's time to finish."

After talking through what still had to be done, Catorso checked the equipment plan with Patina.

"You know, I never really found out why we're going to use the mole anyway," Patina said.

"Rumor has it that The Edge of Darkness is going after POTUS," Catorso said. "That's right, the President of the

US, that horrible loud-mouthed egotistical Flood. You know Flood created new immigration rules and suddenly sent back those without visas or citizenships to whatever land they came from. Some of Juan's family members were sent back to South America on a cargo ship with nothing more than blankets and bottles of water."

"Holy fuck," Lorel said.

"Juan barely got to say goodbye, and that made him incredibly pissed off. I'm not sure if we'll actually get Flood or just threaten to, but either one is bad. Anyway, it's our job to make sure we could get there in one piece with all our equipment and manpower, all underground. And that's why we needed the plutonium from O'Connor."

"Gotcha. Thanks for the run-down." Pedro then unpacked the instructions: "The first thing we need to do is extend the mole about fifteen feet to create a space for the weaponry to be loaded in later. These include one nuclear missile fed on weapons-grade plutonium, a normal machine gun, and inside, machine guns, pistols, grenades, and let's not forget the essentials: sleeping area, a kitchen, and a pee-pot.

"We need to outfit the machine with nuclear blowers that heat the surrounding dirt and rock to such a high degree that it creates a glass tube around the mole. This is borrowed from the Russian technology from years ago, but we'll prove it's viable. One problem with the technology is that the glass-like nature of the tub hardened after the mole passed. And so it's impossible to move backwards or even be pulled backwards."

They walked into the workshop and got to work.

Bzzzzhhhhhh. Saw. Rip. Shred. Pound. Hours and days passed.

"Get that thing in!" Catorso yelled at Dave Patina, mighty lone engineer. They were trying to fit the transmission into the dozer lengthwise. "Wait, try pushing it over to the right."

"Yeah, okay!" Dave was in no mood for getting orders barked at him. "I'm doin' it!"

"Well, just do it right!"

"I am!" In his anger he slammed the sledgehammer on the transmission line, and it snapped into place.

They put treads on the mole, adapted from regular strip-mining bulldozer treads. They also installed guide wheels on the front and back, and in a moment of genius, Dave also decided to put treads and guide wheels all the way around the machine. This would enable it to roll around while chopping away at stone, dirt, and gravel and never get stuck. In addition, they fitted the mole with everything to make it self-sustainable for days, weeks, and even months. The huge beast was capable of cutting through yards of cement-hard rock. It was also an incredibly dangerous weapon. And Juan had serious plans for it.

~

The chair swiveled on its axis, and the folder on the desk was yanked open, creasing the lower left corner. Pages ruffled through with impatience. The reader—pissed. Stop. Pause. Read. A finger underlined the pertinent details, flipped back to a previous page. Finger again. Pages slapped to the right. More reading. *So much stress.*

Dom pulled out the DVD and pushed the open button on the Dell laptop's DVD drive. It took a few minutes to respond. "Friggin' technology."

He sat down and stuck in his ear buds. On the DVD came the message with simple graphics in plain words: *We are The Edge of Darkness. We will Control.* The voice came next, reading the text in a robotic manner with a marble vocal effect:

"Darrera. This is the EOD. We know you know us. And we have this to say to you: all roads lead to The Edge of Darkness. Nothing better happen to us or to anyone we like or do business with. Or more violence than you can imagine will come to you and this area! Worse than the clinics."

"Yeah, got it." The words imprinted on Dom's mouth moments before Greg Stone barged in and messed up his intense concentration.

Greg realized what he'd done and remarked on his backing out, "Scuse me."

Dom glared, but offered, "Wait, Stone ..."

He halted and turned around. "Yep."

"Take a look at this." Dom played the DVD again for Stone, who watched gape-mouthed.

"Holy crap. Some kind of terrorist group behind the clinic shootings?"

"Yep, appears that way. But O'Connor doesn't fit a terrorist profile at all. This thing is very weird and has got me in a ..."

"Pickle?"

"I was gonna say in a bind, but whatever."

"Yeah, I know. It's a tough one. We really need to get to O'Connor."

"We need to find out as much as we can about this group, as well as getting creative with finding O'Connor. Widen the net; talk to everyone," Dom said in a commanding voice, but to be nice, included, "If you can, I mean. That would be great."

"Okay. Will do. Remember those two nut-jobs over in Mount Pleasant? Those search guys who say they can find anything?"

"The ones who posted their makeshift promotional video on our Facebook page?"

"That's it. Should we try them?"

Dom nodded. "Might be worth a shot."

Stone walked back to his desk and the first thing he did was log onto the police Facebook site. He found the Facebook page for The Find Guys. It wasn't too badly done, but they did look a bit far-fetched. One guy, Bobber, wore a cowboy hat with a red rim. His partner, Tombo, wore a baseball cap, had a pudgy face with black glasses and a goofy smile. They both had goofy smiles, actually. Stone 'Liked' the page.

Their "About" section said:

Find Guys! We can help you find anyone, anywhere, at any time. $400 per day plus expenses. Call us at 800-444-5555.

Stone moved down the Facebook page, and read some updates:

June 2: Found – two 5-year-old twin sisters who were kidnapped by a lunatic when they were 3. They were gone, and their parents were frantic. We got on the trail of this bastard, followed him around for 3 weeks, all the while keeping silent, and finally were able to grab the kids and run. We got a very nice reward from the family in addition to our regular charges. (7,653 views.)

May 11: Found – escaped convict Ted Phillips who killed 3 women and raped 7 others. Found guilty in 2011 and sentenced 25 to life. Then escaped by telling a guard he had stomach cramps and sliced his throat on the way to the hospital. We found him by getting his trail, and never letting up. We slept in cars, on the ground without sleeping bags, in tents, going without food for days. We got a hefty reward for it, too! (8,311 views.)

Stone flicked open Messenger:

Dear Find Guys,
Greg Stone here from the Greensburg Police Dept. We have a guy on the loose, and think he's done some pretty wicked things. He says he's being set up, and we at the department are wondering, but we just don't know. Anyway, the point is, we need him. And we need you to find him. By the way, we are professionals, and we're hoping that you are, too. No money passes through this office until we have some proof you've found him.
Greg Stone

Greg searched the net for more on the Find Guys, but found nothing except a Facebook site. *No website?* He paused, then typed *The Edge of Darkness* in the search field. After seeing the video from the EOD on Dom's computer, Greg knew it couldn't hurt. *Darrera will get to it next year.* He pushed the 'Enter' key. Immediately "Error 404" came up on the screen, indicating a broken or dead link. *What the hell?* He went to another browser and tried again with the same result, then he searched for EOD, Darkness, Edge, the Dark, and anything else he could think of, to no avail. Nothing mentioned a group called The Edge of Darkness.

~

By the time Greg Stone woke up the next morning and had grabbed a coffee, flicked on the computer, and signed into Facebook, a message waited for him in Messenger. Stone hated technology. He'd been refusing to do things like download Facebook apps and such for years, but he had to admit this was convenient. He clicked on Messenger and found a message from the Find Guys.

Dear Greg,
Thanks for your message. Wow, the police are coming to us now! I understand you have someone you need to locate. We require a few things to get started. We need recent photos, info on whereabouts, friends and family contact info. Once we get those, we can proceed. After we locate your person, we'll send the police our bill. Let us know.
Peace on earth.
Tombo

Greg sat down and whipped out a response to the Find Guys. This was his chance to arrange the takedown of the most wanted man in America in about twenty years. So what if it was with the help of a service company? Hell, it was better for these guys to take care of it. Stone, Dom, and everyone else had major other things to take care of anyway.

Dear Tombo,
Thanks for your message. You better fulfill your promise if you intend to get paid. We need proof, and we need your promise. Got it? Get it? Got it? Good.

He he, that should get them moving!
A shiver ran down his spine when he realized that this move could make him famous. Sought after. In need. Called to be on TV. Written up in newspapers. He relished that thought. *Damn, I'm good*, a little voice said. Stone

thought this outfit could probably find Brad, but he wasn't going to just let them have it on their own. No, sir.

Greg Stone's life history flew through his mind: He'd had his ups and downs, kind of like his career. He'd started working right after college, married at twenty-eight, probably too early. Had great kids, though: Brandon and Cody and Trish. Divorced at thirty-five. Still working. Just kept working more and more. He'd never had the chance to put his life to use, not in the way he'd wanted. Life went on and then suddenly he was here.

He looked over at the police report still hanging on the wall. The yellowing and tattered sign haunted him:

Missing Person Report of Death. 10/7/1997
Reporting officer: Gregory Stone
Name: Shelly Benfry
Age: 7

Nature of report: Girl kidnaped at age 7. The kidnappers contacted me, set a ransom of $400,000 and requested a Cessna airplane at Latrobe Airport. I arranged the money, the airplane, and a transfer to take place in the parking lot of an abandoned building on Center Street. But at exchanging the girl for the ransom, an accident happened. The group brought the girl in a black SUV. I, the officer in charge, Gregory Stone, walked towards a man in a black hood who brought Shelly towards me. He told me to drop the bag. I proceeded to do so, and I told him to let the girl go. She was walking over to me when one of the kidnappers fired a shot. I ran back towards my car and took cover. An officer opened fire at the group. The man in the

hood grabbed the money bag, ran back to his car, and they took off. I ran over to check Shelly. She wasn't moving. I called an ambulance but she died at the scene. After her death I filed this report on January 14.
Signed: Gregory Stone
Date: 1/14/1998

Dom had been in no mood to see him after that incident, let alone talk to him. He understood. It'd been his fault. The girl, after all, had died when she'd been so close to being saved. Their relationship had hit a wall. They didn't speak for several months, except for usual business. Finally, they did get back to talking as usual, but their relationship had gone back to square one.

A couple of hours later, Greg looked back at the computer, checked the email and found a response from the Find Guys. *That was quick!*

Report #1. Dear Greg Stone,

We called Brad O'Connor's girlfriend, Sally, and went to visit her. She stated that she didn't know where Brad was at the moment. She did say, however, that he told her that some organization is forcing him to do things or else they would blackmail him with bad acts unless he complies. They told him that they would kill her and his friend if he refused. She knew about the abortion clinic shootings.

Stone saved the report to a Word document, thinking it was good they'd talked to her. She'd confirmed what the reporter had told him. He compiled everything he'd found out about Brad, Von, and the EOD and drew a connection map on the whiteboard of his office with Brad in the center circle.

Connection: abortion clinic, *man with birthmark.*

Connection: missed interview.

Connection: talking to Sally and Tom.

Connection: stealing plutonium.

Connection: another abortion clinic massacre.

He had the connections, but he couldn't find out how they went together. He was about to draw another circle when Dom walked in.

"What do we have from those Find Guys? Anything?"

"They got info from Sally, the girlfriend, on Brad, but it's stuff we already have. I'm going out to talk to anyone and everyone from Jeanette to Greensburg to Scottdale to Uniontown, and everywhere in between."

"Okay, try to find out where that DVD was made, too, will ya? Maybe we can get some info ... let the other guys look at the DVD, too. The more eyes, the better."

"I'll get them a copy."

Stone already had Darcy on the case, searching around Brad's apartment and elsewhere, and he'd sent out a crew to search the woods around southwestern Pennsylvania, looking for a needle in a haystack.

He scratched his beard stubble and ran a hand through his hair. He'd compiled a report for Darcy in addition to burning off some copies of the EOD DVD. The report included Brad's background, last known whereabouts, and included his address, picture, and traced a line of movement from his house to where he thought they should be based on reports from TV, Darcy, Peters, the Find Guys, and everyone in the field. He had reports from this, from that, and from everywhere in between, but no O'Connor. Just freaking reports. Life was beginning to frustrate Greg Stone.

Just then, Stone got a call from John Paxton. "Greg, can you come to my office? I think you want to see this."

"Be right there."

Stone took out a newly pressed DVD to give to Paxton and tossed his notes on the desk, then he headed down a flight and around the corner to Paxton's office. He walked in to find Paxton sitting at his desk holding a surveillance camera picture. He handed over the photo.

Greg looked at the image of a guy in a sweatshirt carrying a black duffel bag. "Who the hell is that?"

"This was found on a surveillance camera outside the convenience store on Fourth. Just got it."

"So?"

"Take a look at that bag he's carrying."

"Uh huh. What about it?"

"Look at what's on there."

Greg looked more closely. In small print he found the words *Weston College* in gold letters shadowed in purple. "Weston? Isn't that where our Brad worked for a while?"

"You're right. And a bag like this was carried by the guy who ripped off the plutonium. But who is it? Not O'Connor; there's no birthmark on his neck."

Stone smiled. It was their first major lead in ages. Whoever this was might have a link to Brad and the EOD. *Life isn't so bad after all.*

"We're trying to get an ID now."

"Okay. Did we talk to all the convenience store people?" Stone asked.

"Just the cashier, when we got the tape."

"I'll call the manager. Take a look at this when you have time." Greg handed over the report and the DVD. "It's from a terrorist group, the EOD, suggesting they're behind the clinic shootings. It was sent to Darrera."

130

"Gotcha, will do. We're still lookin' for the van, but there are about a million vans out there just like it."

"I know, too bad we haven't got the license plate."

Greg Stone walked back to his office and closed the door. He leaned back and his mind drifted as he stared out the window at a child pushing his bike up the street.

~

On the morning of October fourteenth, test day, the wind blew hard and cold, about to snow. But they'd be underground, so Catorso thought the weather wouldn't matter.

They'd created the mole in the haven of the prison-like building in that undisclosed location in western Pennsylvania. They'd carefully designed, crafted, and constructed it and left nothing to chance, and no stone left unturned. Today was test day when everything moved forward. Time to yank the mole, their own subterranean monster, out of hibernation.

They started the engine for the first time on October fourteenth at eleven a.m. At first, there was no movement. Turn the switch, nothing. Back to the drawing board. Dave Patina took the engine apart and found a blockage in the fuel line. Once he'd cleared it, the mole started like a dream ... and didn't stop. The thing spewed gravel and dirt right from under their feet, and the beast's huge roar almost deafened them.

"My god! This thing is fulla spunk!" Catorso exclaimed with a grin.

"Somehow I knew you'd put it that way," Patina said from the driver's seat beside him.

"No better way to put it."

The mole lunged forward, sprockets and chewers spinning in midair like a half-crazy, robotic dinosaur coming to life. It roared as it twisted and turned, bucking like a wild bronco. Patina shoved it into first gear, and slowly drove it forward. It inched ahead on its tracks, shimmying back and forth. "Where do you wanna go?" Patina asked.

"Outside." Catorso found the virtual-remote app on his phone and flicked the door open. It popped with a mighty *Thwap* and stopped in open position.

"Ready?"

Catorso grinned. "Ready as I'll ever be."

They inched the mole forward—a behemoth at twenty-six feet long and over eight feet wide. They moved on down the driveway in the middle of rural Pennsylvania, with Catorso thinking it was too bad no one was around to witness it. "I know the perfect place to give it a good run."

Further down the drive, Catorso had them veer off to the side, into the woods.

"I hope you know where you're going," Patina said.

"I do." They moved down along a small path that Catorso knew well. "Almost there." He directed the mole towards a mound and the entrance to a small cave.

"You're not going to do what I think you are, are you?"

Catorso just grinned.

"If that's what you're thinking," Patina said, "then I may be thinking what you're thinking. Right into the ...." He drove the thing forward into the cave opening. "Hole!"

The beast tore away at the dirt on the sides of the opening like a dog digging up a lost bone, and, ever so slowly, moved into the hole.

"Wao! No way." Patina's eyes gleamed like a kid with a new toy as the mole tore up dirt and spewed it out from the edges of its jaws. The head dipped down, and the windshield of the drivers' compartment became covered with muck and slime.

"I can't see anything!"

Catorso didn't flinch as they went down because he'd outfitted it with the latest GPS and computer-generated 3D line images of the upcoming ground, generated instantly as they went along. The images showed up on the twenty-seven-inch Mac monitor mounted directly in the front of the cockpit. He pointed this out to the driver.

"Ah, of course."

The mole took a dip, and the nose turned downwards.

"Here we go!" Catorso yelled, as Patina inched the thing downward, crunching and churning into the deep, dark topsoil. "Let's move it down and really test it."

"It's looking good," Patina said. "I'll try to speed up." The thing sped up to ten feet per second, then thirty. "Woa, that's fast."

"Yeah, things look like they're working like a charm," Catorso said as they went yet further. They soon hit forty feet down.

"Okay, I think we've tested it enough. Looks like it'll work," Patina said.

"I think we should go a tad further, down to fifty feet."

"Okay, but then we're heading back. Enough testing for today."

"Sure thing." They moved further down, the jaws working away. "We should test the nuclear tunnel melt."

Patina hit the nuclear button, and immediately they felt heat. A sucking sound filled their ears. They looked in the back camera at the tunnel created by the machine.

"I see what this thing does," Patina said. "It's practically a glass tunnel."

"Yeah, what a machine!"

"I'll head back up now so we can move back towards HQ above ground."

"Just a sec," Catorso protested, "we haven't hit fifty. Keep going down."

They kept moving down, steaming and twisting with great force. "There. Happy now?" Patina said when the depth gauge read fifty feet.

"Made it to fifty feet!" Catorso reveled in a moment of joy.

"Back up now?" Patina urged.

"All right. We've proved she can do it."

It took a moment to get the mole on an upward trajectory, but finally it inched up slowly.

"Pull 'er up now," Catorso said.

Patina did, and the mole ground to a sudden stop.

"Shit. Stopped in the middle of ... nowhere. We're in the middle of the damn' earth! That's why I wanted to get up to the top sooner."

"Holy shit," Catorso said.

"I'll say." Patina pushed the ignition button, trying to start it again. Nothing. After a couple more attempts, he stopped trying. "I don't wanna break it."

"No, ya can't break it! Shit! Whaddawe do?" Catorso felt like a kid in trouble.

"Try again." Push. Nothing. Patina moved forward in the seat and pried open the engine compartment, easy to get to, as it was a front wheel drive—a sixteen-wheel drive, actually, with the engine lodged in the front compartment.

"Ya gonna be able to get to it?"

"Thinkkkkssssooooo." Patina sighed. He took a minute to find the flashlight on his phone and peered around the engine cove, hoping to find the culprit just like he'd done on the first start when the nuclear fuel line was clogged. He looked here and there, pulled wires, tapped on covers, wiggled fixtures. He tried to start it again and no luck.

Shit, what if it doesn't start ... "Can you fix it?" Catorso tried to sound calm.

"Not sure." Patina continued to check the connections, the links and the wiring. "Try again!" He yelled from underneath.

Catorso took the starter knob and slowly turned it to the right. *Please start.* The engine ground over, trying to come back to life, then it died. Nothing.

"You need to get it fixed soon!" Catorso yelled. His stomach twittered like a hummingbird. "It's up to you to fix it, or else we'll be stuck down here forever! Die in here." *At least Juan wouldn't be on our ass then.*

Patina didn't respond as he searched for the problem, trying the starter and the nuclear fuel lines again. "I just have to find the problem, then getting it fixed'll be no big deal. Let me see. Move, please." Patina moved into the pilot's chair and tried to start it again. *Hurhruhrurhrugggggg.* No go. "Oh shit."

"What is it?"

"I don't know. Still won't activate." Patina wiped the sweat off his forehead with his shirtsleeve, then looked at his watch. "Maybe it's a problem with the nuclear fission trigger."

"Okay, try that. Did you try the starter mechanism? Or maybe it's the electronics!"

Patina glared at Catorso and crawled in the front to check the nuclear fission starter. Catorso watched over his shoulder. Sweat poured off his face; he wiped it away with a dirty towel. "Hurry up, Patina. It's been three hours. You know, we didn't think of an escape hatch. And we're fifty feet under the earth!" He jiggled around in the tiny space of the mole, running his hands through his hair.

"Don't worry, we'll get out," Patina said as he got up and out of the compartment and stretched his back. The stubby but wide man rubbed his arm while he stretched out his neck.

Catorso watched him move to the other end of the mole. He lifted open the compartment and checked the timing switch, then he hit the reset button. He turned around quickly, and Catorso made way for him to get to the cockpit, where he flipped a few more switches and tried again.

Huuurrrrrrgggggghuuuurrrrgggggvrrooom. The thing roared to life.

Thank almighty.

"Told ya we'll get out."

"Yeah! I knew you could do it!" Catorso wiped the sweat off his brow and collapsed into the co-pilot's seat. "Take it up for us, will ya!"

Patina let out a small, "Okay." And inched the machine up to the top. They poked through the earth. Night had fallen.

Catorso felt glad to be out. And alive.

~

Brad looked around at his cellmates. They sat without moving, like stones.

Damn this fucking group. Look at me. Look at my mucky clothes and dirty hands. Look at this fucking mess. Goddamn it! Lives are at stake; I need to get us out of here. These guys have families, lives. People who love them! Got to turn this thing around.

Brad hit his left open palm with his right fist. How did people fight back? Get strong? He had to help these people. But could he do it? And how? Nothing came to mind. He lay down and drifted off to sleep with his back against the gray prison wall.

As he had on many other occasions, Brad dreamed of that day during his Wildlands Outdoor Experience when he was twenty-two.

They were doing an exercise on Vixnard Bay, which required each of them to rig climbing gear onto a huge tree for the next team member to rappel down the hill as quickly as possible. Then they'd had to climb up a steep rock face, race to an abandoned mining cabin, and search for a gun, with which they'd shoot a moving target in the field to score points. They were to do the exercise in teams, and the fastest team would win the competition and be able to claim top ranks. But in the middle of Brad's turn, he'd mistakenly rigged the rappelling line wrong and the team members fell sixty feet still connected to the line, swinging from side to side. During this, the members had inadvertently knocked over the neighboring team's rig, sending all its members to the ground as well.

Commander James Goffrey had been livid. "O'Connor, you fuck-up! Look what happened!"

If he'd only paid more attention to the rigging. He'd stared at the ruckus in disbelief as everyone stood there staring at him ... only him ... and the laughing and taunts began: name calling; fuck up; an embarrassment to them, and to himself. The commander had expelled Brad from Wildlands.

Now Brad had a game plan. But this time he wouldn't fuck it up.

He spent the day reviewing that game plan in his head, and surveying ideas and opinions from the other members, who were quickly turning into fossils. He thought he could give them life. He wanted to take what little sting of hope that remained in their lives and turn it around.

137

Meager portions of food came in small bowls, carried by big, burly men in leather masks, who carried sub-machine guns across their backs. At one point, they brought in a large glass case containing a severed head in some kind of liquid. This shocked everyone and repulsed Brad, although he knew why they'd brought it: to make everyone behave, to make them think before acting on any impulse. Perhaps this was why the men had stopped yearning to be free; perhaps they, too, had high hopes, but after a long period of time, they'd stopped trying, stopped fighting. Brad didn't want that to happen to him.

He surveyed the interior of the room: bare walls and nothing else apart from the benches and a single light bulb hanging from the ceiling by a single cord—nothing useful. That left people. What could he do with these people that would be effective? They were not chained, but, unfortunately, were so weak that they couldn't be of much assistance. And after four days, Brad began to feel weakened himself, but he had to be clear and strong enough to do something. Anything. Though unlike him in normal circumstances, this was far from normal, and it brought out a determination he hadn't known he had in him.

CHAPTER 11

Brad sat most of the night contemplating his plan of action and came up with the winner of all ideas. The next morning of Sunday, October fifteenth, when he was sure everyone could pay attention, Brad cleared his throat to break the silence, and then he spoke:

"I think I may have a plan to get out of here."

The men looked toward him.

"Yeah? How's that, hotshot?" Longhair said.

"Some of you aren't going to like it, especially you, Mr. Longhair, but it's an idea."

"Why? Whaddaya got planned, man?" Reamy squealed.

"When our friend called you fag-go, that got me thinking. When the guy comes in to give us the food, one of you guys calls him over, pretends you're gay and start scheming on him. How about you, Longhair?"

"What the fuck!" Longhair charged at Brad, about to pop him a good one in the jaw, but Frank and the big mouth jumped up and tried to block him.

"Hey, he just said 'pretend'!" Frank Pedron said. "It's actually not such a bad idea! Calm down!"

"Right. All you have to do is say something like, 'Hi, honey,' and be a bit charming. Is that possible?"

"Jesus, whatever."

Time inched on. They looked at each other with a bit of hope in their eyes. The room grew quiet. They hunkered down and fell asleep.

An hour later, the door slammed open, and in walked a six-foot-tall, extremely wide, leather-clad man in a black leather mask. He spoke no words, just carried in a large box and flipped open the lid. On a tray in the box sat the breakfast Brad had become used to: awful hard-to-swallow meals; sometimes of mystery meat with hard, crusty rice; sometimes of soggy bread and some kind of broth, and always bad. But they would sustain his life, if nothing more.

Brad looked around. All the men watched patiently, waiting for the nightly meal. Brad couldn't help thinking how furious it made him that no one was pissed off; no one was angry. Maybe they knew something he didn't.

Brad nodded at Longhair, and the action started. Longhair got up, walked over, and said, "Hi, honey," in his best effeminate voice. "Whatcha got for din-din today?"

The man reached slowly into the box and brought out a long item covered with a blanket. With a quick motion, he yanked off the blanket, exposing a semi-automatic rifle. He brought it up to point at Longhair, as if to aim at his face. Longhair froze and his jaw dropped. Then the leather-clad man suddenly changed direction, pointed the rifle at Rock's head, and fired. The bullet plunged into Rock's forehead, almost directly in the center. A large *splat* appeared on the wall directly behind his head—his brains. A surprised look came over Rock's face, then he slumped over and fell off the bench, on his face.

The prisoners in that cold, dank room gasped in unison.

Should I do it suddenly? Now? Just make a move? Brad wondered.

The man put the rifle back in the box and announced: "He's been here for a year. Didn't need him anymore."

Those words spurred Brad to make a move. He jumped up suddenly and flew directly at the looming figure. He plunged into the masked man with all the force he could muster, knocking him off-balance, but, unfortunately, not enough to tumble him over. The man turned. Brad lunged again. The man grabbed Brad around the waist and pulled him to the floor accompanied by comments and jeers from the prisoners.

"You're an idiot, man! What are you gonna do? They're gonna kill you!"

Leather-clad fell on top of him, and Brad found himself pinned to the floor. While struggling to free himself, he looked to the side and saw Bigmouth staring in disbelief. If he could just motion for them to run, to get out ... Unable to catch Longhair's attention, Brad shouted at the top of his lungs: "The door's open! Run! Run! Go!"

They did.

The masked bandit slammed Brad's head on the hard cement in an attempt to shut him up. Brad all but lost consciousness, then the guard's head flailed forward as if hit on the back of the noggin. He drooped over, but righted himself again, turned, and faced the individual who had whacked him on the back of the head. Longhair stood there holding the food tray. The guard lunged forward, falling on top of Brad, then scurried over and got on four legs. He turned around and, with an evil grimace, tried to grab Longhair. Longhair rushed towards the guard, and barreled into him. The guard went backwards, lost his balance, and struggled to get righted again, but, before he could, Longhair pushed as hard as he could, forcing the guard toward the wall. The guard regained energy and forced Longhair back. Longhair slipped and fell on his face. Moving from inertia, the guard fell over him and landed face first on the floor. Then all movement stopped.

A moment later, Longhair pushed himself up and paused, feeling like a statue, before he made his way slowly over to the guard. Again, he paused. Nothing. He looked closer. A small copper pipe sticking out of the corner of the floor had impaled the guard's eye.

Longhair didn't bother to check for a pulse. He turned to Brad and shook him. "Hey, wake up! Get up!"

Brad finally came to and, with a shiver, propped himself up on his elbows. The two looked at each other and then at the guard.

"We should make sure he's dead," Brad said.

They tried to roll him over, but he wouldn't move. They had to yank his eye free from the copper pipe first, and when they did, blood squirted and dribbled out of the socket.

"Search him," Brad said. "Then let's get out of there! They'll be coming soon!"

"Yeah, I'm with ya!" Longhair fumbled through the guard's pockets. "Hey, I found a cell phone!"

"Great, bring it along! Where are the others?"

They got up, bolted out the door, and took a left, the opposite way from where the guards always came.

"They're long gone!" Longhair said.

Brad hoped they'd meet the others at some point. They ran to the end of the hall. The passageway veered off to the right, and they followed it, the visible light becoming less and less. What the hell was this place, Brad wondered, or was it actually hell? Sure felt like it.

The light grew so dim they had to squint in the darkness, but they didn't slow down. With hearts racing, they kept right on as quickly as they could manage.

Brad ran down the hallway and suddenly slipped and fell. Longhair slid to a stop behind him and almost toppled over as well.

"Come slowly forward," Brad said, peering into the dim light. "Be careful! There are stairs right in front of you!"

"Shit!" Brad heard Longhair trip down the first few stairs, and then stop. "Yeah, just found out! Thanks for letting me know!" More scuffling, and then: "Where are you?"

"Here's my hand!"

"Okay, got it. I can barely see."

Brad felt Longhair grab him by the arm, and they both righted themselves.

"Shit! What do we do now? You all right?" Longhair asked.

Brad sighed, and slowly stood up. "Yeah, it's so dark I can't tell where we are."

"Let's keep walking!"

They walked slowly, and, moving their hands along the wall to find their way, moved down the hall and around a corner. They kept following the wall to the left, further and further, and the way became even darker.

"Let's try to find out where this goes," Brad whispered.

The hall meandered along, and after what seemed like eternity, Brad felt dampness on the wall. His heart sped up. "Do you feel that?"

"Yeah, it's damp; could be water!"

Brad felt they were getting close to a cave or a hall, and, sure enough, the walls eventually gave way to an open space.

"Wait, this is a room," Longhair said anxiously. "Where in the hell are we?"

Brad felt his tension lurking in the air. "Not sure." He looked around, gaping and squinting to see in the poor light. "Holy shit, what is this place?"

They'd found some kind of hall with a huge object—taller than them, at least two car-lengths long, and rounded on one side—on one wall. "Look at that," Longhair said. "Looks man-made. What the hell is it?"

"I don't know. It looks metallic. Maybe it's some kind of boring machine. I'm not sure I want to hang around to find out what it is! Make a mental note of it. Right now we've got better things to do."

"I'm not too good at mental stuff, but I'll keep it in mind."

They looked around the hall, and Longhair announced, "Hey, do you see that little light over there?"

"Yeah. Let's head over there. These fuckers have probably realized we're pretty well gone by now!"

They walked over to the faint light and found a tunnel, too low to walk in comfortably. It looked like it was once a water main or a sewer line. But light, though faint, shone down it from somewhere, and that was a good sign.

"Shall we?" Longhair gestured to the opening. "After you."

"Gee, thanks." Brad got down on his hands and knees and crawled along with Longhair following.

Before long, they came to a break in the tunnel. One way continued straight and one way veered to the right. *Shit. Decisions to make.*

"Shit o'rooney. What do we do now?" Longhair asked.

"I say go straight ahead."

"Okay; I'll follow you, brother."

They kept moving. A bit further down, Brad thought he heard some kind of sound, a faint mumbling with movement. Something. Further on, he heard more small sounds.

"Hey, I hear something," Longhair whispered.

"All right, quiet! Let's move on in!"

They crept towards the sound. Brad realized that it was someone snoring. He thought he saw the top of someone's head, unmoving, in a prone position. They moved closer. Brad saw more people. Something rustled. A body shot up. A head turned.

"Hey! Something's there!" someone said. Brad recognized the voice of Frank Pedron.

Brad came closer to the shapes in the darkness and saw Clem and Frank sitting across from each other. "Hey, guys!" Brad yelled.

"Who's there?" Frank asked.

"It's us! Longhair and Brad!" Brad answered.

"Thank Christ. There you mugs are!"

Brad chuckled at Frank. "Yep; here we are."

Brad and Longhair moved towards the bunch. They sighed and exchanged glances and arm clutches. Glad to be together once again.

"Where are the others?" Brad asked.

"We don't know," Frank said. "We lost them somewhere in the tunnel."

"What should we do?" Longhair asked.

"I'm sure they're all right," Clem said. "Let's wait. They'll be coming soon." He let out a sigh.

Frank yawned. "Gotta try to wake up."

Brad watched them come back to life. "Okay," he said, "let's gather our composure and check our belongings. Maybe we have something we can use."

"What belongings! You have anything useful on ya?" Frank asked.

"Yeah, right, like what?" Clem asked.

"Like rope, tape, anything," Brad suggested.

"Not me," Frank said.

Brad looked at Clem. "Sorry, nothing, man."

"Okay." Brad put his hand on his hips. "Let's chill for a while. Get a plan together. No one's gonna bother us here."

"I'm with you on that one," Clem said as he returned a fist bump.

Brad looked each scapegoat in the eyes to check their composure.

"You know, I could really use a double burger right now ..." Clem said.

"Oh, don't even talk about food ..." Longhair said.

And with that they were gone, deep into their own thoughts. Brad went back to that fateful day at Wildlands. *I'm such a fuck-up. I have to redeem myself.* After about ten minutes, Brad heard snoring coming from a scapegoat. He woke them up about fifteen minutes later.

He couldn't believe the situation they were in. He'd wanted to take what little sting of hope remained in their lives and turn it around, and what a mess it was now! But at least they were in one piece.

"I don't think we should wait any longer," Brad said. "They would've been here by now if they came this way."

"Yeah," the others murmured.

"I just wanna get out of here," Longhair said.

"Okay, I'll go ahead first," Brad said. "Then you guys crawl after me slowly."

"Yeah, but what if something happens to you?" Longhair said.

"Don't worry, nothing will. And anyway, someone has to be first. Everyone agreed?" Brad grew more like the leader every moment.

A meager "Yes" and "Okay" came from the others.

Brad started out on hands and knees, moving slowly in the faint light.

After far too long of crawling on hands and dirty knees, they caught a distant sound, a faint *Ping! Ping! Ping!* Brad's heart pounded. "Do you hear that?" he asked no one in particular.

"Damn right, I do," Longhair replied.

They moved closer, and the sound got louder. It echoed as if coming from some kind of open space, like a cave. They inched further along in the dark for what seemed like hours. The ping got even louder.

"Sounds like water. Where in the hell are we?" Longhair sounded anxious again.

"Sounds, and feels, like a cave," Brad said. "I'm sure we'll find out soon."

Further and further they went on hands and knees. Dirty floor. Dry mouths.

Brad stopped. He thought he felt something touch his fingers. "Hey, did you feel that?" he croaked.

"Feel what?"

"I'm not sure ... it felt like something just crawled over my hand!"

"Holy, shiver me timbers," Longhair said. "Wait. Listen!"

Tiny *chip, chip, chip* sounds grew louder and closer. Suddenly the sounds, and then the feeling, were right on them.

"Holy crap, what is it?" Clem asked.

"I think you mean, what are they?" Frank said.

"I'm not sure I want to find out!" Brad said. "Let's keep going!"

They hurried through the cave faster, still on their hands and knees, not sure how much room they had on each side, even though they could tell the cave was pretty big.

"Ah!" Longhair moaned. "Uh-ha ... aaaa!"

"What is it? Oh, shit! I felt it on my shoulder!" Brad screamed in dismay.

"I just felt it crawl up my arm. Oh God! They're crawling up my leg!" Longhair screeched.

"Oh shit, they're on me, too! I think they're spiders!" Frank spurted out.

"Jesus! I think you're right! Or tiny aliens!" Clem chimed in.

The things ran over their hands and feet, and crawled up their arms—terrifying in the darkness.

"Okay, just don't move," Brad whispered. "If we hold still they might go away."

Longhair retorted with a long sigh. "Okay, I'll try. Let's not move, everybody!"

They stayed in the same positions for what seemed like hours. The spiders, if that's indeed what they were, slowed and finally stopped. They could hear the *chip, chip* of the spider legs running on the ground, getting fainter and fainter. No more running up their arms.

Finally, Brad said, "Okay, I think they're gone." He sighed in relief.

"Yeah, thank God," came a retort from Longhair.

The group slowly ventured on. At what Brad figured was about the center of the cave, they paused.

"Stay here. I'll move on a little, straight ahead. If it's all right, I'll call you over," he said in a loud whisper.

Brad scrambled ahead on his hands and knees, probing the darkness. Further along, some kind of gritty slime covered the floor.

Shit. What the hell have we gotten into now?

"All right," he whisper-shouted. "Come on."

Brad noticed the dead acoustics in the place long before it hit home; nobody was saying a word, no matter how meager, and he'd not heard a breath, not a sigh. He felt around, squishing his hand around in the muck on the floor, and then, as a last resort, whisper-shouted again, "Hey, where are you guys?"

"Yo. Over here," one voice said.

Brad looked around, but couldn't see anyone in the deep gloom. "Who is it?"

"It's Frank Pedron."

"What's going on? Where are you?"

"Over here. Wherever here is."

"Ha! What does the floor feel like?"

"It's all greasy or something. Gross."

"Yeah, same here. Is everyone with us?" There was no response. "Hello?"

"Yeah," came Frank's voice. "Anyone else?"

Brad felt panic rising. "Where's everyone else?"

"I don't know. They were just here. Yo! Is anyone else here? Hey!"

Again, there was no response.

Brad, feeling quite agitated by this time, paused to gather his composure. *What's going on? Only one other person in earshot? Why? What's changed in the last ten minutes?* Again, Brad had many questions, but still no answers.

He moved to the left, still on his hands and knees—the smartest way to travel in this murk—in the direction of Frank's voice. Slowly, he moved, ever cautious, wondering what to do next while he called out to Frank, who answered with short *yeahs*.

"Stay put. I'm coming over."

"Ain't going nowhere."

He crawled over on hands and knees, nervous at the thought of what unknown things might be lurking around the corner or unseen in the darkness.

Suddenly the floor dropped out from under Brad, and a split second later, he found himself in mid-air—falling.

"Aahh! Fuck!" He fell only a short distance but landed hard on his side in never-ending black. *It's blacker than the ace of spades in here.*

Another voice screamed from above—Frank.

"Hey, man! Are you okay?" Brad asked.

"Shit," he gasped, breathless from his fall. "I fell, but I think I'm okay. Where are you?"

"I'm on some kind of ramp. It's going downward. I think we should follow it. Maybe it'll lead us out of here."

"Okay, but where in the hell are you?"

"Good point. Okay, just keep coming towards my voice. I'll guide you. I'll talk for a while, and that way you have a point to focus on. What should I talk about?"

"I hate to tell you," Frank said, "but I don't much care."

"Well, I was married once, you know, really married. It lasted for about five years. I was too selfish, and young, and my wife, well, she had ..." and with a bit of 'audio-navigation' Frank arrived.

"Am I there?" he asked, his voice close now.

"Just feel the floor. You'll feel the lip of the drop off. I'll hold my hand up so you can feel it."

After some time, Frank finally said, "Okay."

"Here's my hand." Brad waved it above his head. "Do you feel it?"

"No."

"Shit. Maybe you're too high up. You might just have to go for it. Just jump. Or let yourself fall off."

"No way! That's nuts."

"It's the only way."

"All right. Shit. Here goes. Aaaah!" Frank landed with a thump, right next to Brad. His leg caught Brad on the side, knocking him over.

"Ouch, goddamn it!" Brad cried.

"Well, what the fuck do you expect, asshole!"

"Never mind. Here, take my hand! Ya feel it?" Brad jutted his hand toward Frank.

"Okay."

They finally connected, and Brad pulled Frank toward him. "Okay. Let's go down this ramp. Or whatever it is. I don't have a fucking clue as to where we're going, but it's the only way. At least it's worth a shot. Stay close. This isn't the time to get lost again."

Again, Brad surprised himself for being the one in control, in command.

A man standing in the shadows. I'll show them. Fuckers.

They crawled down the ramp, the cold cement harsh on their knees, feeling their way down every last millimeter. Finally, the floor began to level out a bit, and they continued forward, until, "Ouch!" Brad hit a wall. "My head smacked into a wall. Let's go to the left."

They continued crawling for a long time on raw hands and knees, and finally, they heard faint noises over to the right. Further down they crawled and eventually saw, peeking its way in ever so slightly in the distance, what looked like light reflecting off calm water.

"Look. And listen," Brad whispered. In the distance he heard what he thought was water running, and one other thing: voices.

They crawled faster, tearing their skin on the rough floor, their only goal being getting to the light, which could mean escape.

The ramp dipped down again, and the darkness eased so they could see just a little. Gradually it curved around to the right, and just after the curve they saw the other four lost souls, sitting huddled in a little group. Waiting.

"Shit! There you are!" Brad exclaimed, dumbfounded, but glad they were alive, well, and apparently in slightly good spirits.

They all looked, and Clem said, "Glad you could make it!"

"Yeah, well, just happened to be in the neighborhood," Brad said. "Listen, how'd you find that ramp?"

"We were just crawlin' like you said; we all must've crawled down it automatically. But then we got to the light here, and we saw you guys weren't with us. So we waited ... we thought you'd be here sooner or later," Skin said.

"That light ahead looks hopeful." Brad stood up straight for the first time in a long while.

"Yeah, I reckon." Skin seemed to have simmered down and taken on more of a positive attitude. Brad admired that.

"What do you suppose we found here?" he asked.

"Looks like it used to be some kind of secret entranceway. From the size of it, I'd say it was used to bring in tanks or freight trucks of some kind. But it's so old. I doubt they know it's even here."

"Yeah, well, I wouldn't count on it. They probably know every inch of this place."

Suardino's gang would be searching for any remnants of the escapees—anything that could lead them in the right direction. But all they'd find in that dirty, empty cell was dust. No survivors, only the dead bodies of Rock and the impaled guard. Brad pictured it in his mind: the leather-clad thugs looking, finding nothing, the head thug getting pissed and telling them to find something, anything, getting more and more pissed that there wasn't anything to find.

Brad smiled, happy knowing they'd tear apart the cell, then fly down the hall, searching high and low, in all the cracks and crevices of that old cement basement. He bet they'd be stumped that they couldn't find not one, not two, but six grown men who were there just minutes ago.

When they'd gathered their composure, the group continued walking down the tunnel to the right, the way growing lighter with each step. The path stopped at an underground river that ran right beneath them.

Clem's fingers dug into Brad's upper arm, pulling him over. "Look over there!" he whispered.

Brad looked and saw a tiny staircase hidden in a crevasse in the wall—another stroke of luck. "Holy shit, good eyes, Clem. I think we should investigate." Brad glanced at the other scapegoats.

They nodded, their eyes gleaming. With Brad in the lead, they snuck into the narrow stairway, trying their damnedest to avoid making any sounds on the rickety stairs. Though stinky and wet, the stairs weren't dark enough at the bottom to lose eyesight, but Brad stopped when he saw that a dark cloud hid the area above.

"What do you suppose is up there?" Reamy asked.

"I don't know," Brad replied. "But whatever we do, we have to be extremely careful."

"I don't think we should even go up," Longhair said. "I mean, why don't we go toward the light? We don't know what we'll find up here, but light says outside to me."

"If we don't, we may be missing something important. It's important to get away, yes. But we need to find out more about this place. What it is? What are they doing?"

"I think it's a very bad idea. I don't want to go any further!"

153

"Come on, Longhair. We need to check it out."

"Well, you can just fuck off." And with that, Longhair stood and crossed his arms.

Brad had to get Longhair involved or someone might find him there. "Listen, Longhair, we can't do this without you. It'll be safer to all go together. What if someone comes and finds you? Then it's all over."

"Fuck, who died and made you the boss, anyway?"

"Someone's gotta do it!"

Longhair sighed. "Fuck, let's go then."

They crept up the stairs one by one, feeling their way as the stairs grew darker. Every time Brad looked around to see if all were following, he wasn't surprised to count everyone present.

At the top he found a small landing and a hanging ladder going up even more. He was about to go up, then remembered the other five below. "Stay here," he whispered. "I'll check it out. When I call, come up. Longhair, give me the phone you found."

"Here ya go." He handed over the phone. "Shouldn't we all go, boss-man?"

"No, this part is too dangerous. Just stay there. I'll be back in a flash." Brad climbed the ladder and, by feeling around with his hands, discovered a small hatch-like door at the top. He righted himself on the ladder, taking care not to fall. What was on the other side, if anything? Could he go through?

He reached around the circumference of the hatch and tried to open it. It felt like some kind of access hatch that had once served the purpose of quick escape. Finally, he found the latches, lifted them, and pushed gently, trying not to make a sound. With a soft *quap*, the hatch wrangled itself from the edges and swung inwards enough so Brad could look in and survey the situation. What he saw astounded him. This outfit was more powerful than he could ever have imagined.

Across the room sat a wall-sized flat screen and, right below, an array of desktop Dells and at least one iMac with icons blinking, software whizzing around and prompts flashing. He checked the phone, turned off the ringer, and started taking photos, putting his thumb over the speaker to hide the shutter sound. Thousands of lights, pieces of hardware, clocks, and counters filled the room. He snapped pic after pic. Clearly it was the control center of some monumental operation, something big enough to start, or end, the world.

In front of the console stood two men and one woman in regular street garb— jeans and t-shirts—but wearing gun belts and walkie-talkies. They stood over the computer monitors and stared at the huge flat screen, which switched to and from different maps, figures, charts, graphs, and written information. A picture of President Frederick Flood, the newest elected president and a businessman who still did business—a conflict of interest as Brad saw it—appeared on the screen.

On the desk monitor, Brad made out the words *Scapegoat Protocol, Edge of Darkness, Kingston, New York*, along with Google maps information on weather and travel. Brad also saw nuclear weapon controlling system graphs, audio surveillance graphs, and independent researcher info.

Brad rubbed his eyes and blinked repeatedly. It was too much for his brain to fathom. Had he not seen this kind of software in his media career, he couldn't have even imagined what it could possibly be used for.

What appeared to be a communication booth surrounded by Plexiglas from floor to ceiling sat in the right-hand corner of the room. A woman who wore a headset with an attached microphone stood inside the booth, her lips moving in conversation.

A small console with a video monitor and a telephone sat in the center of the room. *What the heck?*

He decided he'd seen enough. Now he had proof, in his own mind anyway. He wished he'd had his bag with him, but alas he'd lost it in the scuffle, along with his GoPro camera and Zoom field recorder.

Now he had to find a way out. He couldn't let himself, or the others, get in trouble. All that equipment made The Edge of Darkness incredibly powerful, and Brad figured they wouldn't stop at anything until their escaped prisoners were caught. Or killed.

He started to close the hatch, being careful not to make a sound. He'd just closed the gap when he heard a door open, followed by the bustle of feet and voices getting louder and louder.

"Find these idiots!" a voice yelled. "Then kill 'em."

Brad opened the hatch just a crack and peered through. Inside became a bustle of activity: the men turned and grabbed guns and walkie-talkies; some grabbed notepads and some ran to a computer, immediately pushing buttons and flipping switches.

Brad closed the hatch shut and scurried down the ladder. "We gotta get the hell out o' here," he whispered in a frenzy. "They know we've escaped. I just heard. Let's head towards the light, like right now!"

The men headed back down the steps and raced towards the river. Brad ran at top speed, jumping over ruts, tramping through mud puddles and dank, stale water. He was in too much of a hurry to see if everyone was there. To Frank, who was running by his side, he said, "They've got some kind of control center up there! Looks like they could start World War Three."

They ran down a small tunnel that was rounded at the top, pockmarked and falling apart. They came to a stop at the end.

"Shit!" Brad said.

A large steel gate made of slats about eight inches apart crossed at twelve-inch intervals, forming small rectangles, covered the end of the tunnel, making their imminent escape impossible.

"Oouuch! Damn, my foot!" Longhair cursed under his breath.

Brad looked back. Longhair had gotten his foot stuck in a deep, slim hole near the side of the tunnel.

"Shit, help me! I can't move!"

Brad felt doubly dismayed, first at having a smooth exit plan dashed, and then seeing his comrade's foot stuck in a vicious little ditch. The chances of untoward things happening were great, of course, and the thought entered his mind then of how much easier it could have been on his own, without these dusty old prisoners that everyone had long forgotten about. For a moment he wished he'd left them behind to fend for themselves and had escaped on his own. But then his love for people in general popped back into his head, and he knew there was no way he could do that, no way he could just leave them alone to die.

"Shit, don't worry; we'll get you out!" Reamy shouted as he rushed over and started pulling. Soon two others jumped in and also started pulling. But their efforts proved useless.

"I don't know why you're rushing," Brad said. "We can't get out of here. We might as well just stay here. They'll find us soon no matter what we do."

"Why are you talking like that?" Skin said. "All of a sudden you're giving up?"

I am. It's over. Brad had been through so much, and he'd grown tired. He'd thought escape was around the corner, but now all hope had been ripped from beneath him. He fell silent.

CHAPTER 12

Then a strange thing happened: a face popped up on the other side of the gate.

"Uh!" Brad jumped. "Who in the hell are you?" He turned to the others. "See, I told you we'd get nabbed! It's all over!"

"Jesus Christ, here you are!" the face said. "I've been searching around this whole goddam building!"

Brad didn't know the face, but as soon as he heard the voice, instant recognition shot into his brain. "Wait! You're Von Roberts!"

"Yep. That's right. I looked around this whole place, then I hid in the bushes and saw this little opening here. Thought I'd check it out. And here you are. What dumb luck." Roberts' muddy clothes and scummy hands could attest to the fact that she had, indeed, been looking for them in the woods.

Roberts' short frame surprised Brad. And the fact that she was black surprised him even more. He pictured newspaper reporters as being tall, white, skinny and sharply dressed. But he didn't care what she looked like, he was just happy to see her. Perhaps now they had a chance.

"We gotta get the hell out o' here," she said. "I saw a couple of guys with dogs in the distance over to the left."

"How in the hell did you find us?" Brad felt an inner gleam for the first time in days.

"I tailed you. I pretty much knew what you looked like after the photos on the news. I was in the parking lot of the Stop and Go when I heard a ruckus and saw some thugs push someone in a van. I thought I'd check it out. Remember that car that almost ran you off the road? Who do you think that was?"

"That was you?"

"Yeah. Then I kept my distance. I stopped back a ways when I saw the house, but I saw them take you out of the van and inside. After I saw that, I took off back home and called the police. I told them what I knew, and about your phone call. They said they'd get someone on it, but wanted to get more information about this group, so they could look into it. I didn't know more than you told me, but enough talk. Let's get you out."

Von pulled and then pushed on the gate, but it budged only slightly, so she stepped back and examined the area around it. "Looks like it's an old gate. Rusted around the top and hinges. Why don't you push from there?"

Brad planted his feet, grabbed onto the downward ramp and began pushing while Von pulled. The others watched for a while, and when it seemed as if the gate wouldn't budge, they pitched in to help, led, surprisingly, by Skin, followed by Reamy and Clem.

"Okay! Let's pull!" Skin said. "Longhair, why don't you try to squeeze out of that hole yourself?"

"Why in the hell would I want to take instructions from a fruit cake like you?"

"Shut up!" Brad hissed. "Try to get out. If you can't, then we'll help you. But we need to get this gate off or we'll all be killed!"

They all shut up then, and after a few more yanks, pushes and pulls, the gate cracked, and they lowered it gently to the ground. Von took the top and rested it on a large rock in front of them, and then ran around to greet Brad.

"I'm glad you're alive! After I heard from you, I thought I'd give you a chance. So I got some help from a friend of mine ..."

As she spoke, Brad heard some movement in the distance coming down the tunnel. He looked. Von paused.

"Oh, fuck! Hurry up!" The others were still trying to pull Longhair out. Brad joined in, but the man's leg was stuck up to the knee in a very tight spot. They couldn't budge him.

More noise came down the tunnel—clamoring by more than one man, and definitely nearing.

"They're coming closer. Get me out!" Longhair screamed.

"Damn it!" Brad yelled. But it was no use. He looked around, upset with the way the situation had turned out and feeling bad for the man. He had two choices: either leave Longhair there to get caught, and likely killed, or surrender.

"Get me out!" Longhair pleaded, his voice laced with desperation.

They tried, Brad and two others pulling relentlessly, but his leg was stuck in too deep.

The noises neared—heavy footsteps coming closer.

"Just go! Free yourselves!" Longhair said. "You can't pull me out. I'm too deep. Go!"

"Follow me," Von said in a whispered shout.

Clem, Reamy, Frank and Skin took off out of the gate as fast as their feet would take them. Brad paused to look back at Chuck Jackson, Longhair, who was still stuck in the hole; he nodded his respect and received a nod of acceptance in return. With a sigh, Brad took off after the others.

He'd done his best. He'd wanted to save him, not leave him to die, but there was nothing more he could have done.

As they scrambled down the narrow path in the woods that flanked the building, they heard two noises: one, a group of men and dogs coming around the north corner of the building, obviously searching; the second, a noise in the distance that would haunt Brad for years, the thudding of a volley of heavy punches and a pained gurgle —the sound of Longhair being slaughtered.

Von motioned for them to follow her. "Come on! I've got my car over here!"

They ran until almost out of breath and stopped, shocked and surprised, when Von's car came into view. Brad couldn't believe it. It'd been destroyed: windows smashed; tires gutted; the hood and all its contents smashed to a bitter pulp of metal and oil, like a future warrior downed for the kill.

They stood motionless, without words, and stared at the car, at each other, at the ground. Their escape had been foiled. Brad tasted bitter disappointment.

Fortunately, Von Roberts came to her senses and snapped them all back into reality. "Screw it! We got to get the fuck outta here! Let's go!" And with that they ran at mad speed into the woods and up the nearest embankment.

They ran, panting, and at the top of the hill saw a white building with peeling paint nestled in the woods, apparently abandoned, but worth a look.

Brad looked around at this crew and, as he had on so many occasions, pulled himself back into leader mode. He hated being in charge, but if not him, then who? Somebody had to do it.

They looked increasingly disheveled. The light on them now shed itself on a lot of things, including their futures. Though exhausted, Brad needed to stay on task: escape with a capital E. He waved at them to follow and headed towards the building.

They neared it with watchful eyes. Brad gestured to them to slow down, and they did. At his command, they stopped at the edge of the wooded area and waited. When Brad felt confident that the coast was clear, he waved them on and they sidled up to the building—a shack sitting on the edge of a high cliff.

"Hey," Reamy said, looking through a window, "back in there; what's that?"

Brad looked. Some kind of red, polypropylene plastic had caught Reamy's eye. Next to the plastic lay aluminum tubes with numbers printed on the sides, and other objects littered the floor: a telephone, some loose-leaf binders, scattered papers—tattered and yellowed beyond recognition—piles of ropes, bungee cords, and three bicycle helmets. They walked inside and flipped over the discarded materials.

Frank rummaged through the items on the floor, tossing the binders and ropes behind him, and uncovered two old hang gliders.

"Those look like hang gliders, but they're fucking crap. No good." Reamy the big mouth.

"What do you mean, no good?" Frank retorted.

"Well, look, they're all broken!"

"They're not *all* broken," Frank said in a pissed-off voice. "They're just old and someone's thrown them in here instead of packing them away properly."

"That bar is broken," Reamy said.

"It's a vertical," Frank retorted. "We can splint it. Go find a straight stick or something."

"But there's a rip in that one!" Reamy pointed to the sail on the other one.

"It'll still fly."

"Only an idiot would fly in a hang glider with a hole in the wing!"

"So jump down the friggin' cliff!"

Brad saw the scuffle and smirked. "Can't you two play nicely?"

"Wait; did you say hang gliders?" Von asked from across the room.

"Yeah, why?"

"I used to go hang gliding when I was in college. Became a hobby. Haven't done it in a while, but ..." She paused.

Brad looked around and saw Von in the corner talking on her Android. She had a hand over the mouthpiece, and Brad heard her say, "Five, no, six, including me." Pause. "Yeah, that's right. Anywhere, really. Okay, great. Thanks." She ended the call and walked over.

"Yeah, I've done it a couple of times, too," Frank said. "And I saw this thing on the Discovery Channel that went into the mechanics of it. I think we can do it, especially with expert help." He grinned at Von.

Von snorted. "I'm hardly an expert, but yeah, we can do it. Let's get them outside and get them set up."

"Well, there's not much choice now," Brad said.

Frank hauled one outside and Clem helped Von with the other. Skin wandered through the place checking everything, while Brad collected some rope and looked for something with which to splint the broken strut.

"I've never done hang gliding," Reamy said, looking miserable.

"There's a first time for everything, and I'll be right there with you," Brad reassured him. "Come on. Let's help these guys get them sky-worthy."

"What if we fuck up?"

"Once you get going, it's pretty easy to stay aloft," Von called back.

"Really?"

"Yeah. Anyone can do it."

"Uh, okay." He still didn't look too happy about it.

They followed them out to find that Clem had already snapped a straight branch for the splint. As Brad gave him the rope, Reamy blurted out something that make Brad wince. "I just realized something."

"What is it?"

"There's only two gliders and six of us ... do you think one of those things will hold three people?"

Brad frowned. He wasn't sure how that would work either, but Frank and Von kept working on assembling them, and Clem was struggling to get the rope tight enough to mend the broken strut. At least it wasn't the bar they'd have to hold onto. Brad thought it best not to think about the problems too much. "We hafta try," he said.

Skin raced out of the shack, yelling, "I found some duct tape!" He held several dusty rolls with a little left on each.

"Perfect." Clem held out his hand for a roll. "Hold this while I tape it up."

"Give me one," Von said. "I'll use it on that rip. It might hold long enough to get us to the bottom, and if there's enough left, wrap it around the bars."

Skin helped Clem with the splint while Von taped the rip. Frank stood up and surveyed his work. "The harnesses are a bit sketchy."

165

"How are we actually going to do this?" Brad presumed that each glider only had one harness.

Von grinned. "We forget about the harnesses. The pilots jump on the control bar and the others hang off each side."

Reamy's eyes bugged out. "What if we can't hang on?"

Von's answer was to hand him a roll of tape and point at the control bar. "Wrap. It'll help with your grip." She started wrapping the other end, but the tape ran out before she'd covered much of the bare aluminum.

Frank looked up. "We stand on the bar?"

"Yeah. I've done it," Von said. "It works for short distances, and we don't have to go far, just down. You two ..." She pointed to Clem and Reamy. "You'll come with me."

Suddenly, Brad heard dogs barking, branches cracking, and a man shouting—in the distance but drawing closer. "Whatever we do," he said, "we have to do it now. Listen to that!"

"Okay," Reamy yelled, "let's get freaking going!"

They used up the rest of the tape on the outer edges of the control bars. It didn't cover much on either glider, but they'd have better grip than on a bare bar. The rubber grip on Frank's glider had mostly disintegrated, but only his feet would be there.

"Let's go!" Frank said, lifting his hang glider.

It was time. Do or die.

The dogs and sounds of pursuers drew closer.

Von and Frank carried their flyers about ten feet back from the cliff edge so they could get a run up. Unfortunately, it would be possible to get hung up on trees on their way down, but Brad had no time to worry about that.

"Come on," he shouted to Reamy and Clem as he and Skin ran after Frank. "Get your butts in gear!"

The two men came to life and raced over to Von.

"We'll go first. Watch us and do as we do," she yelled to Frank, then to Reamy and Clem she said, "Grab on. We'll take a run on the count of three and then go over. I'll jump on the bar as we leave the ground so I'll have some control. All you have to do is hold on."

Reamy gulped and wiped his hands on his trousers. "I don't know ..."

"I do," Von retorted. "It's either that or—"

A man's voice soared through the air. "O'Connor! You better stop right there!"

Reamy jumped. "Right. What are we waiting for?" he said. "Let's go!"

Von counted: "One. Two. Three ..." And they ran. "Just follow us," she shouted back at Frank. "Do what we do!" They raced towards the cliff, their sail caught the wind, she jumped onto the bar and they went over.

As they left the cliff top, Reamy's foot caught a rock, and they veered steeply to the right.

Von leaned forward and screamed. "Lean left! And forward. Pull the front down a little!" The glider abruptly tipped left but then evened out.

Brad swallowed. Could any of them hang on long enough?

"Ready, guys?" Frank glanced at Brad and Skin.

Brad nodded. He and Skin took a hold of the bar and they lifted it off the ground.

Frank took a deep breath and exhaled, his eyes flicking over the distance between them and the cliff edge.

Brad figured he was trying to work out when to jump onto the bar. If he didn't get up there, they'd have little control. "You can do it, Frank," he reassured him.

Dogs barked. Far too close.

"Right," Frank said. "Here we go. One. Two. Three ..."

They ran. Wind caught the sail. Frank jumped onto the control bar just before they went over the edge, but he pulled the glider down as he did so, and they plummeted downward.

"Hooooollllly shiiiiiit!" Skin yelled.

Brad closed his eyes and clung on for dear life. He felt Frank struggling to get in the middle of the bar. His foot hit Brad's hand and nearly knocked it off, but he gripped the bar harder and managed to hold on.

"No! Push the front up! Get some air!" Von shouted.

"Lean back," Frank yelled.

Brad wasn't sure how to do that under the circumstances, but he threw his weight back, trying to help lift the nose of the glider. They tipped left and right, but stopped plummeting quite so fast.

Frank laughed like a maniac. It seemed he was getting the hang of it.

"This is awesome!" Skin yelled.

Brad risked opening his eyes, enough to see they were still high above the trees. He closed them again. His shoulders ached and he had to concentrate on holding on. His palms began to sweat. Hopefully they'd hit the ground before he couldn't hold on any more. But even if he fell, a few broken bones would be better than a bullet in the head.

Eventually Frank said, "We're almost there."

Brad opened his eyes. They'd reached the bottom of the hill, and with Frank instructing them to lean this way or that, they managed to head towards an area free of trees. Von flew ahead of them. She tilted the nose of her glider down, and they came down quickly, but she straightened out in time to make a half-decent landing.

Following Von, Frank leaned his weight forward to tilt the nose of the hang glider down, but they came down quickly, much too quickly ...

"Hey, Frank, straighten it out!" Brad screamed.

"Bring the nose up!" Von screamed from below. "Lean back, you guys."

"Friggin' trying," Frank said through gritted teeth.

Brad tried to help pull the nose up, but he couldn't do much, hanging underneath like that. Just before they crashed on top of a pile of rocks and gravel, he let go and rolled out of the way.

"Ouch!"

"Frig!"

"Umpphh!" Brad lay winded for a moment at the edge of the forest, then, slowly, feeling bruised all over, he pushed himself up onto his elbows. "Everyone all right?" he shouted.

"Yeah, seem to be!" Frank said. "Just my leg hurts but not broken!"

"A bit bruised, but I'll live," Skin said.

"Okay over here," Von said.

"I'm okay," Clem said, but he sounded a bit shaken.

"Think so, how about you?" Reamy asked.

"Alive, that's all I know."

"All right. Let's keep going," Von shouted.

They stood up slowly, picked up the hang gliders, and threw them into the woods to hide them. The same familiar voices and dogs barked in the distance, but further away now, back on top of the cliff. They raced into the field before them with no idea of where they were headed. Brad looked at the others and realized that they were all as exhausted as he. Von was the only one showing any real energy. But then she hadn't been imprisoned and half-starved for days or months.

Somebody with a clear head, please help us now!

As if in answer to Brad's prayer, Von shouted, "I know where we're going! Follow me!"

"Don't mind if I do!" Reamy shouted.

They ran after her.

"By the way, where *are* we going?" Brad asked breathlessly as he drew up beside her.

"I made a phone call and got some people set up. They're picking us up at the Eighty-Four Lumber on Route Thirty-One. We gotta hurry!"

CHAPTER 13

Brad and crew hid, crouched over near a thicket of trees off the side of the road, waiting for Von's ride to pick them up. Brad's side ached from the impromptu hang-gliding flight. They were all on edge after being chased, but were happy to be away from Suardino and his thugs.

"That control room was crazy," Brad said after he'd filled Von in on what he'd seen. "I took some photos, but I was in a hurry so they might not be that good."

Von's eyes lit up. "That's great. Let me see."

Brad gave her the phone and she flicked through the images. "What do you think they're going to do?" she asked. "Blow up the world? Why was Flood's picture up there?"

"I don't know, but they wanted plutonium, if that's any clue. I wouldn't put anything past them now."

"We're in deep shit!" Bigmouth Reamy said. "Hope we get out of this alive."

"If I have anything to do with it, we will," Brad said firmly.

A moment later, he stood, cocked his head, and listened. A car was heading in from the distance. "Here comes something!"

Von handed Brad back the phone and peered through the bushes at the road.

"What is it?" Reamy asked.

"Who? Is probably the better question."

"Right on."

"You know, if it's not Von's friends, we could be in a lot of shit ..."

"Hey, Reamy. Think positive," Clem said.

Von retorted, "Don't you mean, think *positively*?"

"Come on, woman; this ain't no time for a grammar lesson."

"She's a newspaper reporter," Brad said. "Grammar's part of her job. Anyway, be quiet. They're almost here. Get down!" Brad almost scream-whispered. "Don't anyone move a muscle."

The crew did as he asked, and soon a car drew close and slowed down as if looking for something. Von peered at the car, about two football field lengths away and slowly moving their way.

"Is that them?" Brad asked.

"Uh ... I'm not sure ... wait."

The grey Vandago van crept down the road. She peered again. The van inched closer, then stopped, turned around and drove off.

"Shit, no! Where are you going?" Von whispered. She pounded her fist on her thigh.

"Maybe it's not them!" Brad said.

"Guess not, but I thought it was a—"

"Where did you tell them to meet us?"

"Around here, somewhere." She fished her phone out of her pocket and looked at the screen. "They're here. It must be them."

The van inched back down the road.

Von peered at the van again, then looked back at her phone and nodded. "Yep, it's them." She got up and walked out. The van stopped, and she talked to the driver. "Okay, get ya butts over here!" Von motioned for the group to get into the van.

With everybody safely in, the van sped off down the road. Brad leaned back against the seat and breathed a sigh of relief. He hoped Von's friends knew what they were doing.

~

Juan and the goons were half way down the hill when, through the trees, they saw a car take off. It spewed dust as it turned the corner.

"It looks like they flagged down a van!" Juan grumbled.

"What's that goddamn van doing out here in the middle of nowhere?" one of the goons asked in surprise.

"Well, I don't know," Juan yelled in frustration, "but don't just stand there! Get your ass in gear! Find them!"

The little goon dressed in black flung the rifle on his shoulder and ran down the hill.

"Wait! What in the hell are you doing?"

"I'm going to find them, like you said."

"You'll never find them on foot, you fool! Go get the fuckin' car!" *This guy might be loyal, but he's also three bricks shy of a load.*

"Oh. Right. Will do." He took off up the hill again, heading back to the headquarters.

"Hurry up!" Juan yelled after him. He sat down to wait, and the others did the same. No one said anything, likely too scared he'd bite their head off.

After far too long, a car drove up with the goon at the wheel. Juan ran over and jumped inside. The others tumbled into the back seat.

"Let's get this crate moving!" Juan slammed his fist down on the dashboard, and the car took off, squealing tires. "Goddamn it! Where are those freakin' freaks?"

"Don't worry about it, Juan, we'll find them," one of the goons said.

They sped down the road, looking from side to side for a white van, and searched several smaller roads that turned off the highway, but with no sign of the van.

"Where the hell did they go?" Juan asked, gritting his teeth in frustration. "It's like looking for a booger on a beach full of sand. Fuck, they could be anywhere." He felt a vibe on his phone and pulled it from his pocket—a call from Suardino.

"Our scapegoats, they escaped!" Juan told him before he could speak. "We had 'em locked up, and they got out."

"Holy shit. How'd they do that?"

"Killed the guard!" Juan rubbed his chin.

"I didn't think they had it in them to do something like that!"

"Me neither. We're following them, but I'm just warning ya ..."

Juan knew Suardino would probably be able to track them down. And he waited for an eternity for an answer.

"I'll see what I can do to find them!"

"Good!" Juan grunted. "So what were you callin' about, anyway?"

"I was tailing that Sally yesterday, you know, the girlfriend? I was hiding behind the bushes across from her place, and two guys showed up in a green SUV. They talked for a while, and then I followed them. They went to this small office in a warehouse in Mount Pleasant."

"Yeah? And?"

"Well, I snuck up behind them when they went in. I couldn't get a peek in the place, because it looked really secure. No windows."

"Uh huh. So what good does that do us?"

"Just a sec ... I'm getting to that ..."

"Better be good."

"I went back after hours and got into the place, saw their whole operation. There wasn't much there, but I did find notes on O'Connor. They were hired to try to find him."

"Are you fucking serious? How do ya get in?"

"Basement window, and, yeah, I'm serious. It looks like they're on his trail. They were hired by the Greensburg Police Department. Someone you know well."

"Greg Stone."

"Hit the nail on the head."

"Jesus Christ."

"I should stay on top of this and find out what's going on."

"Not *should*, you'd *better*. Find them or your butt's grease. No question."

"Yep, I'll get it done. I will!"

~

Suardino realized that he'd better get some things done or he might get a bullet in the brain. He had to find out quickly if things were on track. The mole had just been tested in a Pennsylvania town in the middle of nowhere, and now the plutonium needed to be ready to arm. He had to get people ready to work.

Suardino raced back to the office with one mission in mind: track down O'Connor. That meant contacting the Find Guys, avoiding the cops, and doing it all without getting killed. Killing, though, he didn't mind.

Of course, every other group on earth was also looking for O'Connor. The actions The Edge of Darkness had taken to get O'Connor to do their bidding had stayed in the headlines, not faded quickly from the public eye as they should have. The EOD didn't want that kind of scrutiny. *Did we go too big? Is there no turning back?*

Suardino and Juan knew about the other scapegoats, but no one else did, except the police. They were still looking for those who'd committed the other crimes, but the other scapegoat cases had been drying up and were even now turning cold. Suardino hoped. If the scapegoats disappeared and no evidence was found, then the cases would be dropped. Poof. Finished! That's how it should work out. Except for that one lingering case, O'Connor. He just might shove those plans in another direction, which was exactly what Suardino and Juan wanted to avoid.

Suardino had to find him before the cops did.

~

Brad, Von, Reamy, Skin, Clem, and Frank came around the bend into downtown Jeanette, making their way across the southwest end of Pennsylvania on Route 130. The driver, dressed in black and wearing a ski mask to hide his identity, inched slowly down the road, paying attention to every traffic light, stopping at every stop sign. No speeding, no taking chances of getting caught. Not a sound came from the people inside the van, save their breathing.

Brad found himself in the mountains, climbing upwards, towards a plateau on top, where he was supposed to be. He clawed the vines and dirt, gripping small trees for support as he ascended. His foot sank into the dirt, and Brad had to yank to free it. He dropped to his hands and knees and crawled, but the more he crawled, the harder it became to make it to the top. He saw light from above, but it wasn't getting closer. Brad made one last-ditch effort to get to the top, crawling and clawing. He blinked and realized he'd been dozing.

He looked around the van. The other scapegoats were in shut-eye mode as well.

"Welcome to the land of the living," Von said with a grin.

"Yeah, thanks ... I think." He peered through the window. "Is this route 130?"

"Yeah, we made good time. It's two thirty."

"Where are we off to, by the way?"

"To my friend's place in the hills over by Ligonier. Then we're going to make a document and a video about your experience, and give it to a Mr. Greg Stone of the Greensburg Police Department. I've been in touch with him."

"Really? So you asked him for help."

"Yeah, I called him. He is the police, after all. It's their job. But they only have so much manpower and aren't quick to believe every story."

"You came and got us. So you believe me, then?"

"What? Are you kidding? I risked my life to follow you, come and get you, lead you to freedom, and you're gonna ask if I believe you?" She glared at Brad, staring directly in his eyes, unmoving. "I just want to find out what's really going on."

"You're gonna find out, then. Because I am telling the truth. You do believe me, right?" Brad stared back.

"Here we go again. I'm here to find out the truth. So I guess the answer is yes."

"Ah, sorry. It's a little hard to know who to trust these days."

"No sorry necessary. Point taken."

A police car with sirens blazing came around the corner, up from behind.

"Holy shit, can you get off the road?" Brad shouted.

"They don't know this van," Von said, but she told the unnamed driver to turn off anyway.

"What's going on?" Clem asked, waking up. "Are we getting busted?"

The cruiser came closer as the van slowly pulled off into a Dairy Queen parking lot. The police car slowed down behind them.

"Oh my God," Reamy said. "Just tell them the truth. We're scapegoats, we were set up."

"Not sure if they'd believe us," Von said.

But then the police cruiser sped up and pulled on past the Dairy Queen and down Route 130 without stopping. The crew let out sighs of relief and relaxed in their seats.

"Holy crap," Reamy said, folding his arms.

Brad and Von glanced at each other but said nothing, then they stared out the windows as the van drove on. They passed the Greensburg Country Club and got onto Locust Valley Road heading towards Route 66. Thirty-three minutes later, they arrived at the traffic light in Ligonier.

"Hey, you all awake back there?" Von asked.

"Where are we?" Reamy sputtered. "Planet Xenon?"

"Up your nose with a rubber hose," Frank responded, grouchy from just being woken up.

"No, Ligonier, Pennsylvania, population sixteen hundred, give or take."

"Damn small town," Reamy grumbled.

"A small historic town that saw action during the French and Indian War in 1763," Von said. "Right over those hills there's not much but wilderness and woods. Makes it quite easy to disappear. For a little while, anyway."

"It reminds me of those little New England ghost towns like ... shit, can't remember the name ..."

"Salem?" Frank chimed in.

"Yep, that's the one. Same kind of small-town spookiness."

"You're right; it's a bit eerie. Good thing we're not there yet," Von said.

"There? Where's that?"

"Erie, Pennsylvania."

"Haha, Miss funny britches."

They drove on Route 30 and eventually turned left onto Route 28 in the hills of the Laurel Mountains.

About twenty minutes later, Von said, "Okay, almost there. Keep going ... Wait, turn left here. Go down that little dirt road." Von pointed to a tiny path between the mighty evergreens.

"This one?" the driver asked, slowing the van.

"No, sorry, the next one." The van drove on, tires crunching in the gravel. "This is it."

"Gotcha." The driver yanked the car over to the left and drove slowly down the path beneath low overhanging trees. The edges of the woods encroached on the path, making it hard to see. They continued on.

"We're almost there," Von said.

Wherever there is, Brad thought. He guessed it would be home for a time, but for how long, the wind only knew. Brad watched the driver as the car ambled further down the dirt road. *Feels like we're riding on air.*

Finally, Von whispered, "Slow down ... slowly, and yep! Stop here. Wait, drive up a bit, I need to see if I can see it through the trees." She got out of the car, closed the door, then race-walked up to the edge of the trees and peered through. She turned back with a grin and gave a thumbs-up. Those in the back of the van sighed.

She opened the sliding door and whisper-shouted, "Let's go."

"Don't mind if I do," Skin retorted.

"Grab your stuff and let's get going."

They took what few belongings they had, opened the doors, and got out, warily checking the surroundings. The hidden fortress surprised Brad. He found it unreal that someone could live this far back in the woods, miles from contact with anyone—a home for a true back-to-the-woods woodsman. He thought of the movie *Deliverance* when four friends looking for people to drive their car down to Antry wound up in a surreal little town in Appalachia and barely made it out alive. Being in southwestern Pennsylvania, they weren't that far from Appalachia, actually.

Hope we don't run into any freaks.

They walked through the trees, following Von to the destination: a leaved and thatched wall, obviously camouflage, and impossible to find unless you were Von Roberts.

"You said this guy is a friend of yours?" Brad was amazed that she'd found it at all.

"That's right."

"What exactly is this place, and who is this guy?" Brad inquired as he looked around at the other faces. Though non-verbal, the men looked relieved that they'd arrived there unscathed.

Clem nodded. "Yeah, I mean, we barely know you. What if this is a trap?"

"Right," Brad said. "Before we go in there, we need to know more. For our own safety."

"Okay, gotcha. He used to be a Navy Seal but retired after Desert Storm. He was a cameraman for Channel Six News when I was a reporter in Greensburg, and that's where I met him. He retired from the news and basically became a prepper, you know, one of those guys who thinks the world's gonna end and he and his entourage need to find a way to survive."

"Oh yeah, I've seen the TV show," Clem said. "What does he think's gonna destroy the world?"

"He thinks the government will become more powerful, shrink the dollar value, and stock money in its own vaults, which will lead to a civilian uprising. Everyone will go crazy and take the law into their own hands. That's why this place is so hidden and has the security of a military base."

Von reached through the leaf-swathed panel and ripped open the thatch that lay on top of it. From somewhere inside she pulled open a little door on a small wooden box hidden inside the foliage. She pushed a security code on a very modern keypad, and they heard a click. Von again slid her hand into the thick leaves, just to the right, and moved some kind of lever to the left, exposing another steel box. She opened the door, revealing a small fingerprint pad. When she put her thumb on the pad, a door clacked open, and she slid the foliage-covered door to the left.

Brad and Frank looked at each other in disbelief.

"Are you sure you're just a reporter?" Frank asked. "C'mon, there's gotta be something else under that reporter guise!"

"I'm a lot more than you think," Von replied with a gleam in her eye.

"I'm not sure if that's good or bad," Frank said.

"Oh, all good, of course."

"How'd you know how to do that?" Brad asked in amazement.

"He taught me all this because he trusts me."

"Well, that's good to know."

They walked down a path and arrived at a large brown and green house with two barred windows on either side of a simple wooden door. Von marched onto the front porch, and the group, led by Brad, followed.

Suddenly a voice rose up from a small walkway on the left of the house. "Tha she izz!" A big man in his sixties with a wispy white beard walked over.

The two hugged, obviously happy to see each other.

Von looked around at her gang and started to introduce them, but her friend said, "Don't worry about formalities now, hon! They look exhausted. All they gotta know is that I'm Barry. Nice to meet everybody."

They all nodded in unison.

"Who is this, again?" Brad asked, glancing at Von.

"Oh, this ole barn door?" she said while patting Barry on the stomach. "We go way back. Helped me on about a thousand and one things I was working on as a reporter. Has a lot of info on everything and everyone, and what he doesn't have, he can find."

"Sounds like the kinda guy you wanna know." Clem stood with his hand on the railing.

Von grinned. "Oh, he is!" The two laughed in unison.

Brad coughed. "Uh, do you have a bathroom?"

"No, sorry. You have to use mother nature." Barry cackled, the laugh of a proud man.

Though curious about him, Brad didn't smile.

"Don't all look so glum! I'm just jokin', fer cryin out loud!" Barry said.

Brad relaxed and, along with the others, let out his first laugh in days.

"Not only do I, or we, rather, have a bathroom, we have a state-of-the-art security system around the premises, satellite communications, and a bug-out den.

It'll hold about eighteen or twenty people for six months. Call us the Pennsylvania preppers."

Brad guessed they were in good hands and was, once again, stunned at Von's resourcefulness. *This woman is amazing.* He spaced out for a moment, memory falling back to Sally. He wondered how she was doing and hoped she was okay. *We have to get out of this in one piece.*

"Brad!" Frank jolted Brad out of his daydream.

"Yo!"

"Go to the bathroom, will ya?"

They walked down a ramp to the left of the entrance and disappeared into the bowels of the hidden den in the middle of the woods.

CHAPTER 14

Monday, October sixteenth.

Just when he thought it was safe to think about Brad again, Tom Ratner was called to the front desk to meet two people who called themselves the Find Guys, whoever the hell they were. Tom walked to the main entrance of the construction firm and stuck out his hand mid-stride as he'd done on a million other occasions.

"Nice to meet you, Mr. Ratner. I'm Tombo from the Find Guys. This is Bobber. We're here to talk to you about a Mr. Brad O'Connor."

"Oh, yes; I've heard his name on the news. But I don't know him. Never met him. Now if I can help you in any other way ..." Tom shot a glance into both men's eyes, first Tombo, then Bobber.

"Ha, come on, Tom," Bobber said, "or should I call you Rat? We know you know him. We're the Find Guys after all."

Momentarily shocked, Tom let out a short gasp. *Fuck, they know I was called Rat during high school.* He wanted to forget those times, and wanted everyone else to forget as well. Rat, of course, came from his last name, Ratner. He'd always hated that name. That they knew his nickname, one he hadn't used in more than thirty years, froze him to the core. *Hate these guys.*

"Rat, listen. We just need to find O'Connor. If you know anything at all about his whereabouts, we're prepared to offer you a tidy sum as a reward."

The offer was plain and simple ... and enticing. Although Ratner Construction was making money, there never seemed enough to go around. Tom's wife wanted a new car. The kids were approaching college age. The house loan, the car loan, the ... *But why would they want to talk to me? Who in the hell are they?*

"Well, the last time I saw him ... it was in Jeanette ... at the ..."

"Yeah? Where?"

Tom hated these pushy two. Was starting to hate people in general. He hoped Brad had gotten out of there.

"We're professionals, you know. Helping to get to the bottom of this," Tombo said. "We won't let anything happen to him, you can rest assured about that."

Tom glanced from one face to another, then spurted out quickly, "I think it was around the Seven Eleven, on ... no, maybe the Shell station on Fifth."

"Okay, now we're getting somewhere." The man in sunglasses glanced at his partner. "Anything else you can tell us?"

"That's all I know. Haven't seen nor heard from him in weeks. I hope he's still alive."

"Okay, thanks for your help, Mr. Ratner. Call us if you have any questions, or any more to offer. Don't forget about the reward. The offer continues to stand."

"Okay, gotcha."

They all made the required eye contact and said their pleasantries. Tom held out his hand to offer a goodbye. *Now get the hell out of my company.* They shook it and left.

~

Although Von helped the crew tremendously, Brad was still unsure of the direction they were taking. Three months before, Brad had been a nobody—he'd been, as that guy Suardino had put it, a man who didn't stand out in the crowd—but now here he was in the middle of the Pennsylvania woods with a bunch of fugitives, men like him, nobodies who'd become somebodies, wanted for crimes they'd been framed for or forced to commit. The only thing he could do was to hang on for the ride and stick with it to the end, wherever that might take him.

The morning after they arrived in the bunker, Brad, just up and groggy, walked out of his bunk, and nearly bumped into Barry, who was walking down the hall.

"Oops! Whereya off to there, partner?" The big man asked.

"Uh, just getting something to eat."

"Okie smokie. You know where the kitchen is. Say, listen, Von told me a lot about you and your background. She told me you were caught up in some kind of weird scapegoat thing, is that right?"

"Yeah. This terrorist group is framing people, the people I came with. I know I didn't attack those abortion clinics. And these guys didn't do their deeds either. We were taken advantage of. Used, compromised, blackmailed."

"Well, that's what *you* say. And Von, she's a real good gal. You seem like you're on the up and up. But you never know these days ... terrorism, lies, cheating, stealing ... Von may believe you, but others won't."

"I know, but I have the word of these guys, I have threats by the guy from The Edge of Darkness, and I have photos of their control room. If we can find someone or something that points to the fact I was home that day, or that something else happened ... that's all we need. I've thought about it over and over in my head, and can only think of contacting the neighbors. Contacting everybody."

"Well, that might work, but ya know it ain't gonna be easy gittin' in there. You certainly have to lay low, ya know. Don' even think about goin' yo'self!" He uttered all that in one breath, which added to the emphasis. "Lemme check it with Von. *She* believes you, or at least she wants to find the truth. And these guys you helped might help you prove it, if they're willing to put it on paper."

"Yeah, well, let's figure out what to do. And how to do it."

"Oh, that we will, my friend. You can rest assured."

Barry's seriousness haunted Brad. He realized that not everyone was enrolled in Brad's story as easily as Von.

Von walked up the ramped hall. "Mornin', ya'll."

"Morning."

"Why so quiet?"

"We were just talking about how to approach fixin' this thing." Barry, a burly dude, didn't mind getting to the point.

"We need to plan it out on paper first," Von said, "and I suggest we start yesterday. Then we see what we need to do to put it together in rock form. I say write it on paper and make a video. Then ..." Von looked around and swiped her arm across her mouth.

"What?"

"Get the weapons and make a plan," she whispered in a loud, almost cat-like tone. "But not just any plan, *the* plan."

Brad narrowed his eyes. Weapons wasn't a word he'd heard coming from Von before. Her tone indicated a plan that was either devious, conniving, or which stretched legal boundaries, likely all three. At this point, however, he didn't really care.

His mind went back to the fateful day he'd seen the newspaper article and had that sinking feeling inside. He recalled touching base with Arrow, the headhunting firm, then Tom, then Sally. He retraced every footstep, every move. He remembered the time the EOD caught up with him in the woods, and retraced his lucky escape. He remembered dropping the bag of plutonium at the EOD's feet and running away. He remembered being caught again, then the prison, his comrades, and his escape just a few days before. What would happen to them now? He had to pull them through, with the help of Von and Barry, hopefully. He had to. If not, who would?

Never-ending questions lingered: How was Tom doing? Had he been dragged into this, too? How about Sal? Was she involved now? Would they stick up for him? Did they know what was going on? Were the cops still looking for him? He had to find out what was going on. And quickly.

~

Sally was just on her way out the door on the same day when the phone buzzed in her back pocket. She stopped, yanked it out, and saw an unfamiliar number. "Yes, who's calling?"

A low and static-filled voice came on the line. "Sal, hi, it's me."

"Oh my God, Brad! Where are you? How are you?"

"Listen, I can't tell you that right now. But I'm safe. I need you to talk to someone ... tell her about the things I've been through ... tell her ..."

"Tell ... *her*? Who's this ... her?"

"Oh, Sal, don't worry; she's helping me, us, get out of this thing."

"Us? There are more of you? Brad, what's going on?"

"I can't tell you everything now, honey. Just trust me. With your and Tom's help, we can beat this thing. Please!"

"Okay, okay. What do I need to do?"

"I'm going to put her on the line; just answer her questions. Her name is Von, and she's a reporter."

"Okay."

After a pause, a woman said, "Hi, Sally, is it okay if I record this conversation?"

"Yes, but … who are you again?"

"My name is Von Roberts. I'm a reporter for the Latrobe Press. Do you remember when Brad first told you about the incident at the abortion clinic? When was it, and what did he say?"

"It was Monday last week. He told me he got contacted by this group, The Edge of Darkness, and they said they needed a favor."

"Which was?"

"Brad had to steal some plutonium for them from this nuclear reactor and give it to them or they would do another one. And even kill me and his friend Tom."

"Do another one, meaning attack another abortion clinic?"

"That's about the size of it."

"Okay. Anything else you can remember? Did you ever meet these people? See them or know what they look like?"

"No, I'm sorry, I didn't. They could be anybody."

"Okay, thanks for your time, Sally. I'll need this in writing. Could you write up a short scenario of what happened for me?"

"Sure, okay. Could you put Brad back on?"

"Sure. Talk soon."

Brad came back on the line. "Hi."

"Hi, Brad, I'm sorry I doubted you. I'm glad you're safe, and I'm glad she's helping you through this thing. I hope they find these people!"

"Me, too, Sal. Thanks for believing in me. Miss you. Bye."

And with that, the conversation was over.

In Barry's place in the woods, Brad looked at Von to see her reaction.

She nodded. "Could be true, but she's repeating what you told her. Let's see what Tom Ratner gives us."

Brad recited Tom's number from memory, and Von dialed. Brad prided himself on being good at remembering numbers, although with modern technology, that feat was getting much harder.

The phone was answered with a quick, "Yep."

"Hello, Mr. Ratner?"

"Who wants to know?"

"This is Von Roberts from the Latrobe Press. I have someone you know here, and I need you to speak to him."

"Uh huh, who might that be?"

Von shoved the phone in Brad's face. "Hi, Tom, it's me."

"Jesus. Where in God's name are you?" Tom's concern touched Brad.

"I can't really tell you that. And, actually, I'm not even sure. But that doesn't matter. I'm gonna give the phone back so you can tell her about the abortion clinic thing and about the few days after that. Can you do that? It's the only way I can be saved."

"Uh, okay, sure." Brad handed the phone over to Von. And Tom continued with trepidation.

"Mr. Ratner, uh, I need to ask you some questions, and record the conversation. We need to compile evidence to support your friend here. Is that okay with you?"

"Sure, I'd do anything to help Brad."

"On the day after the first abortion clinic shooting, where were you?"

"I was here at work. And I got a phone call from Brad saying he didn't remember the day before. He went to a job interview and they said the interview was actually the previous day."

"Okay. Did you hear about this group, this gang, The Edge of Darkness, who was after Brad?"

"Yeah, Brad told me that. It sounded crazy, but I would have to say I believe him."

"Did you happen to see anyone from this group?"

"No, I haven't. Don't you wanna let me know where you guys are? I could always bring you something to help if you need. I could let the police know, too. They can help."

"I don't think that's a good idea. We're alive, though, that's all you need to know. Please don't tell anyone you spoke to me or to Brad. I ask in confidence, okay?"

"All right."

"Thank you, and we'll be in touch. Bye." Von stuck the phone in the breast pocket of her jean-shirt and turned to Brad. "Well, looks like you have a couple of players in your court. But it's not exactly proof. We're gonna compile more of this kind of information and *then* we have some firepower."

"Okay, sounds good."

"One question: did The Edge of Darkness tell you why they wanted the plutonium?"

"No, they never said. I'm sure it's something no good, though, and big, considering all the equipment in the command center. Looked like state-of-the-art stuff, too."

"Where was that? In that place I got you out of?"

"Yeah, in that tunnel there was a set of rickety stairs, like a fire-escape. I snuck up and took a look."

"Okay, I'm gonna print out those photos, but I think what we need to do right now is to go through that mind of yours and draw a floor plan of that place from what you can remember."

"Sure, I can do that." Brad wondered why she wanted a floor plan. *Does she want to go back there?* "Why am I drawing this?"

He looked into Von's eyes and saw a fiery gleam. He couldn't pull his eyes away. And then he knew why she wanted the map. She wanted to go back and find that room.

~

Suardino packed the car to go on the hunt for O'Connor. He threw in a spiral notebook, his phone charger, MacBook Pro, iPad, walkie-talkie, Go Pro, and some clothes. He also tossed in his 357, and a 22 caliber, then he got in, slammed the door, and was off. First stop, the woods. He parked at the small cleared area at the base of the hill the scapegoats had successfully hang glided down and walked around. Even at one p.m. the fall air felt crisp and cool. He combed the area for anything that might lead him to O'Connor and the others, but found no physical evidence. Next stop, back to the Find Guy headquarters in Mount Pleasant, Pa.

He pulled the car into the parking lot of a Big Lots discount store, then rushed to the back of Big Lots and into the woods to circle round behind the Find Guys' headquarters. A car sat in their parking lot, so he waited, checking info on his phone. After what seemed like an eternity, he checked the car; it hadn't left yet. Hoping to hack into the Find Guy computer system, he set up his charger, pulled out his MacBook Pro, and logged on.

Once logged on, he found his way to the Dark Net, opened Terminal and typed in *FindGuysXXAeroleater Link. Nexus.* Enter. More script. *Run? After, punch, 45544.* Then a few more commands. He looked for anything regarding mail on the desktop and finally just decided to check Find Guys on Gmail. He bypassed the password, and found their message from Stone and the chat history—he was on the right track. All he needed to do now was find their physical whereabouts. He lay low, waiting for the Find Guys' car to pull out. Then he would follow.

Ten minutes later, Suardino checked his watch and his iPad on which he had his schedule, contact info, notes, maps, and the like. His goal was to locate O'Connor, find the rest of the scapegoats, kidnap them, and use them as barter ammo when the EOD went to get the president. After all, they'd have in their possession five men who had committed very serious crimes. They could be used to make deals.

As he went over these plans in his mind, the door opened to the Find Guys' headquarters. Out walked the two faces he'd seen before. They got into the Find Guys' car, started it up, and pulled out of the parking spot. Suardino got out of his own car and sneaked up to the side of the building flanking the office, heading to the same window he'd entered by before. He cracked it open and squeezed through, then crept to the top of the stairs and slipped through the basement door. Down the hall on the left, attached to the office, he found a little plastic sign:

Find Guys. Location Services. 800-444-5555.
Findguys.facebook.com.

He stopped to listen, to see if anyone was in the room. No movement. He yanked the small packet of lock tools from his pocket, the same ones he'd used to get into Tom's apartment the morning he drugged O'Connor.

He stuck in the long tool and twirled it around, listening for the telltale pop. Finally, a click, and he turned the knob. The door opened. He entered slowly, pulling out his flashlight. The computer workstation sat on the left, surprisingly still on, just in sleep mode. Hacking in would be easy. He pulled his Remote Desktop Connection device from his backpack and put it next to the computer, then opened his MacBook Pro and found the device on Bluetooth.

The start-up came on: IOD Remote Desktop Connection. He searched for the link to the Find Guys' computer and clicked it, then punched up the documents folder and copied everything to the MacBook. As a mark of good measure, he included the music, movies, and downloads files as well, all copied with the touch of a button.

To his right sat a filing cabinet. He looked in that and, under 'O', found the file on Brad O'Connor. He yanked it out, opened it, and used his phone to snap pictures of each page, then closed the file and put it back in the cabinet.

The file copying completed, he closed the file on the Mac, disconnected the remote desktop, unhooked the cable, and placed the device back in his bag. Finally, he punched the sleep button on the Find Guys' computer, and made sure everything was in its right place, then Suardino slunk out the door, making sure to lock it again.

He was almost down the hall when he heard male voices and the front door of the building jiggle. The Find Guys were coming back. He scooted down the hall towards the basement door, but before he could get there, the front door burst open. A small clunky man came in the front hall and caught Suardino standing there.

"Who the fuck are you?" the man asked as he ran over, gun drawn.

"I'm on a mission," Suardino said slowly, then he turned and gave the fatty a whack on the side of his head with the butt of his revolver. The man fell down and Suardino kicked him in the head. He lay still, unconscious. Suardino reached down and felt the man's carotid artery.

Nothing. Shit!

Suardino took off down the hall and yanked open the basement door.

"Hey! Not so fast!" the other man yelled. "Who in the hell are you?"

A shot rang out and a bullet ripped over Suardino's head. Suardino turned, tucked in his head, and charged, ramming the man in the torso. The man fell, and Suardino repeatedly bashed his gun into the man's temple, drawing blood, until he lay unmoving. With that, Suardino walked out the front door and checked for any unwanted attention. The coast was clear. He got in the car and backed up, almost careening into the mailbox. *Fuck me! That was close!*

~

The next morning, Von searched the Internet for The Edge of Darkness. Unfortunately, her searches produced nothing but Error 404's. She then searched every possible combination of the words—Darkness, Edge, Edge of the Dark, Dark Edge—but still without luck. Knowing they were illicit, she clicked on the green circular globe for the Tor browser, going dark, then she searched for anything related to plutonium, nuclear reactors, Brad O'Connor, and Chimerton—the only things she had to go on.

What the hell would they need plutonium for? A bomb, she guessed. Was there something else Brad knew but had forgotten? Was she exhausting all possibilities? If she could convince Brad to go back to the prison, they'd be in a lot better position. From what he'd said, that was the heart of it all. The only problem was getting Brad to go back in there.

Tor didn't lend much help because it took too much time and she didn't really know what she was looking for, at first. She tried every combination of words again, and some links popped up leading to an organization in Mexico that investigated kidnappings. She clicked the first link on the page and found a story about a blond man wanted for the murder of his family—the wife's father ran a multi-million-dollar jet sales company. Soon after the killings, the man had disappeared until someone hired the organization to track him down. According to the man's story, he'd been forced to do the murders to avoid even worse bloodshed.

Von's jaw dropped. The case was remarkably like this one. A picture at the bottom of the page showed a Hispanic man with sunglasses and a mustache. The article didn't say whether or not anyone was searching for the kidnapper, but the photo was of one shady-looking character.

The next best course of action was to try to break back into that place she'd broken Brad and the gang out of two days before. Crazy or not, she knew one thing: if Brad's story was the truth—*if*—then this group was aiming to take a piece of the world and do who knows what with it.

"Hey, Brad, wake up!" Von said into his left ear.

Brad rolled around on the upper bunk and his right arm flailed out. "Whaaa," he grumped.

Von suspected that six-ten a.m. was a bit early for Brad's liking. "We have things to do. Come on." She grabbed his arm and yanked, almost pulling him out of the bunk. "Hurry up!"

"Okay! I'm coming, jeez." He sat up, put his legs over the edge of the bunk, and jumped down with a thump. "Where to?"

Von handed him a cup of coffee with milk, and he took a sip, feeling life pump back into his brain. He took another sip and thought it was the perfect cup, not too light, and not too sweet.

She took him into Barry's den on the first floor in the back, and there they found a large leather swivel chair, two other armchairs, a sofa, and a long desk along the wall. On this desk sat two computer CPU's, two twenty-five-inch monitors, a MacBook Air, and professional TV camera and audio equipment.

Von sat him down in the swivel chair and let him finish his cup of coffee. "More?"

"Please." He was beginning to feel that he could conquer anything.

She left the room and went to fetch another cup. While she was gone, Brad, unable to stop himself from being curious, looked in the closet at the back of the room. What he saw made his heart jump. The closet housed a huge cache of weapons: rifles, machine guns, a grenade launcher, infrared goggles, and radio equipment. This guy was prepared for anything. He returned to his seat, just in time.

Von came in with another cup of perfect coffee and handed it to him as she spoke. "Today we have to make a video detailing everything you told me, every little thing. I might ask you some questions, but otherwise, just talk.

Cover the whole thing, from day one. We've got plenty of memory, so we can do numerous takes."

"I guess you really are a good reporter. Just tell me what to do, director," Brad said as he righted himself in the chair.

"Hmph," she responded, and a little smile formed on the edge of her lips. "Flattery will get you nowhere."

With that, she aimed the camera at Brad and pushed the record button. Brad started to talk, telling everything from that moment when he woke up on the day of the interview to find that he'd missed a day, right up to the present. At the end, he pleaded with whoever would be on the other end of the video: "I'm being set up by a crazy outfit. I didn't do those abortion clinic shootings. I only took the plutonium to protect myself or something else would happen. I do know one thing: this group has to be stopped or something even more serious *will* happen." Brad paused, staring into the camera.

Von shut off the machine and looked at Brad. His weary and stubble-crested face gave the perfect undertone to the video. "Excellent. Now let's get the others."

Slowly but surely, each scapegoat told his story. Reamy, Skin, Clem, and Frank, and they all shared the heartbreaking tale of Longhair, caught in the hole and being slaughtered. After they were finished, Von checked the file on the iMac and saved it with the title: 'Scapegoat Story 1'.

After the recording, she began to put the whole story down on paper to give to Stone. Hopefully, she'd be able to put all of her ducks in a line to, at least, have a convincing story. She typed, backspaced, corrected. Thought. More typing. Checking with the others, checking roads with Barry. Finalizing details. The morning grew into evening.

Finally, the report was finished—thirty-three pages, and the only thing they had to prove their innocence. At five fifteen she walked into the living room where everyone was watching TV.

"Finished. Next stop, police headquarters where we will present this, the photos, and this copy of the written stories to a Mr. Greg Stone."

"Yeah!" Clem said. "We'll show them."

"Oh yeah, them buggers better believe us," Skin, always the negative one, said.

"Don't worry, all we have to do is be careful," Brad reassured them.

Von caught his eye. "Us three need to do something." She pointed at herself, Brad, and Barry. "We have an important mission."

"Whaddaya mean?" Clem asked.

"We have to go back to that place," Von explained. "We have to see that room and at least document it further if nothing else. The pictures Brad took aren't that clear and could be of anywhere. We need better proof. You guys stay here. We'll go ourselves. Barry, me, and Brad."

"That's crazy!" Skin said. "You don't know what they've got going over there, and who knows if you'll be able to get back in. They definitely have it guarded. You can't just waltz in there."

Von glanced at Barry. Barry walked over to the closet and opened the door to the weapons cache. "That's why we have these," he said, motioning for everyone to go over and have a look.

They did. Mouths opened; jaws dropped. They weren't prepared for such an arsenal of shotguns, machine guns, and pistols.

"Holy shit." Skin turned to the others. "I'm not sure if I like this one. Do you all like this?" He looked around at them. "I mean, this might bring on World War Three. You guys could get slaughtered!" The muscle between his eyes tightened. "I don't even know how to use a grenade launcher."

"Yeah," Clem agreed. "I'm not so sure it's a good idea. You really shouldn't take any chances. We should take a vote on whether we allow you guys to go on with this plan. Whaddaya think?" He looked around.

"Yeah, that's a good idea," Skin said. "You can't just decide by yourselves. We're all in this together."

Brad, Von, and Barry looked at each other. Brad hadn't anticipated resistance from the group. But they still needed to go.

"Thanks," he replied, "but if you vote against us going, you might be doing us all a great injustice. I think we can head these guys off if we need, and we can win this. But it's imperative that we go back in there. These are just weapons; we're not saying they'll be used. They're purely for protection, and we'll review how to use them."

"I have another idea," Clem said. "Say we all take a vote, yes? But we'll vote on *us going with you*. If we get voted down, then you can't go either."

Skin's face turned red. "What? What the hell are you doing? I ain't going in there again!"

Brad shook his head. "Just us going is much easier and smoother. We escape quickly if we need to. All of us coming might impede the mission."

Frank nodded. "Yeah, Clem, we could all get wiped out. Someone should stay out here."

Clem chimed up again: "But we can't let them go alone. It'd be three against the world. We have to help them. Brad and Von saved us. Would you rather still be in that shithole?"

"That's true," Frank said. "I guess I'm okay if the weapons are for protection only and if you teach us all how to use them."

"Right on," Barry said. "I know damn well how to use the weapons, and I've already taught Von. And Brad's had some gun experience. It'll only take a few minutes to get you all up and running."

"Skin?" Frank inquired.

"Uh, well, okay, I guess, if you're all in." Skin looked around at the others.

"It might be our only chance," Von said.

"Come on guys, if we're all in this together, then we should fight it together," Clem said.

Brad no longer cared who came, he just wanted to get going. He and Von looked around and finally they saw slight nods from the group, glances at each other. They had agreed.

Over the next few hours, Barry taught the group how to load and unload quickly, aim, and fire their weapons.

"Okay, this is an AK 47 assault machine gun, with a magazine. To load, turn on the safety, click the release button, and slide the magazine out. Slide in a new one. Click the safety. Aim. And pull the trigger," Barry demonstrated as he taught. He picked off a coke can perched on top of a fence post. "Here, you try, Skin."

Skin clicked the magazine release but forgot to hit the safety.

"Hey, don't forget the safety button."

Skin's mouth dipped into a scowl, and his mustache went up on the left side.

Barry looked at the group and scratched his beard. "Everyone, this is probably the most important switch on the entire weapon."

Skin picked off a can and gave a smile of satisfaction.

They took turns shooting at an old barrel Barry had outside the back door. The last thing he taught was how to clean their weapons. "This is one of the most important parts of owning a gun."

"Yeah, and it's also one of the most dangerous," Brad chimed in. "A college buddy of mine was accidentally shot and killed by his roommate during gun cleaning. Be sure to get very comfortable with that weapon, be scared of it, careful with it, and above all, respect it."

The gang looked at each other and nodded in silence.

CHAPTER 15

On Tuesday, October seventeenth, Stone sat in his office searching the criminal database. The person in the surveillance footage they'd received a few days before wasn't O'Connor, but carried a bag just like his. So far, he'd found *nada* on the network. Picking up the phone, he dialed the number for Stop and Go.

"Stop and Go food and gas," the raggedy voice on the other end said—sounded like a California surfer.

"This is Greg Stone from Greensburg P.D. Is the manager in?"

"Just a minute." He heard the call from the muffled phone. "Dave! Some police dude is on the phone!"

Two seconds later: "Yes, this is Dave, the manager."

"I want to talk about the video and pic from your store cameras we got the other day, remember?"

"Yeah, I do. But I already told the police everything I know."

"I know, but I want to clarify a few things. Did anyone you talk to see or hear anything outside that night?"

"We only had two people in the store that night. They didn't hear anything. One staff member did say she saw some dirty dude using the payphone behind the car wash. He had some kind of bag with him."

"Okay." *Probably O'Connor.* "Anything else you can tell me?"

Greg knew what he would hear: "No, sorry, that's all I know."

Stone hung up the phone. His shoulders slumped. "Why are the cops always this late to know anything?" he said into the air. "The last to hear anything? Fuckin' stupid!" The air didn't answer back.

The doorknob jiggled and then banged, startling Greg out of his trance. "Yo! Come on in."

The door opened and Darrera walked in. He tossed a pile of papers onto Greg's desk. "Take a look."

"What's this?" Greg started thumbing through the 1982 printouts.

"Stories about claims by some blond guy in a small town on the coast of Texas that an organization made him kill his family after someone from the organization masquerading as him had slaughtered a whole store full of people. The wife's father was the president of a multi-million-dollar jet sales company," Darrera said in a matter-of-fact tone. "The man claimed the group wanted three planes free of charge or else they'd kill many more."

At the bottom, there was a picture of a Hispanic man. The name under the picture said Juan Gabriel; he was noted as a personal friend of the family's. Greg's face contorted as he continued to read aloud: "Robert Billings, forty-three, was convicted in the slaying of his wife's father, mother, wife and two kids. A life sentence was handed down by Judge Harold Warner yesterday for this brutal crime. The attack on the store remains unsolved. All the man had to say was that he doesn't remember the first crime, and claims he was set up to take the fall for it. He told the press later he was forced to turn over three jets to a secret organization or his family would be killed

... holyfuckittome," Stone finished reading and stared up at Dom, who was looking down at Stone over his glasses.

"Howduya like that one?"

"Freakin' unbelievable."

~

Von decided to drop off the video and the documents they'd spent hours making to Greg Stone herself in a secret drop that only she and Stone would know about. She yanked out her phone and punched the contact for G. Stone. The phone rang around ten times and then went to voicemail.

"You've reached Greg Stone. Sorry I missed your call. Leave a message and I'll get back to you."

Von didn't know what to do at that moment. The choices went through her head like rapid fire. *If I leave a message, I risk being found out and tailed. If I don't leave a message, I risk losing what could be a good contact. He has my number anyway ... maybe he'll call back ...*

She punched the red phone icon to hang up and banged on the steering wheel twice. "Fuck."

She'd just driven off when her ringtone started playing. She slammed on the brakes, veered onto the berm, and glanced at the phone—Greg Stone. Shaking, she slid the answer bar over to the right. "Von Roberts."

"I thought I recognized this number." Stone sounded bewildered. "You know you and your friend there are highly sought after. And in some serious fucking trouble."

"Yeah, I know. Just listen to me for a second, can you?"

"I'm listening."

"I know where O'Connor is. I have proof that this guy didn't do it. He's innocent."

"Where is he, then?"

"I know, but I can't tell you. I believe—no, I know—he has been set up, and not only him. There are others.

They're all in trouble. I've compiled some things to show you that'll make you change your mind about all this."

"Hmm, spoken like a true private detective or newspaper reporter or whatever the hell you are. We have a lot of sources on this, and a lot of our own manpower. I'm sure the truth will be known soon without your help."

"No, listen; I have some things I need you to see. This will show that this guy is being set up, and I can help bring justice to this whole mess. Just meet me so I can give them to you, and you can make the final decision. I know what you'll decide. Just promise me you only meet me, get these things, and let me go. I need to do what I need to do. And then I'll be back in touch with you. Please, I'm begging you."

A long pause came, during which she heard nothing but breathing.

"I had a feeling there was more to this than meets the eye," Stone finally said. "I don't have proof, no pictures, no witnesses, and no reports from anyone. But I have a gut feeling about this case. It stems from the way people talked about Brad, the things they found in his apartment, the video from The Edge of Darkness. For all I know, I'm being played by O'Connor. What if O'Connor is The Edge of Darkness? What if O'Connor created the whole thing himself? But I found this report about a blond guy years ago saying the same kind of things. So who knows? Anyway, played or not played, I have to get to the bottom of it and find out the truth. We need to right this whole sinking ship. So all right, for Christ sakes, I'll meet you."

Von straightened up in the car seat, stared straight ahead, and focused one hundred percent on the communication. "Great, thank you. I think we should meet at the square in downtown Ligonier. In the gazebo. Tomorrow, October eighteenth at three p.m."

"Right, gotcha."

"You will let me go? You won't follow me? Take me in?"

"I'll let you go. I give you my word. There are too many unanswered questions in this case."

Greg probably had to grit his teeth to say that. He's putting his entire trust in me, something he's not used to. Nothing like stretching the comfort zone. "Fantastic. You won't be sorry. See you then."

"Okay. Yep. Done."

~

The next day, Stone got into his red Ford and headed for downtown Ligonier to meet Von in the gazebo. He arrived at the square at one fifty-three and parked alongside the square in front of Valley Dairy. Glancing around, he walked across the street and aimed for the gazebo. The trees were beautiful that time of year, and the sun reflected off the pines in the gazebo. Stone lost himself in the moment, admiring the gorgeous day, wishing he'd have more of these kinds of days, being lost in the sun, having no problems except what to have for lunch. Maybe someday.

He made his way up to the gazebo and, realizing he was early, pulled out his phone to check Messenger.

Someone called his name. "Mr. Stone!"

He looked around. Von Roberts strode up the walkway from the other end of the gazebo. He nodded as she walked up and motioned her to come closer.

"Thanks for coming," she said.

"You think this place is safe?" Stone asked.

"Well, Ligonier's pretty far from the action ..."

"Yeah, I guess so. Let's get this over with."

"Sure." She sat down, opened her brown rucksack and pulled out a DVD, a folder with a thick document, and a collection of pictures. "These, Mr. Stone, are a collection of evidence that I'm sure you will find very interesting. This"—she waved the DVD—"is a series of interviews with four men who have the very same stories as O'Connor: they were set up and blackmailed by The Edge of Darkness to provide a service for an outcome."

Greg took the DVD. "Uh-huh. It's just a DVD. Just interviews, guys talking. Doesn't mean a thing."

Von gave him a look of exasperation before handing him the folder. "And this is a detailed document that explains each story in depth and describes a prison in which these guys were housed for months. It describes scenes, voices, and happenings."

"Yeah, same deal. A written document without any proof attached. I think you should be going back to—"

"But this," Von interrupted, "will surely get your attention." She took out some blurry pictures, obviously taken on a smartphone camera in a hurried and haphazard fashion. "They were taken by O'Connor during his escape from that fortress. He said he saw this room from a ladder that led up from the sub-basement when the group was on their way out."

The pictures showed some kind of control room, complete with monitors, maps, gadgets, and control personnel. Greg frowned. "Wait. What group? What men? On their way out where? This is all hearsay! You could be the biggest brunt of a huge—"

"Just read it! It's all in there!" Von, almost livid, jabbed her finger at the DVD and the document. "Every last minute of each one's encounter with that group. Every last second, every last word. Just watch it; read it. Then you'll know. Sure, it's just DVDs and words. But it's all true!"

"Can't you just tell me about it? I don't have time to sit there and watch things and read things."

"No, you have to watch it and read it. You promised me, gave me your word that we'd do it my way. Watch it. Please!"

Stone was indeed intrigued, but wasn't sure how much. He got up, nodded, and took the rucksack, then he paused and bit his thumbnail, looking Von directly in the eyes.

She stuck out her hand. They shook. And not another word was said. He walked out of the gazebo and across the street to his car.

~

At seven in the evening, Greg Stone got a scotch on the rocks, then sat down on the lumpy sofa, perched Von's thirty-three-page document on his lap, and started the DVD. "Okay, Von Roberts. Let's see what ya got."

He pored over both the homemade DVD and the document, trying to figure out if this stuff was actually true.

"What are they trying to do here? It sounded like the stuff was actually true. The contents of the video slowly sucked him into the situation. The talks from each person seemed to be honest, and with that Stone felt the stories were on the up and up. He tried to find inconsistencies and discrepancies in each person, one by one, but couldn't.

Does this story read like fiction or non-fiction?

He combed the document from cover to cover twice and watched the DVD three times. It compelled him, made him think. Made him wonder. And he came to see it more as non-fiction. Why would those people lie? Would they go to the trouble to look disheveled and exhausted only to lie?

The freaking Edge of Darkness put those guys through a hell of a ringer.

Finally, at eleven-thirty p.m., Greg Stone decided he believed Brad, Von, and the others, whomever they might be. He punched the note function and the microphone icon on his phone. It dinged— ready to record. He recorded some notes for the morning, hoping it would do voice to text well:

October 20 0600 hours assemble team at HQ ammo, grenades, bulletproofs, Darrera, Paxton.

The note function took time, but worked. He pushed DONE at the top right corner.

His plan was to get everyone together and follow Tombo's lead to wherever that took them. His crew had followed every lead they'd got, from asking neighbors to following the lead for the duffle bag with the gold and purple logo on the side. That's where their luck had stopped. Stone felt empowered to be on the case now. He had a deep feeling that he'd play a major role in ending this whole thing. And for that, he decided to believe Brad, Von, and the rest of those people. He had the Find Guys on the case. Darrera was even under his watchful eye, for the time being. He was ready to go in for the kill. Two minutes after taking the note, Stone fell asleep with the DVD on and the document still in his lap.

~

The next morning before dawn, Brad, Von and the gang got into camouflage clothes Barry had given them and began loading up the black Toyota Rav 4 with serious weaponry.

"Be careful with that!" Brad instructed as Clem fumbled a grenade launcher.

Skin didn't fare too much better at hoisting the huge machine gun out of the closet and onto his shoulder. "Shit, this beast is heavy!" he yelled.

They planned to leave early enough to get to their target around seven a.m. the following day, while the guard was low. They could sneak in then, and if that idea failed, they'd have a little more prep time.

"Not sure if I like this idea, but we have to do what we have to do," Frank said.

Brad stared at him. "You're right, Frank. It's the right and only thing to do, and it'll all work out in the end," he said with conviction, then he handed Frank two shotguns, a night scope, and seven bulletproof vests, and nodded for him to go to the car.

Frank sighed. "Yeah, that's why I'm here."

When they'd finished loading equipment into the Rav, it was seven fifteen.

Von walked out. "You almost ready?" she asked Brad.

"Yep. We should leave soon."

"Listen, I know this is my idea, and things may turn out to be a total nightmare. I just want you to know that I am trying to help, and I think this is in our best interest. We need to see and document exactly what's going on in that place. The last thing I want to do is to put you guys back in there."

"I'm not arguing. I think we need to do this, too. We could be helping to stop a disaster of immense proportions."

Brad and crew walked to the car and climbed in. Brad looked around at the weary faces. "Okay, everybody, this could get serious. We know we're not warriors, gang members, drug lords, none of the above; we're just normal people, trying to make things right." They stared into each other's eyes. "Everybody ready?" Heads turned and nods were given.

"Yep."

"Me too."

"I gotcha."

"Our plan is to take it slowly today and canvass the situation. No rushing. Everybody agree?"

They all nodded wearily.

"Okay. Let's go put an end to this thing."

Barry, who was driving, started the car, and they crept slowly down the gravel drive, back towards Morley Heights on the other side of Uniontown, back to that ornate house in the woods, and back to that terrible prison.

"We should stay on the back roads," Brad said. "It's doubtful that any cop cars would normally be on this road, but with this manhunt on, the cops might be out in droves." *But if we get stopped, we could always ask for Greg Stone.*

They left the driveway and picked up speed. Taking back roads was Barry's specialty. He was, after all, a Pennsylvania prepper. When rounding down around New Stanwick, they heard a siren and saw a mass of police cars zooming down the road towards them from the opposite direction. Barry, quick as a cat, turned the car left onto Sewickley Street and stopped in a yard behind one of the houses.

"Okay, get down! Put these over you." Barry handed them two worn but clean blankets, and the scapegoats hastily pulled them over their heads.

The police cars slowed down as they passed through the borough.

"Don't even breathe," Barry said as the gang waited beneath their blankets. "We don't want to give the cops any reason to investigate."

Brad heard cars turn down the street they were in. They came closer, and closer, but then faded away again. Brad's stomach seemed to have lodged in his throat. They waited longer, and when they finally heard the cars head out of town, Brad and the others moved for the first time in minutes.

"I think it's safe now." Barry started the car again and backed out of the yard.

"Phew, that was a close one," Skin exclaimed, pushing off the blanket.

Clem popped up beside him, his eyes wide. "Shit, I'll say."

They got back on the road to Uniontown and drove on towards Morley Heights, where they'd head back into the woods.

"You sure you know where this place is?" Barry asked.

Von nodded. "Pretty much. The events of last week had a big impression on me. I'll find it again."

"Ya know, I just thought of something," Clem said.

"What's that?" Brad asked.

"What if we get down there, and nobody's there? What if the whole place is gone?"

"You saw the place! It's a fortress, undefeatable. The first floor is not all there is to that building."

"I know, but what if it's just a façade? What if they can move it? Just a thought, but what if?"

Brad fought back a sigh, reminding himself that this was coming from the mind of a man who'd been locked in a cave for months. No light of day, no TV, no reality. Of course, his mind would wander ... perhaps to places beyond. This was the imagination of a caged man.

"I guess we'll just have to wait and see," he said, and looked at Von in the front seat, who peered back at him.

The car kept driving, not too fast, not too slow. The last thing they needed was to attract attention. No one knew their car, no one knew their whereabouts, and no one knew their next move. For that, Brad was grateful.

~

Juan was finally satisfied. *All the parts in play, pass go and collect two hundred dollars.* He'd spent around two months checking the mole from head to toe, sparing no expense to get it outfitted with everything he could think of for a relentless underground weapon. Now it was locked and loaded. Ready to go.

Official launch day, October nineteenth, had finally arrived. Lorel Hudson started the mole and moved it out onto the ground under the trees where he saw daylight for the first time in months. Lorel stopped it there and stuck his head into the engine casing in the front of the machine.

"Let's get that thing underground, where she belongs!" Juan yelled. Things were never done fast enough.

"We're almost ready to go," Lorel said from deep inside the engine casing. "Just tightening up a few more screws."

"What's the plan, boss?" Catorso asked with caution. "Same entry point as before?"

"That should do. Are we set? Is the nuclear reactor safe? Do we have the warheads intact?"

"Yes and yep, four warheads on each side. You operate with the remote control. Push the lever up, hit the switch to the up position. Push the number corresponding to the warhead you want to fire, and push the red square button on the bottom. That will send the missiles up through the ground and into the air."

"Gotcha. Don't forget to say goodbye to your loved ones. Ya might be gone for a while. By the way, Catorso, good job."

Catorso gave an elated grin. Juan saying he'd done a good job was as rare as winning a gold medal in the Olympics. "Thanks, boss!"

Juan glared at him and barked, "Call Patina to get over here! Let's get out o' here. We are The Edge of Darkness, and we're almost ready to take on our next mission under the guise of the scapegoat protocol!" Juan looked at both of them with a sneer and motioned for them to come along.

They went to the back of the fortress, where they'd stored their gear two weeks ago.

"This shit's been here so long I forget what I packed," Catorso complained.

Patina chuckled.

Juan pulled his pack out of the back closet. "Always ready, right here with me."

Juan got into the mole first and went up to the cockpit. Though little more than a cubbyhole, it had to do. Ten feet across, it had chairs placed in a circle under the windshield, a dining area towards the back, and behind that the barracks. Then came the tiny bathroom and an equally tiny shower, and in the very back of the beast sat the firing room with the warheads loaded on the top.

The others got in and took their places in the command center. Catorso started the mole, and it came to life with a mighty rumble. They let it warm up, then inched it out along the path to the entrance to the tunnel they'd created when they'd tested the mole previously.

Catorso turned to Juan. "Ready?" After seeing nods from both men, he pointed the nose down the hole and jettisoned forward.

The thing wiggled and made its way down, and further down, spewing soil and rock and jiggling all the while. For a moment, Juan thought it might jiggle them right out of creation, but it kept going down and moving forward—into oblivion. *Next stop: Washington, D.C.*

The twenty-second century mole with nuclear capability slowly but evenly churned its way through the hard bedrock under western Pennsylvania, a difficult feat. The mole took a tremendous amount of energy, and the interior grew hot. After being underground for two hours, tempers flared easily.

In the cockpit, Catorso, Patina, and Juan examined the underground scan of Washington, D.C., rife with subways, sewage systems, electrical cables, waterways, and the like. Continuing straight to D.C. would not be an easy task.

Catorso went over the plan. He had to get close enough to attack the Capitol building, then move to the White House to capture President fucking Flood, the vice president, the first lady, and the defense secretary.

Juan looked over Catorso's shoulder.

"Yes?"

"So what's happening here? Where in shit's name are we? The computer says we're still under Uniontown? What the hell is taking so long? We shoulda been at least to Maryland by now!"

"Yeah, well, things take time. This fucking machine isn't perfect." The beast punctuated his statement with an extra loud rumble. "We had some problems with the melting and movement. But it seems to be making progress now."

"How about the warhead? Is it still intact and ready?"

"Yeah, of course. We wouldn't let anything happen to the precious warhead!"

"Just be careful they don't go off in your face!"

216

"Don't worry, I'm not stupid!" And with that the mole pushed forward inch by inch.

They made progress during the next half hour, but still not up to Juan's expectations. Even so, excitement bubbled up in him at the thought that they were making the goal a reality. When the EOD got the president, they would be the most powerful organization in the world, and no one was going to stop them now.

~

On Thursday, October nineteenth, Tombo from the Find Guys stood in the downtown office of the Latrobe Press. He'd discovered that Von Roberts first broke the story of the abortion clinic shooting—over two weeks ago now. Tombo identified himself as Tim Richardson, attorney. His story was that he had a client who had some beef with Von after she'd done a story on him and he wanted to sue for slander.

He spoke to the chief editor, Darin Blank. "Well, she took a leave of absence about a week ago. Said she was going to try to uncover this mystery. Haven't heard from her since."

"Okay. Do you happen to have Von's address or contact information? It's crucial for our client to get this resolved. And it's best for her to stop it going to court."

"Sure, just a minute." Darin Blank went to fetch her file.

While Blank flipped through the filing cabinet, Tombo reached over the desk and slid open the top drawer of Blank's desk, just out of curiosity. The story of the abortion clinic shooting, with Brad on the cover, lay directly on the top. Tombo moved the paper and saw the story of the second shooting. *So here's the stories about the guy. Never had a chance to see the articles.* Tombo read the first few lines of the top paper. A few moments

217

later, sensing Blank was about to come back, Tombo stopped reading and slid the drawer quietly shut—just before Blank walked in.

"I really appreciate this," Tombo said as he handed him the information.

"I'm not supposed to be doing this—privacy and all." Blank looked directly at Tombo's face for a moment. He must have decided that Tombo looked trustworthy because he wrote down Von's address, home number, cell number, and affiliations. "I trust that in return you'll make sure your client doesn't sue."

"I'll do my best." Tombo thought that Blank himself must have more questions than answers.

After his meeting at the Latrobe Press, Tombo worked his way to Von's address, a little two-story, red-brick house on Chestnut in Youngwood. Didn't look like anyone was home, but one never knows. Tombo got out of the car, strode up to the front door and punched the doorbell. No one came. He was about to leave when an elderly white man opened the door with the safety chain still attached. He peered out over grandpa spectacles, white hair glistening in the sun.

"Hello, I'm looking for a Ms. Von Roberts," Tombo asked.

The man flinched. "And who might you be?"

"I'm a lawyer. And I need to talk to Von about a story she did a while ago."

"Don't give me that crap! I know Von like the back of my hand. She never said anything about any lawyer."

Tombo was sunk. He felt like an a-hole and an idiot. This man was obviously smart as well as observant.

"What's your real story?" the man asked.

"Okay. I was hired to look into this nuclear theft case. With the guy, you know, the guy—"

"Who stole the plutonium ... for that group who blackmailed him?"

Tombo blinked. He felt as if he'd been slapped hard on the back. *So many people already know.*

The man slid the chain off the door and opened it slowly.

"Yeah, how did you—"

"Know about that? I just told you, I know Von like the back of my hand."

"Would you mind telling me who you are?" Tombo asked, wondering why the cops hadn't made it here first. Maybe they had. Maybe it was Tombo's goofy and trustworthy face that led him this far.

"You're looking for Von, then?"

"Yeah, I really need to find her."

"Why?"

"Well, if what this O'Connor guy says is true, this could be the start of World War Three. The cops are looking for them, but haven't zeroed in on anything yet. I'm working with them on this."

"If I tell you anything, I want complete assurance and reassurance."

What's this guy getting at? Does he want money? "Well, we'll give you all the assurance and every credit you deserve. We'll try to make it a hefty sum."

"What do you mean?"

"Reward money."

"She's my daughter we're talking about! I want reassurance for her safety and security, not mere money!"

"Of course, sorry. You'll have it!" *Not a greedy bastard after all.*

"Well, maybe I can help you. Come in."

"Thanks. I'm Tombo." He stuck out his hand to shake, and then presented his business card.

The man gave a quick shake and stared at the card. "Tombo? What kind of a name is that?"

"It's a nickname. Means dragonfly in Japanese."

"Does that name suit you? Are you a dragonfly? Don't look like one to me."

Tombo didn't like the way the man peered directly into his eyes. "It's just a nickname. I don't like to use my real name on my card."

"Maybe it's a name your father used to use for you. To make you feel, well, more able. Come and sit down. Have some coffee." The white chap led him inside and motioned for him to take a seat at the dining room table.

Tombo was getting ticked off with this guy now. How could he see so much in such a short time? "So, by the way, you didn't tell me your name. What's your relationship to Von?"

"Sorry, I was getting to that. I'm her stepfather. The name's Nick."

"Okay, what can you tell me, Nick?" Tombo shot back.

"Just over a week ago, Von said she was leaving to search for this guy after he called her saying he didn't do it. She went to track him down and later texted me, saying she'd seen him being thrown into a van and had followed it to Uniontown."

"Holy crap, do you think that's where she is now?"

"Not sure, haven't heard from her. I've texted her numerous times, though. But no response. She knows this guy Barry who is kind of a prepper in the Laurel Mountains near Ligonier. She could've gone there."

"Hmm. Okay, thanks for your time." Tombo pushed out the chair and stood. The white chap made him nervous.

"You're not leaving so soon, are you?"

"I don't want to take more of your time."

"Time, my son, is all I have."

"Uh, can I ask ... what kind of relationship do you have with Von? A good one?" Tombo sat down again.

"Yeah. Sure. Being her stepfather, she looks up to me. Her mom and I hooked up after her father left when Von was seven. He was kind of a disgruntled guy. Her mom died when Von was sixteen. She had nowhere else to turn."

"Sorry to hear that. How did her mother die?"

"Murdered. A young black woman in Pennsylvania with no future except drugs and violence sometimes ends up like that. And that's why Von became a reporter, I think. She never said so, but I think she had a yearning to report these things, to turn bad into good. She had to work mighty hard to keep a job and get respect."

"Yes, I can imagine. That's why I really need to find her." Tombo's demeanor softened. "My partner and I were the Find Guys, but he was in an accident ... he didn't make it," he said sadly. "We, uh, I, can find anyone, anyplace, anytime." *I think I still can, without Bobber.*

"Here, have another cup of coffee." The white chap laughed and slapped Tombo on the back.

Night fell as they drank more coffee. Nick's phone dinged and he checked it.

"What's up?" Tombo asked.

"I think you and I had better stay somewhat close," the old man said. "I've been around and can always help a dragonfly."

Tombo frowned. *This guy is a bit creepy.*

"I want to come with you. On your hunt for Von."

Tombo stood. "I'm not sure if that's a good idea. I wouldn't want anything to happen to Von's relative."

221

"Yeah, well, you let me worry about that, will ya? I just got this." He stood and showed Tombo a text that read: *Just want to let you know I'm safe. We're heading to Uniontown area because that's where we think a terrible terrorist group is. Just wanted to let you know in case something happens. We're planning to get there in the morning.*

"Whoa!" Tombo exclaimed as he read the text. "We need to get down there. You can ride with me."

"Hehe, not so fast, Tombo. We've got to make sure we have our provisions set." The old man walked to the closet and got out a 12-gauge shotgun and a .44 magnum. "Hope you know how to use these, just in case." The man shot him a glance over the glasses balanced on the end of his nose.

"I'm licensed." Tombo reached for his wallet.

"I trust ya. I say we leave at dawn. There's no sense going down there now when we can't see anything."

"Okay, probably a good idea. I'll check it out on Google maps. Do we know where we're going exactly?"

"Not exactly. But we can, at least, head off in that direction."

"Are you sure you know what you're doing? I mean we could get caught up in some crap here."

"I know as much as you. And you're supposed to be the 'Find Guy', right?" The old man-made quotation marks in the air.

"We can find anything!" Tombo said, going back to Superman mode.

~

The day after meeting with Von Roberts, Greg Stone got a hot cup of coffee, picked up the stray *Herald*, and randomly started reading The Born Loser. In it, Wilbur asked his father why they couldn't watch the movie they'd both voted for and whether or not majority rules. His father responded with the fact that his mother is always the majority no matter how many votes they had. Greg chuckled. *A page out of my own life.*

He opened the Internet and got on Messenger. The Find Guys had sent a new message. "About time, Jesus."

New Message
Find Guys   4:16 p.m.
Greg Stone,
Getting closer to nailing this on the head. In Youngwood and may have news soon.
Tombo

Stone closed Messenger and sent a quick email about the message to Dom.

At seven forty-two that evening, Greg Stone hit the police department's app to link up with police radios. His goal was to find Paxton. He located him in Car Forty-Five on route Lincoln Highway East past Barnes and Noble and gave him a call.

"Hey, Pax, can you get over to Youngwood? Got word from those Find Guys that something may go down there. Not sure what, when, where. Just be on the lookout."

"Will do. It'll take me a few to get there, but I'm on my way."

"Ten-Four."

"Hey, Stone? Did O'Connor really do it?"

"Not sure yet. He says he didn't, says he was set up, and I guess it's possible. Anything is. Anyway, go to the Knight's Inn, check in, and stay put till you hear from me."

Next, Greg Stone called Dom Darrera, who was probably still in his office even on a chilly Thursday evening. Darrera picked up the phone on the first ring. "Hey, Stone."

"Dom, I got a message from the Find Guys. They tracked down Von Roberts to a place in Youngwood."

"Yeah, I just got your message. Why didn't I get it sooner, Stone?"

"We've been a bit crazy over here. There are a million things happening right and left. Anyway, they're following up on it and are about to let us know the next move, whatever that may be. I've got Pax over there now."

"You know I am a police lieutenant, the chief here. I expect to be told these things and to be kept in the fucking loop. You might want to get over there yourself by the way!"

In his mind's eye, Stone saw Dom stare out the window, as he usually did.

"Don't worry. I'm on the case," Stone replied. And the phone went dead.

He suspected that Dom was losing some pride. He was a police lieutenant who'd given away their power to some small private outfit that was doing a better job at finding bad guys than the police were.

Stone bit his bottom lip and ran a hand through his shaggy hair. *Fuck. Am I going to let him go down like this? Will his career end with everyone knowing that he's a useless police lieutenant who couldn't get the job done? And who leads a useless department?*

~

Carmine Brant and the EOD's only female member, Debra Stiles, manned the fortress control room during the night and early morning.

Stiles, seated at the control desk in front of the computers, said: "The mole's progress was pretty slow and bumpy at first but it's steadied out now. After all that fixing and upgrading, it's supposed to be ready for action."

"It has no problem with the top layer of soil," Brant responded. "The going gets tougher when they hit bedrock. It's programmed to go at thirty feet per second, by the time they get up to speed, but it takes a bit of time to get there. That'll get them to Washington in ten hours. Let's hope they don't run into any problems in the bedrock."

Stiles put down the manual and looked back at the computers on the desk. The monitor in the fortress showed the progressing movement of the mole underground in Pennsylvania. She stared at the movement and the trail they'd programmed it to take through the bedrock, moving southeast and then east, towards Washington, D.C., then opened the Comm to Patina in the cockpit. "Comm A to Comm B, your engines show a bit of heating up—slow it down to twenty feet per second briefly, can you?"

"Ten-four. What's the nuclear rock-melting device say? We're okay getting through the bedrock, right? Is everything turning to glass correctly?"

"Checking glass burn and rock melt ... just a sec ..." Stiles checked the monitor. "Glass melt looks good. You're paving a virtual underground glass tube. Can be used for centuries to come." She looked over at Brant, who was busy programming information into the computer. He looked over and smirked.

"Ten-four, Comm A. My question is," Patina said from the mole's cockpit, "am I going to be able to get on the same path back to the fortress after the deed?"

"No. You have to come out at some other point."

"Shit. All right."

"We'll just move to some other point and come up at coordinates. It should be okay."

"Better F-in' hope so."

"We'll get you back, don't worry. For now, I need you to descend to one hundred and eighteen feet, speed up to twenty-five feet per minute then to thirty-three."

"Roger, descending to one hundred and eighteen feet, then nuclear speed up to ten feet per second." Patina paused, as if waiting for the mole to catch up. "Now up to twenty," Patina said.

The mole finally kicked in, and began working its way through the soil, and finally into bedrock. Catorso's voice came over the comm. "Jesus, this thing is a swift and nasty beast."

Patina laughed. "And it's taking us to the top of glory world."

Catorso gave a snicker loud enough for Stiles to hear over the comm. "We'll either be glorified or vilified," he retorted.

"Ten-four, Comm A. Over," Patina added suddenly, as if he'd forgotten Stiles was still listening in.

"Comm B. Out."

CHAPTER 16

The day grew into evening. Brad, Von and the crew were making headway through the Pennsylvania woods, where leaves, already turning orange and red, glistened in the evening sun. They veered off the road several times with Von exclaiming, "Wait! I think it's around here!" only to have her say later that she was wrong.

The woods stretched for miles and, seemingly endlessly, took on a similar view. It was difficult to know where one was because the woods all looked the same, and this fortress was not something you could put into the GPS navigator. Brad, too, from time to time, thought he knew where they were, but alas, no. They kept driving.

All of a sudden, they came to a small bridge and a fork in the road. "Hang on," Brad said. "I remember this. It's where the driver looked around and asked me if I'd learned that I was theirs yet. Holy crap, keep going ... uh ... to the left!" And further on: "Wait! This is around where Von almost drove us off the road."

"Oh my God, Brad, you're right. I remember that little dip off right there!"

They kept driving.

"Jus' tell me where ta go!" Anticipation laced Barry's voice.

"Don't worry; will do!"

They kept looking, relentlessly searching the woods for anything that would lead them in the right direction.

Barry made good time through the woods on a narrow, windy road. By six forty-five, being late October, in the woods it was already dark. Matted leaves lay on the side of the road, appearing black in the moonlight, which made it hard to tell where the road ended and the woods began. Brad feared Von was losing track of where she was.

He glanced over at her in the front seat. "Are we getting close?"

"Uh, I think so," Von said with a frown as she peered into the dark.

"Concentrate," Barry said. He glanced at Brad. "This look familiar?"

Both Brad and Von studied the surroundings. Fortunately, the fall moon was quite bright that night.

"Just keep going really slowly," Brad said. "And everyone look through the woods. Maybe we can see that fortress through the trees. Remember what it looked like? I do. It was a freaking veritable castle." He grabbed the army binoculars from Barry's camouflage bag and scanned the area.

"I remember, too," Von said. "It was scary, and weird. It's hard to see in the dark, but that day I followed you I parked alongside the gravel driveway, and I could see it through the woods. And there were still leaves on the trees then. I remember coming around a huge bend to the left ..."

Just as she said that, the van took a big bend to the left.

"Slow down! This looks familiar. Wait, look through there!"

Brad lowered the binoculars, squinted through the branches of the trees, and then raised them to his eyes again. The turning leaves made it hard to see anything distinct that was of the same color, but he caught an angle, a shape unseen in nature, reflecting moonlight. "Stop," he said.

Barry brought the Rav 4 to a quick halt.

"Look." Brad put the binoculars down and pointed at the right side of the road, to the left of the rearview mirror. All eyes followed. Through the trees they caught a view of the side of a brown-brick building, a sight that let them know they were on the right track. "See? There it is." Brad handed the binoculars to Clem, who peered into them like a pro.

"Holy fucking cow," Clem muttered. "There it is."

"Let's go on further and stash the car," Von said.

"Gotcha." Barry put it into gear and pulled forward slowly. A little farther on, Barry drove the car between a bunch of pine trees to the left of the road, a spot where they would be unseen and, hopefully, safe.

"Let's wait here until close to morning to see if anything comes or goes," Von suggested. "Then we can make our way to the back of the building and see if we can find that tunnel entrance."

"Sounds good." Brad figured they were about half a mile away.

"I'm ready." Skin sounded like he was trying to have confidence.

They surveyed the situation without a word spoken for around three hours, then Von said, "I think I should get some back-up on this. Just in case. I'll text Stone."

She typed in the following, then showed it to Brad:

We are at the fortress where The Edge of Darkness has their headquarters. I'll turn on my location finder so it's visible. Please try to locate us and send back-up.

Brad shrugged, but didn't object, and neither did anyone else. Now they were here, anxiety rose in his gut.

He remembered the bullet in Rock's head and the sound of Longhair's execution. The worst they faced with the cops was prison; he didn't want that, of course, but if The Edge of Darkness caught them, they'd be slaughtered.

Von pushed the 'Send' button.

Nothing came or went, and around four a.m. on Friday, October twentieth the gang got out of the car and grabbed their gear. It was barely dawn. After walking for several minutes, they came to a pine with a huge trunk that angled in two directions. They put down the gear and looked at each other.

"Shhh," Barry whispered. "Looks like this is a good place to gather. Anything happens, let's make this the meeting point."

"Sounds good to me," Clem whispered back.

Von whipped out a plastic spray bottle and started spraying the ground.

"What the hell is that?" Skin exclaimed. "Fine time to be bug spraying!"

"It's not bug killer," Von retorted. "It makes the leaves wet so they won't make noises while we're walking around."

"It's fall; leaves crunch when you walk on them," Brad said with confidence.

Von looked over with a grin. "Only someone who's spent a lot of time in the woods in the fall knows that one."

"Yeah, well, I lost a lot of time playing army in the woods when I was a kid. Anyway, if we get separated or if we run into gunfire, come back here." Brad looked around. "Everybody in?"

"Yeah, I'm good."

"Me, too."

"Let's go, then." Brad moved to take the lead but Barry stepped out in front of him.

"Brad, wait. If you go first, there's a chance they may see you and recognize you and those other boys, too. Von and I will take the lead, if it's all the same to you."

Brad stopped and put his hand up to halt the group. He wanted to be the one to save everyone and everything, but he knew Barry was right. "Okay, you're right." He motioned Barry and Von in front, and they set off, creeping into the dark woods.

It took about forty-five minutes for Barry and the crew to get to the east side of the building. They stayed about one hundred yards from the structure, aware that being seen by those inside might suddenly screw up their mission.

"This place looks dead," Clem whispered. "I wonder if anyone's in there."

"Just because it looks dead doesn't mean there's no one there," Brad said.

Just then the gang felt the earth shaking from somewhere down deep and heard a distant rumbling. They stopped in mid-step.

Brad frowned. "What the ...?"

"Holy shit, what's that?" Skin's voice rose in pitch.

"Feels like an earthquake," Frank said. "I was in Japan during the 1995 Kanto earthquake long before The Edge of Darkness and this whole mess started."

"There aren't usually earthquakes in Pennsylvania," Barry said.

"Let's wait a second," Clem said. "It seems to be going away..."

They waited.

"There; it's stopped," Von said when they could no longer feel the shaking or hear the rumbling. "Okay, let's take this slowly and creep around to the back. I remember this ... don't forget, I've already been this way once."

They crept around the building with Von spraying the dry and newly fallen leaves before every foot step. The wet leaves emitted less sound, but with every step they were still in danger of cracking small twigs, kicking a rock, or attracting attention from the dogs they knew must be in there somewhere.

They continued downward and parallel to the building. Once they cleared some rocks, they realized that the gate where Von had picked them up loomed below them to the right. They paused and gathered their composure.

~

Tombo sat at the table on the early morning of Friday, sipping the fresh coffee he'd just received from Von's stepfather. "What role is Von playing in all of this, do you think?"

"My guess is that Von, with all of her reporter's drive, made friends with the guy who stole the plutonium; what's his name?"

"O'Connor."

"Right. I think she believed he was in serious trouble and decided to help him. I don't think she'll stop until she succeeds."

"Is that the kind of girl she's always been?"

"Oh yeah. She's a trooper."

"How do you mean?"

"When she was about sixteen, she had this friend Julie, who was overweight. Nice enough gal. She started to get bullied in school and the bullying got relentless. You know how nasty kids can be. Von stuck by her side and told her to ignore it, that she was better than that, that she was a great girl. Well, the bullying never stopped, and after graduation Julie took her own life. Her parents found her hanging in the basement. Von was both devastated and livid when she heard that. She elicited the help of several friends, made some protest signs, took a video camera to school and confronted the kids who'd teased Julie. They hounded them for months, trying to interview them every time they saw them, asking why they bullied Julie like that, loudly and in front of everyone. That drew major attention to the issue. It embarrassed the kids so much that one boy quit school, and a girl's grades dropped so badly she was taken off partial scholarship. That made Von happy. It was the first time I knew what power the combination of devastation and anger can have."

"That's an amazing story. I guess being a reporter's in her blood."

"Yeah, I guess so. Anyway, let's get this show on the road! I think if we leave now, we'll have plenty of time to find Von." Nick pushed in his chair and grabbed his jacket and knapsack with the equipment. They headed out to the driveway, where they got into Nick's old red Chevy Nova. "Hope she's okay." Nick turned away as he loaded his knapsack into the car.

"Well, she's your stepdaughter," Tombo said.

"Yeah, what does that mean?"

"I think she's probably fine."

"I guess that's a compliment, then. I'll text her. You text your friend, Stone, and let him know what we're doing."

Phones in hand, they started texting:

Von! Where are you now? We're coming to help you. Dad

Mr. Stone,

*We're going after Von and crew. Will text our location
soon.*
Tombo

   They drove down the highway leading out of
Youngwood and sped off towards Uniontown.

~

At five-forty-two a.m., the gang made their way down the
hill, making as little noise as possible, with Barry leading.
However, Clem stepped on a twig, and a loud crack
ricocheted into the air.
   They got to the bottom of the slope and peered
through the trees at the tunnel opening. It looked the
same as it had when they'd broken out in wild run. Brad
suddenly felt apprehensive.
   Brad put a finger to his lips and then motioned for
them to move on carefully. He stopped them some way
back from the tunnel, walked up alone to check the
opening, then returned and made an 'O' with his thumb
and forefinger before gesturing for them to follow him.
   Barry stopped at the entrance to the long, dark tunnel
and whispered, "Well, folks, here we are. We've got to get
this done with and move on to the next level. All ready?
Brad?"
   Nods from everyone. Brad gave a thumb's up.
   "Let's go, then. I'll go first," Barry said with confidence.
He made a come-on gesture with two fingers.
   They squeezed through the opening they'd exited
from five days earlier, sneaking in with guns drawn. Von
almost tripped over a ragged shirt that lay bloody and
frayed on the side of the tunnel. She gasped and everyone
stopped, wide eyes turned to her.
   Brad walked over. "That was Longhair's," he
whispered, remembering the horrible sound of poor

Longhair being beaten to a pulp. He swallowed, took a deep breath and took the lead, continuing on down the tunnel, gun drawn.

A sound came from farther in, beyond their line of sight. They paused and Barry and the gang watched as Brad stepped cautiously forward. A man suddenly appeared from the left and flipped the rifle he wielded directly at Brad's head.

"Thanks for joining us, Mr. O'Connor!" he hissed.

Brad flinched, but, trusting that Barry would keep the group, now about fifteen feet behind, quiet and out of sight, he turned and looked at the man.

"What in the hell are you doing here?" he asked.

"Sorry, I must've gotten lost down here," Brad lied smoothly as if he'd been doing it all his life. "I was doing some sightseeing and my car broke down. So I was trying to make it back to town, when I thought I'd ..." Brad looked around and let out a short laugh.

"Yeah? You just accidentally found this place, huh?"

"Yeah, you know, just came upon it, and ... uh..."

"Ha! This place is in the middle of nowhere and hidden in the woods. You can't just find it."

Suddenly Brad heard a noise from behind him.

The man turned towards the sound. "Hey, who's that back there?" he asked, peering into the darkness.

Out of his peripheral vision, Brad caught sight of Barry's greying hair and realized that Barry was racing for the man. Barry grabbed the man by the neck of his shirt, and pulled him over.

Clem also ran up and launched himself on the man, his octopus-like arms folding around the man's waistline.

The man fell on his side. "Ump. Ow!" He struggled to get free. "Arrghh! Let go of me!"

Clem pushed the man farther to the ground, yelling, "You're not going anywhere!"

Barry stood. "Guys, get over here! We need help." The rest of the crew raced forward and landed punches on the stranger. "Hey, don't kill the guy! Get a sock in that mouth!"

"We don't have an extra sock, Barry!" Brad yelled.

"I do." Barry took off his shoe, yanked off his sock and stuffed it into the man's mouth.

"Von, do you have any rope or anything?" Brad asked.

"Not really, just my belt, and my ..."

"What?

"My bra." She brought her hands inside her shirt, unclasped her bra, and dragged it out from one of the shirtsleeves. "It's a girl's trick," she said. "Here ya go." She tossed over the bra.

"Good. Let's tie him up." Barry pointed at the man being held down by the knees of Clem, Skin, Frank, and Brad. "The belt on his hands, and the bra around his face and through his mouth."

The man kept struggling, trying to break free, and screaming through the sock, but to no avail. He hacked with the sock stuck in, as if gagging. And then the bra went on.

Brad glared at the man. "We should keep him with us. We can use him as a pawn."

"Hey, that's not a bad idea." Barry looked at Clem and Frank. "Take him; keep him close. Do not let him go!"

"We won't," Clem said.

The eagerness with which they held the man amazed Brad. He looked almost mummified.

This guy ain't goin' nowhere.

The men yanked their captive close, and Clem tied the man's hands behind him. "Just for good measure," Clem said as he turned back to the group.

"Thanks, Clem," Barry said.

Brad motioned to the group to gather around him. "After that, I think we really need to be on alert." He looked around the group, noting their eager assent.

"Let's get to that staircase," Von prompted. "It's now or never."

"Yeah, but stay close, and keep quiet. Especially him." Barry pointed at the stranger. "Brad, you lead."

"Okay, everybody. After me."

They kept moving slowly, inching their way down the tunnel without a sound. The only light they had was a dim glow from the morning light seeping in from the entrance and a tiny light bulb down the tunnel.

After about fifty feet, Brad stopped them. "I think it's best if you guys wait here, and only I go up there and see what's going on. Just in case." He looked around to make sure everyone was paying attention. They were, and they nodded in agreement.

They stayed put, and Brad kept going, not stopping until he reached the rickety staircase that led up to the landing with the ladder at the top. Brad looked back at the crew, motioned them to stay where they were and pointed to the top of the stairs. They gave a brief nod. Brad ascended the staircase.

Quiet as a mouse, he made it to the landing he'd stepped onto five days prior, then climbed the ladder to the top. Once there, he listened for a moment—nothing— then slowly and quietly cracked open the hatch. He heard fans, no doubt used to cool the computer CPUs, and waited with bated breath in case someone had heard the hatch open, but no other sounds emerged.

He peered through the crack at the huge left-hand monitor on the wall facing the control booth. A picture of the interior of what looked like some kind of cockpit came on, the camera located at the top looking down. Brad saw hands moving a joystick and fingers pushing buttons and swiping commands on a screen. The cockpit appeared to have a window that looked out to something dark.

What is that? Not water. What? Soil?

What on earth was he seeing? The monitor on the right showed stats. Brad squinted to read the labels: fuel, water level, burn, reactor, glass tubing. A map on the right side showed a dotted line in Pennsylvania that followed no road. It went across West Virginia, part of Maryland, part of Virginia and all the way to Washington, D.C. The map clearly showed the Pentagon, the Capitol building, the Mall, the Ellipse, and the White House. The dotted line curved across the Potomac where no bridge existed, and then crossed Route 395 and continued right through, cutting through suburbs and ignoring roads as if no buildings existed, to stop at the White House. A dot moved slowly along the line—the vehicle whose cockpit showed on the monitor? Such a route could only be followed in the air or beneath the ground. Day would be breaking outside, so the darkness in the window of that cockpit could only mean that the vehicle was underground. Was that even possible? As far as Brad knew no tunnel ran that route.

Suddenly, on the left monitor, a picture of President Frederick Flood appeared with his open mouth and pointing finger, as he'd been portrayed in the media on so many occasions. Flood hadn't made many friends with his matter-of-fact rhetoric and his pompous, arrogant style of speaking or "Flood Talk" as news-show hosts referred to it. He'd made many enemies, in fact, and had brought to the presidency the okay for normal Americans to be as racist and arrogant as he was. He was ripping away at the heart of the nation. But why was his picture on this screen?

More numbers appeared on the right monitor; they looked like some kind of weapon stats. A sudden shiver raced up Brad's spine. If what he was seeing was what he thought he was seeing, the world was in deep trouble.

Just then, a figure popped up from behind the monitor and walked around the control table—a woman, late thirtyish, wearing some kind of vest. She passed the hatch and went to the front of the console.

The screen flicked again. More movement. Brad knew that at least one person manned the controls in that room, but now he heard voices, indicating more than one. His heart raced. He slowly closed the hatch and retreated back down the ladder to the rest of the crew, who gathered around to hear his report.

"I saw some stats on a monitor up there," Brad whispered as quietly as possible. "And a picture of Flood."

"The president?" Von looked bewildered.

"The very one. You have to see this, but, shhhhh," Brad half mouthed, half whispered. He took off his backpack, pulled out a Ricoh sports camera, and attached the pistol grip. Then he motioned for the others to stay put and pulled on Von's shirtsleeve to get her to follow him up the stairs.

"Look out for us here," Brad told the others before he left. "Don't let that guy get away." He pointed at the tied-up man being led around like a dummy. "If anyone, and I mean *anyone* or *anything*, comes, bang on the stairs quietly twice." His eyes widened, asking if they understood.

"You got it," Clem whispered, then turned to watch the tunnel as Brad and Von began their ascent.

They crept up the staircase, got to the top, and were about to inch open the hatch when Brad looked at Von and mouthed, *"Are we okay?"*

She nodded and mouthed back, *"We are."*

He opened the hatch.

The stats were still there, and this time there was not only a picture of Flood and his pointing finger, but also printed lines after bulleted points under the picture: immigration, nuclear, abortion, and other explanations too far for Brad and Von to see. Brad aimed the Ricoh at the large screen and scanned it over the computers.

Von's face contorted as she squinted to read. She looked over to Brad. He nodded, joining her in disbelief, then pointed the Ricoh at the monitor and moved it around in an effort to get as much of the room as possible on camera. He pointed it here, there, and in every direction, then they clambered back down the ladder and joined the others at the bottom.

"Something's going on up there," he whispered. "Something bad. We have to get this information out. We have to try to stop this thing."

"What is it?" Clem asked. "What are they doing?"

Von chimed in. "It's about Flood. It looks like they want to attack or kill President Flood. And they have this weapon—"

"That moves underground."

"Like that huge, torpedo-shaped thing we saw in the basement of this place!" Clem said.

"Yeah, you're right."

"The thing you told me about, Brad?" Von asked.

"Yep, that's it."

Von turned and looked around and said, "Brad, me, and Barry are going up there to stop this. We need your support."

Frank, Clem and Skin looked at each other and then back at Brad.

Their captive yelled in the sock. It muffled the sound but didn't stop it completely. Barry shoved the bra deeper into his mouth and tightened the bra holding it in place. "I know another way to keep you quiet," Barry hissed. "Wanna push me?"

The man said nothing more.

~

Stone woke up with a start at five-forty-five a.m. He rubbed his stubble and knew he had to get not only his ass but also his crew into gear. He glanced at the phone and sent a message off to Paxton, ignoring the crappy way he felt.

R U there? Haven't heard from the Find Guys yet. Stay put till further notice.

A buzz came in at five-fifty, a text from Darrera.

Where do we need to be? This is taking way too much time.

Stone replied: *We are on the move to Youngwood. I'll text when I know more.*

He grabbed his phone, .357 magnum, badge, and jacket and rushed out the door. He jumped into the Honda and backed out of the driveway, almost running over a stray rabbit. After flooring down the street, he turned left at the corner, and then waited impatiently at the red light, tapping on the steering wheel.

He checked his mail and found a note from Tombo sent at 12:30 a.m.:

Stone! We will depart for Uniontown tomorrow morning at 7:00 to rendezvous with Von, a Mr. Brad O'Connor, and a few others. I believe you'll want to be there with us when we do. Meet us at Sheetz where 119 splits.

Stone glanced at his watch—already six thirty. He had to hurry. He called Paxton.

"Yeah." *Mumble, mumble.*

"Paxton, wake up. I'm coming there now. We got a mail from the Find Guys. Meet us at Sheetz at seven. We're on the trail of O'Connor and Roberts!"

"Holy fuck."

"Get out of that fucking hotel room and get over to meet us. And don't crash the car on your way over."

"I'm on it!"

~

The old man pulled down and adjusted his homemade bulletproof vest, then continued loading the car. "These should work even if they're homemade," he said referring to a box of what looked like some kind of grenade. "Might be the only protection we have."

Tombo glanced up and nodded, but he didn't think they'd need armaments, homemade or otherwise. All they were doing was finding a reporter and a guy, who by all accounts wouldn't harm a fly. "You are sure you know where to go, right?"

"You know, if you're the dragonfly, I'm the master," Nick said.

Tombo looked over and saw Nick give a smug smile. *What a pompous ass. You only think you're the master.*

"Of course, I know where to go!" Nick said. "The way Von talked about this whole mess, I had a feeling someone would eventually come here to search for her, so I got prepared." He checked his mail again and grinned.

"What is it?" Tombo asked.

"Instructions on where Von went and what she saw along the way." He read the mail aloud: "Pops, we went into some wooded area beyond Uniontown near Somerset, and then through some forest and along, I think, Route 423. We made another turn over a bridge. Then we got to this place. It looks like a stone mansion in the middle of the woods. Von."

"No address? No map?" Tombo asked.

"Nah."

"Okay, well, I can program Von's number into the Find Friends app and hope I can locate her that way."

"Yeah, try it," Nick said.

Tombo punched in the details and waited. After a moment, he shook his head. "No, it's not linking up. Can't find her."

"I'll text her and ask for more details."

Tombo climbed into the Honda. "Let's get going."

Nick walked around to the passenger side and slid into the seat, all while typing into his phone.

Tombo reversed the Honda out of the parking lot and flew down the street like a bat in a hurricane.

"Relax, Dragonfly," Nick said. "We'll get there." A little further on, he said, "You know this might be the end for both of us, but I'm sure we can find Von and that O'Connor guy."

"Don't worry, it won't be the end," Tombo assured him.

Tombo had just pulled onto Route 119, east of Sheetz, when a car with a police light on top came around the corner doing around sixty miles per hour. It pulled into the Sheetz parking lot. Out climbed a tall man with a mustache who walked briskly into the Sheetz shop. Tombo noticed his license plate: 711Stone.

Holy crap. Looks like I'm finally going to meet the famous Detective Stone.

Tombo parked the car and turned off the motor. He looked over at Nick who was patiently staring at his phone. "Hey, Nick, look at that. It might be that detective I told you about. Greg Stone."

Nick and Tombo waited.

CHAPTER 17

Brad, Von, and Barry glanced at each other, speechless. Something horrific was about to go down. Their return glances shared an all-knowing agreement: they had to stop the mess before it got started.

Brad gave one quick nod, and all three of them took their guns out of their holsters. Following Brad, they climbed up the stairs to the hatch. At the top, he took a deep breath, exhaled slowly, then cracked open the hatch without a sound and peered inside. A woman sat in front of the closest monitor while a man stood on the other side of her, fiddling around with the second monitor. Brad looked back at Von and Barry, pointed at the fortress control room, gestured, one, two, and three, then burst through the hatch like wildfire, the others following hot on his heels.

"Hands up! This is an ambush!" Brad yelled, pointing his gun at the woman. He trusted the others would cover the man.

"Holy Jesus! How the hell did you get in here?" The woman jumped up, spilling coffee down the front of her tan and white checked sweater and onto the front of her jeans, which sent her into a swearing and hopping frenzy while she tried to wipe the coffee off. The man just stood there blinking while the woman calmed down. She took a step forward. "Who the fuck are you?"

"Who are we? Who are you is more the question," Brad replied.

She took another step forward.

"Get back!" Brad gestured with his gun. "I'm done messing around. The Edge of Darkness had taken too much from us already. We're here to get revenge and to stop you people."

The woman stopped moving, but she didn't step back. "Yeah, right." She sneered at Brad. "That'll never happen! This organization has too much power. Oh, wait, I know who you are; you're the scapegoat who stole the plutonium, Mr. O'Connor."

"Yeah, we'll see who has the power." He trained his gun at her head. "Where's Number Two; Suardino, isn't it?"

"Who? What are you talking about?"

"Don't give me that shit!" Brad stepped forward and poked the gun into her temple.

"We don't know where he is," the man at the monitor said, eyes wary, "but he knows where you are."

"Oh yeah? Good. And who in the hell are you two?" Brad looked at the man and pointed his gun towards him.

The man pursed his lips and pointed at nothing. "Ha! Wouldn't you like to know?"

Just then, the hatch opened and in walked Barry holding the stranger. He must have left when he realized Brad and Von could handle these two.

"We found this bastard downstairs," Barry said. "Who is he?"

The man at the monitor looked at the bound man and smirked. "Fuck, Mediate! Can't you do anything right?"

Barry ripped the sock out of his captive's mouth. "Got a first name, Mediate?"

Mediate swallowed. "John. John Mediate."

Brad turned his gun on him. Von kept hers facing the other two.

Meditate put up his hands—Barry must have unbound them so he could get up the ladder. "Wait! Don't shoot!"

Barry tightened his grip on the man and he stopped struggling. "I got him."

Brad returned his gun to the man by the monitor. "And you? Who in the hell are you?"

"Me? I'm a do-gooder," the man replied, his eyes on the monitor.

"The hell you are," Barry chimed in. "And what name would that be?"

Silence.

"Speak up, boy," Von said. "Can't hear you."

Brad stepped forward and jammed his gun into the man's temple.

"Uh, name's Brant," he confessed.

"Gee, thanks," Barry said. "Now, get over there!" He shoved Mediate towards the corner and trained his gun on him.

"You too, Brant." Brad gestured with his gun. He glanced at Von. She had her gun aimed firmly at the woman's head.

Brant reluctantly joined his colleague in the corner.

Brad turned back to the woman while Barry kept his gun aimed at the men in the corner. "What's your name?" Brad demanded.

She just glared at him.

Brad took one shot at the wall above the monitors and accidentally took out a light.

"Okay, okay! No need to get fussy," the woman exclaimed. "It's Stiles. Debra Stiles."

"And who's in charge here?"

"Wait a minute." Keeping one hand in a surrender position, she used the other to click something on the computer, then pick up her headphone microphone.

"Stop," Brad growled. "And step away from the computer."

She raised both hands. "You want the boss, I'm gonna call him for you. That's all."

"Yeah, you sure about that?" Brad narrowed his eyes.

She stepped away from the console, hands spread, glaring at Brad. "You wanna talk to him? He's underground. Our comm is the main way. But we all also have UHF two-way radios that use a repeater signal for communication." She pointed to the radio sitting on the console.

"Fine. Do it. But make sure we can hear every word."

"Sure." She put on the comm set, turned to the computer, and pressed a couple of keys.

A voice rang out from the monitor speaker. "Comm B here."

"Juan?"

"Just a sec. Juan! Call from Comm A!"

Stiles clicked something else and the cockpit view changed to show a man sitting at some kind of console. Another man came into view, a shifty-looking Latino. He stared into the camera. "Yeah, what is it?"

"We have a small problem here. Take a look." Stiles pointed the remote camera towards O'Connor and the other two.

The man looked down slightly, presumably to look in a monitor. "Holy fuck," he said, staring in disbelief. "There the bastard is! You make life difficult, O'Connor! *I'm* Number One, by the way!"

"Juan is the mastermind of this whole operation," Stiles said.

"Yes, I am. And it's nice to finally see you, Mr. O'Connor. Now what are my assistants doing letting you in there? Stiles, get him down below."

"He broke in. He's got two other people with him. And they've got guns on us."

Brad grinned, raised his gun and aimed at the camera. If the bastard could see his face, he could now see the gun. He quickly aimed it back at the woman.

Juan pounded on the dashboard in the mole. "I can't believe you, goddamn, fuckin' people!"

Brad looked around the room at everyone. Von and Barry stood motionless. Von had her gun on Stiles, and Barry covered the other two.

"Where's Suardino. Jesus. Wait till I get a hold of him!" Juan yelled.

Brad tried to remember the names being thrown around. "Not much you can do from underground, ha!" he said, gloating.

"Goddamn it!" Juan pounded on the console again, and the connection went dead.

"Keep an eye on her," Von said. "I have to check my phone."

"Now?"

"My stepfather has a private detective friend who can get Stone and the rest of the world on our side." She pulled her phone out of her pocket and started typing.

"You're sure? Does he know where we are?"

"I'm mailing him that right now. He has firepower; I know that much."

Brad approached the console, keeping his gun trained on Stiles. "What's going on with that thing down there? They have a bomb?"

"Yeah, uh, there's a … a bomb," Stiles said.

Shit! Plutonium makes nuclear bombs.

"What are you planning to do?"

"I'm just a helper, I don't know many details."

"You know how this console works, though, so show me." He motioned for Stiles to approach the bench. Brad knew the ins and outs of video documenting from his career and was adept enough at computers; with a few pointers he'd soon know what was going on.

"Uh … this is the comm button." She pointed limply at the console. "Here are the coordinates of the mole. The trajectory of the … the …" Stiles glared up at Brad, a snarl on her lips.

"What? Spit it out! What do you have? A nuclear bomb, right? Isn't that why they wanted me to break into Chimerton?"

"Why should I tell you anything?" Stiles suddenly turned and ran towards the door. Barry jumped to block her, but tripped and fell, and only grabbed her by the ankle. She kicked at him, struggling to get out of the door. Von dropped her phone, raced over and grabbed Stiles by the waist, then yanked her down onto the floor and sat on her. Stiles continued to struggle. Von slapped her hard and she calmed down.

"You see this? It's called a gun!" Brad ran over, yelling, and pointed the gun at Stiles' face. "Don't move."

Stiles grimaced beneath Von. "I won't."

"Get up," Von said, climbing off the woman.

Stiles glared at both Von and Brad, pushed herself up onto her elbows, and then spat in Von's face.

"Bitch!" Von yelled and slapped her again.

"Get up!" Brad yanked Stiles up by the arm, while keeping his gun trained on her face, and dragged her over to the control panel. "Tell us about your plans. About the bomb, that underground thing. The picture of Flood on the monitor. Now!"

"Fuck you. You'll be sorry." She wiped her mouth.

Brad jabbed his gun into her temple. "I really don't have anything to lose at this point," he growled in his most menacing tone.

She sighed. "The warhead information ... is right here." She pointed. "And the mole operational info is ..."

"Keep going."

"The thing was modeled after the Subterrene, a Russian ground dozer designed in the 1950's. It uses nuclear power to melt away rock, and then creates a glass tube behind it as it moves. When it gets up to speed, it can go about thirty feet per second in rock; that's twenty miles per hour. And it can go at forty feet per second in soft soil."

"Jesus," Von said.

"Unbelievable," Barry whispered.

Brant made a run for the door. Barry sprang into action and tackled the large man from behind, catching him off guard.

"Ahhh, let me go!" Brant yelled.

"Hey, calm down, buddy." Barry squeezed so tight, Brant couldn't move. The fight went out of him, and Barry dragged him back to the corner with the other guy, who leaned against the wall, watching it all with a grim expression. "On the ground, both of you," Barry said.

"Keep going," Brad said to Stiles, as the captives did as Barry commanded.

"The warhead is attached to a small rocket drill that exits from a slot on top of the mole. And that's all I'm saying!" She jutted out her chin in defiance.

"Oh yeah? How does it arm? How does it detonate?" Brad poked her with the gun.

Mediate mumbled something under the sock that Barry had replaced in his mouth. "Ey, ey, ta zi so ou."

"What's he saying? Brad asked.

Mediate repeated it again. "Ey, ey, ta zi so ou."

"Sounds like he's saying, 'Hey, take this sock out,'" Brad said.

"You might be right." Barry yanked it out.

Mediate's drool ran down his hairy chin. He swallowed, then began talking: "Our system uses a series of dual-end timers, a remote-detonating device, and a radar fuse. To arm, a numeric safety code is entered into a keypad in the mole. Next, the mole and the control room both have access to the timers, which must be set in order to launch. Our system is designed with ..."

Stiles turned and shouted, "Shut the hell up, Mediate!"

"Yeah, what the hell are you doing, Mediate?" Brant yelled.

"Shut the hell up," Barry growled, glaring at them in turn, his eyes blazing. "Just what I thought," Brad said. "Bombs, warheads. Where are you planning to take that thing? Does it have something to do with him?" He pointed to President Flood on the screen.

"That's classified." Brant eyed Barry's gun, but didn't make a move.

"Oh yeah? Too bad. 'Cause one way or another you're gonna tell us what you have planned!" Brad shoved the gun into Stiles' chest.

"Uh the, wh ... wh ..." Stiles began.

"Stiles! Shut the fuck up! Don't tell him shit!" Brant screamed. He clambered to his feet and tried to run, but Barry lashed out with a right hook that sent him sprawling onto the ground.

"Tell us or you die." Brad grabbed her around the throat with his left hand, while holding the gun to her chest with the other.

"Okay, okay!" She wriggled around, but that just made Brad squeeze tighter.

"It's no use struggling. I'm not letting go." Brad surprised himself with his determination and the strength of his grip, but this thing was bigger than him, bigger than all of them; he had to rise to the occasion.

Suddenly, she relaxed. "We're going to the White House." She could barely speak because of the pressure around her throat.

Brad let up his grip. "You're planning to kill Flood? Is that what this is all about?"

"Not kill, capture. And blow up the White House." Stiles breathed heavily, wheezing out of her nostrils.

"What? Are you out of your minds?" Brad yelled.

"Fuck, Stiles!" Brant leapt up and over towards Brad.

Barry grabbed him by the forearm and yanked him back with such force that he sprawled onto the floor again. "Not so fast there, mate!"

Brad realized that Stiles wanted her life more than she wanted to protect The Edge of Darkness.

It all came pouring out: "We're planning to go to the White House and capture the president, the first lady, and the secretary of state. From below. Never know what'll hit 'em. Then we'll blow up the White House itself."

Barry let out a slow whistle.

"Is that so?" Brad said. "Just one question: why?"

"That damned president Flood had caused Juan so many problems. He's dished out a lot of shit for a long time. The worst is that he sent back relatives and friends to Mexico with that illegal immigration policy, even though they'd been living here for years. They're

Americans. He changed laws to suit himself and banked millions illegally! He needs to be stopped!"

"Yeah, he's an a-hole, but that's no reason to do this!"

"If it's not us, it'll be someone else. We're going through with it. Now get the fuck out of here and out of my way!" Stiles suddenly shoved Brad to the side and lunged for the upper side of the console.

Brad could take no more. He aimed the gun at Stiles' right thigh and pulled the trigger.

Brant let out a gasp.

Stiles fell over frontwards onto the console, screaming: "You shot me, you bastard!" She slumped onto the computer chair, eyes gleaming and staring fiercely at Brad. "You're going to be sorry you did that," she hissed.

Brad smacked her across the face with the back of his hand. She fell to the floor in a slump, grabbing her wounded leg. Brad stepped over her and pointed the gun in Brant's direction. "It's just superficial. She won't die. But it'll hurt like hell. Take it as a lesson or the same will happen to you."

Mediate and Brant glared at him.

"I got them covered," Barry said. "And my finger's itching."

Brad glanced at Mediate. "He knows what's happening."

"Yeah, and he's gonna tell us. Ain't that right?" Barry poked his gun into Mediate's side.

No response.

"I'll make sure of it," Barry said in a threatening voice.

Von was texting again.

"You didn't tell me you had a stepfather," Brad said. "Is he coming?"

"Didn't think it was important. He's old. Anyway, yeah, he's on his way." She shoved the phone into her jeans pocket.

Brad sat at the console, taking a deep breath as he settled into the chair, then pushed the comm button for contact with the mole. "Hey down there, Juan. It is Juan, right? Uh huh. Just so you know, we're in control up here, so you'd better not try anything fishy!"

"You ain't gonna tell me what to do!" Juan stared into the camera, his stubble-filled face taking up the whole picture. "O'Connor, you have just messed with the wrong group!"

"Yeah? Tell that to her." He yanked the webcam off the computer and focused it on Stiles' anguished expression as she gripped her wounded leg. Silent tears streamed down her face. Brad lowered the camera to show him the gaping hole in her leg.

"Why, you fucking asshole! We'll get you; mark my words," Juan yelled into the comm.

"I know what you're planning to do, and I'm going to stop you," Brad said. "There's no way in hell you'll take that mole under Washington D.C. to get the president and blow up the White House."

Brad searched the console for any control that would be useful. "Timer, remote detonation device, radar fuse ..." he muttered to himself. "Von, call up the others, and get them to help Barry tie our captives' hands behind their backs, then help me over here."

"Will do."

Brad scanned the information on the screen while Von yelled down the hatch to the others. He noted nuclear tunnel-melt stats, what might be the trajectory control and a numeric keypad.

Von joined him and peered at the screen. "Clem's staying down to make sure no one disturbs us from below."

"Good idea."

"Yeah, he thought of it."

Brad chuckled. *What a team.* "She said the remote control was here," he said. "I expect this console has a device for operator control of everything with a manual override switch, and for safety, a way to control the speed and action from here." Brad looked to and fro.

"She said the manual controls need to be activated from the mole before they work up here," Von reminded him matter-of-factly.

"You're right. She did say that."

They searched the desktop for any software that might be useful and scanned the console from end to end. Seconds passed.

"You know what we could do ..." Von turned towards Brad.

He grinned. "Are you thinking what I'm thinking?"

"We could detonate the device from up here."

"That way we'd spend the nuclear energy. Then we go down and get them."

"Yep, we launch it and detonate it far enough underground where nothing, or no one, would get hurt. Hopefully, that is," Von said.

"Right. Where's that detonation button? But let's warn Mr. Juan first." Brad pushed the comm button again. "Juan, sir. We're going to detonate that nuclear warhead you have on board. Oh, but you'll have to punch that numeric code into the keypad down there, and—"

"Now that ain't gonna fucking happen!" came the response, but his face didn't show up on the monitor.

A banging came on the hatch. Brad turned to see what the ruckus was all about.

Clem climbed through the hatch, followed by an old guy.

Brad released the comm button so Juan couldn't hear what was going on in the control room.

"This guy here says he is Von's stepfather," Clem said.

Von turned. "Oh my God, Nick! What on earth are you doing here? I told you not to get into any trouble." She strode over and hugged him.

"Just as long as you're safe."

A young man climbed through the hatch behind him and righted his glasses as he stood up.

"This here is Tombo," Nick said, "which means dragonfly in Japanese."

"Oh, Jesus, family reunions now?" Brant scoffed from the sidelines, his hands now tied behind his back, same as Stiles and Mediate, and under the watchful eyes of Frank, Skin, Reamy, and Barry.

Brad shot him a glare before turning back to shake Tombo's proffered hand.

"Nice to meet you," Tombo said. "I'm in a detective unit called the Find Guys."

"How ya doin'?" Brad said quickly, not taking time for formalities. "Just to fill you in, these assholes have a nuclear warhead on a tunnel-boring machine and are planning to blow up the White House and kidnap the president."

"My God!" Tombo said. "Sounds like a real-life thriller. Anyway, we were hired by Greg Stone from the Greensburg P.D. to find you."

Brad and Von glanced at each other.

Von grinned. "That means Stone believed me when I met him last week."

"I don't know about that," Tombo pointed at Brad, "but we've been looking for this guy a while now."

"Really? Where is Stone, by the way?" Von asked.

"On his way," Tombo said proudly.

Brad pushed the comm button down again. "The cops are on their way, Juan," he said into the microphone, then he turned, covering the mic with his hand, and whispered to those in the control room. "Let's see if we can hear what's going on down there."

Sure enough, they could hear Juan and two other voices bantering at each other.

"Bloody hell, Juan! What should we do?" one voice asked.

"Fuck him," Juan said. "We're going on with our plans, damn it! We have plenty of firepower."

Brad looked at his team and rolled his eyes. "You all heard it. He's crazy and will stop at nothing to get to the president."

"Juan, we should really think about this."

They heard someone pound on something, and a rumble like a machine starting up.

"Look." Von pointed to the console, where the words START UP – MACHINE ENGAGED blinked in red letters.

"How fast does that thing go? Brad asked. He looked at Mediate, but he only shook his head. Maybe he didn't know. "Do we have time to stop it before it gets where it's going?"

"Hopefully," Von replied. "Let's continue on with our last idea."

"But we don't know the implications, do we?" Brad said. He turned around and looked at Tombo. "So you're a Find Guy. You found me. Know anything about computers?"

"I do, actually." Tombo stepped closer. "I have an advanced degree in computer science."

"Good." Brad pulled him to the console. "Take a look here. These mad men are under the ground with a fucking nuclear bomb or warheads. The future of the Earth may rest in our hands. See if you can find something here." He glanced at Tombo. The man looked petrified: his eyes widened, lips pursed.

"Uh, okay. I'll help as much as I can."

Brad stared into Tombo's eyes. "We need to know if we can take control from up here. Can we detonate the warhead remotely, safely? And if so, would it rock the surface? Cause an earthquake? Should we even try to blow it up?"

Tombo paused with a thoughtful frown on his face as the seconds ticked away. He rubbed his left arm once and pushed up his glasses twice. All eyes focused on him. "Uh, I'd say that it's probably not a huge warhead if it's in a tunnel-boring machine. The earth down there, if they're deep, is probably bedrock."

"Uh huh, so?" Barry asked.

"Bedrock is tough, hard as nails," Tombo said, glancing around. "But it depends on how big the warhead is and how far they're under—"

"If they were to spend that warhead, it would be all over, right?" Brad asked.

"I'd think so, but I don't know the details ... I'd have to see the software, and hear more about the warhead and the situation..." Tombo looked down.

"Well, look what we have right here for you," Von said gleefully, pulling him down onto the chair of the console. "Here's everything you need to know, right on the computer."

Tombo stared at the monitor, flicked things back and forth with the mouse, and opened and closed windows, checking files. He found the device's home folder and clicked it, and then clicked a mole icon. Up came all the technical information. "Hmm, no override controls," he murmured after a quick scan of the information. He clicked on Terminal and opened it, then punched some commands. The terminal scrolled down.

A prompt came up: *Action >*

Tombo typed: *entersys.*

Another prompt: *pswd?*

Tombo typed, *yes*, then pushed 'Enter'.

Yet another prompt: *reveal pw?*

Tombo typed *yes* and hit 'Enter'.

A new window came on the screen. Tombo's eyes widened, and he turned to Brad and Von with a grin. "I think I can help you."

Brad, Von, and Barry all looked at each other.

"Well, let's get to it, then," Brad said. "Get comfortable, Tombo." Brad pulled Tombo's chair further towards the console.

Tombo struggled a bit as if he didn't want to be there.

"You need to help us; you know that, right?" Brad stared directly into Tombo's eyes. "Please. There's nowhere else you need to be right now, right?"

"Uh, right." Tombo nodded meekly. "I'm a Find Guy." He stationed himself in the control seat, and moved the mouse back and forth on the screen. "On the left twenty-seven-inch screen are three windows: they look like comm, mole stats, and mission information. On the right screen ... see those other three windows?"

Tombo's eyes lit up and his voice became more animated. "And here's the terminal." He pointed towards the black screen containing prompts. "This is how we get into the system from the backdoor. Ah ha! Here's Flood's information, including a video from YouTube ... a mission statement for this trip, it looks like, and more info, but where's the ...?" He searched here and there and found a small icon in the lower left corner. "Okay, here it is ... the weaponry folder."

Juan's voice blasted over the loudspeaker. "Comm B to Comm A. I hope you're still there, O'Connor, 'cause I want you to know we're going to Washington D.C. to complete our mission. And by the way, my right-hand man, Suardino, is on his way to you right now. And you can't activate that warhead without me switching it from down here. You're all sitting ducks in a pond with no water!"

Brad scowled and turned to Barry. "Can you get Frank to monitor that door? We need a guard on there twenty-four seven." He pointed to the door on the opposite wall. "Has Clem gone back downstairs?"

"Yep."

"Good. Nothing had better get through those doors!"

Barry gave Brad a stern look. "Don't worry; nothing will."

Frank walked to the other side of the room to take up his post.

"Juan," Von said, "we have the police on our side now. There's no way you're going to get away with this. It's impossible. You'd best give up while you're ahead!"

Tombo examined the weaponry folder. "It looks like there's about ten to twenty kilotons nominal yield of warhead on that thing. That means it's equivalent to ten to twenty kilotons of TNT blowing up—like the MX warhead the navy designed in the fifties, similar to, but smaller than, the Fat Man of Nagasaki. Small, but deadly. Near the surface it would rock the top and send debris upwards, causing a cave-in and breaking the surface of the earth, shaking it quite a bit. It would feel like a M4 or 5 earthquake. Far enough down, it still would rock topside noticeably. They did underground tests of these things in the sixties and seventies. Radiation was contained, but it still rocked the surface."

"Right. Thanks." Brad glanced at Von, then turned back to the Find Guy. "Tombo, can we control that thing? Can we launch it from up here?"

"If we launch, it'll cut through the dirt and bedrock. We'd need it to be away from populated areas before we can do it safely. But it can be done."

"Well, that maniac down there has a nuclear warhead on that thing," Von said, "and he's planning to take it to Washington to blow up the White House and kidnap the president. I say we do it." She looked around; scowls on every face stared back.

"I agree! I'll do my best to help," Tombo said.

"With Tombo helping us, I think we should try," Barry agreed.

Skin and Reamy nodded their agreement. The old man just blinked, looking as if this was all a bit much for him.

"You know, this group is evil," Brad said to Tombo. "They went to a lot of trouble to make the mole, and they made a warhead to boot."

"And they might want to do a lot more than kidnapping and blowing up the White House," Von added.

Brad nodded. "And that's a chance we can't take. Can we detonate this thing, Tombo? Or disable it? Now?"

Brant groaned. Everyone ignored him.

Tombo gulped, then turned back to the screen and opened the weapons icon. "Okay, here it is. Hang on, I'll check the terminal ... let me see ..."

Brad and Von looked at each other. Brad pushed the comm button. "Juan, we're going to detonate your warhead. That way you can't use it anymore, for anything. I'm just letting you know—"

"What? What the hell? No, you can't. I need it, you bastard! And you can't override it from up there anyway. Right, Patina?"

"Actually, Juan," came another voice, "you can override it, but there are safeties it needs to get through before it can be fired. The system has to be armed by an operator code and an environmental code. An operator code is basically numeric. An environmental code is a natural event, like wiggling that would be caused by a launch."

"Did you hear that, O'Connor?" Juan yelled into the comm. "You need the code in order to do anything. And there ain't no way you're getting that!"

Brad glanced at Tombo, who stood to his left.

"You're fucked, O'Connor!" the man Juan called Patina yelled gleefully.

"Yeah, they're right. Technically," Tombo said quietly, turning to Brad. He turned off the comm before continuing. "But I may be able to do a little fiddling and see what I can do about bypassing that whole set-up."

Brad nodded. "Great. Go for it." He turned the comm back on. "Got news for ya, Juan and Patina; our man says he can do it." Brad glanced at Tombo and caught sight of the old man, who was sweating profusely, rubbing his face.

"The hell he can!" Juan yelled. "It's impossible. Weren't you listening, O'Connor?"

"Okay, here's the terminal ..." Tombo said as he typed in some commands at the prompt. "Okay, hit any key to activate, then push 'option', 'command', 'F5', 'delete' buttons together," Tombo recited. He watched the tracking simulator on the screen. "Here goes." He clicked and pushed the mouse to the left. "Push the 'command', 'delete', and 'shift' buttons together which opens the launch prompt ..." The red icon signifying the warhead sputtered on and off.

Activate>? *Y*

Launch sequence> *1,2,3*

Trajectory> *7-0-114*

Tombo fiddled with codes and pushed buttons on the keyboard. The weaponry icon flashed, blinking red on and off. "Done. Looks like we can control the launch of the warhead, but detonating it is a whole different story."

Brad grinned at Tombo. *This guy is a genius.* "But if we have control, that means they can't do anything on their end, right? They can't detonate the warhead?"

"It looks like they can't, if it's in admin mode, which means it's under control room movement up here, but if they try to detonate it, then they'll know we've been tinkering with it and might turn off admin mode."

"Right." Brad rubbed his head. He looked at Tombo, then back at Von and Barry. "That's a chance we have to take. You know what's at stake here. He ..." he turned to Stiles and glared, jabbing his first finger in the air at her, "you ... have to be stopped!"

"O'Connor! You still don't know who you're messing with, do you?" Juan demanded into the comm.

Suddenly Mediate said from the shadows, "Our system is designed with a foolproof, double-arming and fusing system."

"Well, look what we have here! He's alive," Barry said.

"You have to enter a special numeric code into the keypads," Mediate continued. "After launch, the environmental safety gets tripped. Then you can detonate the warhead."

The group looked at each other.

"Shut up, Mediate," Brant growled in a dangerous voice.

"But you can't control the movement of the mole," Mediate added.

"What?" Brad grimaced. "Why the hell didn't we know that earlier? You must know the code."

"No, I don't. I can't remember it."

"Bullshit! What's the code? Tell us!"

Juan came on the speakers. "What are you doing, Mediate? Don't tell him! You're dead meat!"

"Yeah, why should I tell you?" Mediate stared and bared his teeth at Brad. "I'm on the bad team, remember? I'll only tell you if ... uh ..." he paused, his muscles freezing in place.

"Tell us!" Barry demanded.

"Only if ..." Mediate paused again.

"If what, for Christ's sake?" Barry took a step towards him, glaring down at the man.

"If you let me go. I had nothing to do with this. I was used, just like you, O'Connor." He glared at Brad. "I was forced. Used! If I give you the code, I'm out, one hundred percent."

"Wait," Brad said. "How were you used?"

"They forced me to help drug you, and move you from one place to another while you were out."

"Did you all hear that?" Brad looked around. "They did do it. They drugged me. I was set up."

"It's true," Barry said. "Wow."

Brad, Von, Barry, Skin and Reamy looked at each other as if in telepathic communication. Nick retreated to a vacant chair and sat down heavily.

"That's fine," Barry said. "I can agree to that."

"Yeah, okay," Von agreed.

"Fine by me," Skin said.

Reamy nodded. "Yeah."

Brad turned to Meditate. "Okay. You tell us and you're out, one hundred percent. Never heard of you. Now give me the code. Von, can you write it down?"

"Don't do it, Mediate!" Carmine Brant yelled and struggled against whatever the team had used to tie his hands.

Barry reached down and grabbed off the floor the dirty sock that had been in Mediate's mouth. "Here, buddy. Why don't you put a sock in it?" He shoved the sock into Brant's mouth. Brant shook his head violently, trying to shake it out.

"Got it." Von grabbed a pen and paper.

Mediate looked around at everyone, and the memorized code spewed out: "35460713, space, 409888, space, 21334786."

"Wait, what? Slower!" Von said.

"35460713, space, 409888, space, 21334786," Mediate repeated more slowly.

Von wrote frantically as he spoke, then reread the number out loud. "Okay, that's 35460713, space, 409888, space, 21334786, right?

Mediate nodded. "Correct."

"Can we activate the warhead with the code?" Brad asked.

"Yes, after you enable the timer and the radar fuse, and disable the three safeties. I'm not in this, right? I won't be used?"

"Of course not. How do we enable the timer and fuse?"

"You have to enter the code and set a time for the warhead to go off. And then start the launch sequence. The thing will take off and then travel for as long as you set the timer. But ..."

"Yeah?"

"This thing is designed to dig through the earth, but moves pretty quickly. You have to set the timer for long enough that it won't affect us here."

"Holy shit. How far would that be?" Everything the man said raised questions.

"Uh, probably about six to eight hundred feet straight out. That's quite a long way. Could take a long time."

"Okay, thanks." Brad looked around; all the faces said *let's launch.*

Brad turned to Barry and Von and raised his eyebrows. They nodded. "Let's go; let's launch it!"

"Okay, it's now or never," Barry said.

"Where does the code go?" Brad asked.

Tombo brought something up on the screen and then pointed to the keyboard.

Brad entered the code himself. "35460713, space, 409888, space, 21334786."

"That it, Von?"

"Yep, you got it."

Brad hit 'Enter'. "Now we have control. Now what, Mediate?"

Brant screamed something against the sock in his mouth, but it came out as an unintelligible mumble, and he shut up when Barry raised his hand as if readying for a punch. The woman Stiles had her eyes shut, her mouth set in a grimace.

"Now you set the timer," Mediate said, undeterred by Brant's protests. "At a rate of three feet per second, I'd say, for thirty minutes. But you're going to have an explosion on the surface."

"How much?" Brad asked.

"On the surface, my guess is it'd be a relatively small magnitude, like a four or five or so. But there's a possibility it could be more. Which would mean people would feel it."

"People may be shocked, but it shouldn't cause any major destruction. Dishes might fall off shelves. It may just be doable." Brad looked around at the others. No one disagreed.

"Thirty minutes would give the warhead a good time to get away from here, anyway," Mediate said. "Then you can blow it."

Brad pondered Mediate for a moment. "Why are you doing this? Helping this group? You're pretty smart, I'd imagine, so why engage in something so destructive?"

Mediate looked up, his eyes weary, bearded lips dirty, face creased with anguish. "'Cause I was used, like you. I'm just like you."

Brad frowned. "A scapegoat?"

"Yes."

"You could have run. But you stayed around. What the fuck for?"

"Hey, when you're from a broken family, with no money, what are you supposed to do? Rob banks?"

"Of course not. What did they make you do— something other than drug me?"

"Yeah. I don't really want to talk about it ..."

"Brad," Tombo said. "I just checked the angle of the warhead and thirty minutes would put it under the Laurel Mountains. Less population. Might do very little damage."

"Let's hope so. Set the timer. Thirty minutes from our present time is five-fifteen."

Tombo typed in the time. "Done."

Von grabbed Brad's arm. "Brad, are you sure about this?" She looked back at Barry.

"Come on, Von; don't have second thoughts now. We made our decision already," Barry said. "How else are we

268

gonna stop these guys? And it's better than having that maniac use it on the White House."

"We have to do it," Reamy said.

"It's the only way," Skin added.

"And it's a yes from me," Frank called from the other side of the room.

Von rubbed her eyes and squeezed her temples, then glanced at her stepfather. He gave her a nod. She sighed. "Okay. Let's do it."

"Now get the radar fuse ready," Mediate said. "Click the weapons folder. Click on manual detonation: radar, fuse."

"Holy shit. Radar, fuse," Brad said, glancing at the clan.

Tombo followed the instructions. "Here goes." Click.

They waited. Nothing at first. Then the mole icon flashed briefly on the monitor. Brad and Tombo both looked at each other.

"That small yellow light there must be the warhead," Tombo said.

"Right, gotcha." A small rumble came on the monitor.

Shortly after that rumble, Brad heard Juan. "Comm B! O'Connor, what the hell did you do? This thing rocked back and forth. What's going on?"

"Don't worry about it, Juan. You're right, we can't do anything from up here. It's probably just a glitch in the mole."

"Hahaha! You're useless, O'Connor," Juan said.

"Yeah, it was your imagination." Brad looked over and winked at Von and Barry, who were both smiling. They kept watching the monitor. The yellow icon signaling the warhead moved quite quickly to the left.

The mole moved, too. No words were spoken.

Alarm bells suddenly started ringing. Brad shook his head, jolted out of his trance. Everyone with hands free covered their ears; the captives winced. "What the hell is that?" Brad yelled.

He looked at the monitor.

MOLE = position – stalled for detonation.

Initiate = go? Y   N

"Shit, this is it," Brad said. "Here goes." He pushed 'Y'.

"Get this thing moving!" They heard Juan scream at Patina. "We need to make as much time as possible! Hurry up! What's going on?"

Tombo pointed to the monitor. "He's trying the power-up sequence again."

"They can't move it when detonating," Mediate said. "It's a built-in safety feature."

Suddenly, the warhead detonation device tripped, and a robotic female voice came over the speaker, both in the mole and in the control room: *"Warhead armed. Detonation ready. Ready! Three, Two ...*

"Uh, Juan, looks like they took control of the—" They heard Patina say to Juan.

"I don't wanna hear it, Patina!" Juan screamed. "Hey, O'Connor! What the hell did you do? Turn it off. Reset the controls."

"Sorry, Juan, but there's not a fucking thing I can do," Brad said with a smile on his face.

"Fuuuuuccckkk!" Juan screamed.

"... one!"

A second later, an explosion rumbled and the topographical map on the second monitor showed the ground lifting up around a mile from the control room.

"People are probably going to think it's a small earthquake," Barry said from the back of the room.

Brad smiled. "Yeah, if they only knew what was going on here, I think we'd all be forgiven."

"What the hell was that?" Juan screamed through the speakers. The mole had stopped at detonation, but started up again right after. "What the hell happened?"

"You've been disabled, Juan," Brad said.

Brad and the gang listened to the conversation in the mole.

"Tell me, Patina, damnit!" Juan said.

"Yeah, they detonated it," they heard Patina reply. "Our warhead is gone."

"How did they do that without us knowing?

"Must've overrode the system. Fuck, we're screwed." He sounded defeated.

Brad and the others looked at each other. Cheers filled the room.

"Yeah, wooo!" Brad shoved his fist into the air.

"All right!" Von seconded it.

When the cheers had died down, Brad said, "Okay, Juan. It's over. I think it's time you turned that machine around."

"Don't be stupid. We're carrying on. I'm sure that's not what you want to hear right now, but it'll take more than that to stop us. A lot more."

Brad pushed the comm button. "Continue on with what? You're finished. Come on." Brad and Von looked at each other, mouths agape.

"Damn. What are we gonna do if he continues?" Von asked as an aside.

"Stop that thing now!" Brad commanded.

"No fucking way! Not in your wildest fucking dreams!"

Brad clicked off the comm.

They monitored the computer screens in disbelief, watching the mole continue on.

Tombo, looking at his phone, said, "Greg Stone is on his way here right now."

"Okay, keep me posted," Brad said. "We've got to find out how to stop that thing!"

CHAPTER 18

Stone rounded a corner, hoping that Tombo's directions and coordinates were right. It was slow going on Google maps using a phone. Paxton was in the car behind him, but they spoke on their phones, through Bluetooth.

Suddenly the ground lurched. "What the hell was that? Did you feel something?" Stone asked Paxton in disbelief.

"Um ... maybe a large truck accident? A building collapse? I don't know."

"Who knows? Where do I go?"

Paxton checked Google maps. "Take a left, then keep going for about another forty miles."

"Right." Stone and Paxton kept driving. "You know," Stone said after thinking for a while, "Von told me and the Find Guys texted me that The Edge of Darkness had this mole underground mining thing they were planning on taking to Washington to kidnap the president. When she told me, I didn't believe her ... but now I think I do."

~

Suardino was ready to head out of Youngwood but not before stopping at McDonalds drive-through for breakfast.

"Ah, kin I taka yo orda, please?" came the question from the clerk.

"Yeah, an egg muffin, hash browns and large coffee."

"Okay, das one egga muffin, hash, and large cofay. Das foa-tweni-sebun. Drive roun please."

Suardino wondered where they'd hired this staffer. When he drove up to the window, he found out—the large black woman with dreadlocks who gave him a toothy grin looked like she'd just arrived from Jamaica.

Suardino paid, flipped open the coffee, took the egg out and munched while driving with his right pinky. Suddenly the car bounced slightly some coffee slipped up through the mouthpiece, burning the tip of Suardino's nose and dribbling down his shirt. He slowed to forty-five, put the coffee down, and gathered his composure before taking another sip and increasing his speed again.

Just as he reached sixty miles per hour, the UHF two-way radio crackled on the seat next to him. "Fuck." A piece of egg muffin dropped out of the corner of his mouth. He slowed the car, put the muffin down, and grabbed the radio. It was Juan. "Yeah," he said, still chewing.

"Suardino. Where in the hell are you? They found us. They broke into the control room and maimed Stiles."

"What?" Suardino nearly choked on his muffin. "You've gotta be kiddin' me! I'll get over there right now and—"

"No! They activated our warhead and blew it up."

"Crap! That must've been the shaking I just felt!"

"I need you to meet me at coordinates N45, E63. We're bringing this thing up, and then we're going to Chimerton to get more plutonium. I need you to pick me up and get us over there as soon as possible! Those coordinates are a little mom and pop farm in Kecksburg."

"Okay! Got it. Just tell me when to get going."

"Patina! How long will we need to get up there?" Juan shouted.

Suardino just caught the reply: "Not sure, but he should get going now. We'll take the thing up as fast as we can. I'm guessing six, seven hours at max."

"Okay, I heard that. I'll head over there now and wait. Let me know when you come up and I'll pick you up."

"You'd better be there!" With that the line went dead.

Suardino popped the last bit of egg and muffin into his mouth, grabbed the steering wheel, and yanked the car around in the opposite direction.

~

By this time, Brad and his team had been in the control room for almost twelve hours. Brad, Von and Tombo sat at the console; the old man had found a sofa to rest on, and the others had either found chairs or sat on the floor with their backs against the wall, their guns still trained on their captives.

"Mmm ..." Tombo broke the silence.

"What is it?" Brad asked, sensing his concern.

"It looks like they're bringing it up, towards the surface!"

"Damn. What've they got planned now?"

"Not sure, but according to the trajectory calculations, if they come up, they'll be around here ..." Tombo pointed to the map. "Around this spot, here, around Kecksburg"

"Gotcha ..." Brad pushed the comm button again. "Where you going, Juan? What you planning now?"

"You stole our plutonium, O'Connor!"

Brad couldn't believe what he heard.

"Take two guesses where we're going. The first one doesn't count. You can try to head us off, if you have the guts. Hey, why don't you? We'll turn you into dog meat."

Brad and Von looked at each other, and then at Barry. All three of them said, "Chimerton."

275

Brad pushed the comm button again. "Oh, yes, Juan, you can rest assured we will stop you, don't you worry. I hope you have a good plan this time coz we'll see who the dog meat will be!" And with that, Brad hung up the comm again. "I've got to get over there," he said to the crew. "I can head them off at Chimerton."

"You'll do no such thing!" Von retorted. "You could get killed!"

"I'll be okay."

"But we're not letting you go alone," Barry said. "Clem can come with me, and everyone else stays here, guarding these guys and making sure no one surprises us. Von and Tombo need to stay here to keep contact with Stone and check on the mole."

Von looked woebegone, but nodded. "Okay, but be careful!"

Barry went to the door, called Clem up from downstairs, and filled him in.

Clem frowned. "I'm not sure if it's a good idea, but I'm in."

And with that, Brad, Barry, and Clem climbed down the ladder.

"I'll take Clem's spot," Skin said, following them down.

Brad ran down the tunnel to the van with the others close behind.

~

Stone and Paxton drew closer to the fortress. They rounded the first corner in the woods when Stone got a text from Tombo:

The terrorist group is bringing the mole up towards the surface. They will come up at coordinates N45 E62 near Kecksburg. Please get there and head them off.

"Paxton!" Stone said. "They're bringing the mole up. We've gotta get over there!"

"Where?"

"Near Kecksburg. Stop and turn around."

"Okay."

Stone stopped his car and Paxton stopped behind him. After executing five-point turns on the narrow road, they sped up and headed for Kecksburg. As they drove, Stone voice-typed a message to Dom using Siri. "Hey, Dom, we got news that our group here is bringing up the mole. They're planning to surface around Kecksburg. Meet us at the entrance to the bypass on Route 31 ... Siri, done ... Send."

Stone drove like wildfire, doing a hefty eighty-seven miles per hour. He felt a buzz from his phone, yanked it out while trying to keep his eyes on the road, and tapped the message icon.

Glad to be included in these things! Why didn't you tell me this earlier? Will be there in a flash. I'll mail when I get close.

"Sorry Dom, the world doesn't revolve around you!"

Paxton asked, "Darrera, huh?"

"Yeah, pissed that I didn't mail him earlier."

~

Von and crew focused on the mole in the monitor. The computer image showed it slowly moving upwards towards the surface. Another hour passed, then Tombo got an email that made his mouth drop open.

"What?" Von asked.

"It's Stone. He wants us to call him."

Von's eyes lit up. "I knew he'd come around. We should ring him."

"But do we really know he's on our side?" Reamy asked.

277

"If you haven't noticed, there's an underground dozer heading towards the White House; I'm pretty sure Stone will want to help us save the day!"

Reamy grimaced. "Right. Give him a call!"

Stone answered the call almost immediately. "Greg Stone here."

"Stone, this is Von Roberts. Thanks for helping us."

"The video was quite compelling," he said. "And we've got something much bigger on our hands."

"I know. I guess you're on your way to Kecksburg."

"That I am. I've got Dom and my crew heading over there, too. And we're almost there now."

Von ended the call, and she and Tombo turned to watch the monitor as the mole inched further up, almost out of the ground now. "What's gonna happen when they reach the surface?" Von asked no one in particular.

"Brad and Barry will stop them before they get to Chimerton," Reamy said.

"We can only hope. I have faith in them, but this Edge of Darkness group is evil. Never know what they might do. Right?" Von looked over at Stiles, who was in the corner. Her wounded thigh had stopped bleeding, but she wore her pain on her face.

"Juan may be a little crazy," Stiles said. "But he's committed to this mission, and I'm not sure anyone can stop him now. Do you know how much drive he had to make that mole? It took years and millions." Spittle came out of Stiles' mouth as she said this. "He won't stop. Mark my words."

Von looked over at Reamy. She pursed her lips and her brow furrowed.

~

Suardino sped along on Route 119 back through Greensburg, heading to Kecksburg when a green Honda accord whizzed by, followed by a red Toyota Prius—Stone and Paxton, heading towards the coordinates of the exit point.

"Assholes, run me off the road, why don't you!"

Later, Suardino waited in his car in the middle of a small farm near Kecksburg, Pa. A mound of rocks rose from the ground before him, followed by a volcano of dirt. The mole pushed up even further, dirt spilling out and falling off the nose of the mole as it worked its way through the soil.

Suardino shook his head in amazement as the huge, alien-looking monster broke through the topsoil. Looking like a giant cucumber, it rose straight up, eventually arrived at its tipping point, and then dropped forward onto the ground, where it came to a stop.

The hatch opened, and Juan climbed out and perched himself on top of the mole, looking around.

Suardino got out of his car. "Hey, Juan! Glad you could make it. I'm here to pick you up," he yelled.

"You and me both. Hey, look who's coming." Juan pointed to a green Honda coming down the road.

"Yeah, probably Stone. And, of course, back-up."

"Fuckers. Let's keep our guns on them. But I wouldn't bet they have a lot of people in that car."

They watched the car skid to a stop on the gravel. Juan squinted to see inside the car and smiled, proud of his achievement, when he saw Stone staring with his mouth open at the giant cucumber lying on the ground.

A red Toyota pulled up behind it, both angled sideways to the mole and directly in front of it.

Stone got out, using his car for cover. "Juan, I presume!" he called out. "Can't say I'm pleased to meet you."

Another cop got out of the second car in the same way. He stood by the hood, where they could see the gun in his hand, and yelled, "Get down on the ground with your hands up! And tell anyone else in that thing to come out here with hands raised."

Juan snorted. "Fuck you!" He climbed down and took cover behind the mole.

Suardino pulled out his revolver and crouched behind his car.

The second cop joined Stone behind the Honda.

"Is that Stone?" Suardino called.

"Who wants to know?" Stone replied.

"Put your weapons down and get down on the ground, you mother."

"No, *you* get down on the ground," Stone yelled back.

All Suardino could see of the man was a rifle resting on the car, barrel low, aimed his way.

Juan popped his head around the corner of the mole and yelled, "We don't take orders from you, Stone!"

Taking advantage of Juan's distraction, Suardino jumped up and ran towards the mole. He fell in mid-stride.

"Hey, you okay?" Juan asked.

Suardino climbed to his feet.

"Get the fuck down or we shoot!" Stone yelled.

Two gunshots flew over Suardino's head. "What the fuck! You're going to be sorry you did that!" He took off, jumped over a mound of dirt, and raced to the edge of the mole, taking refuge behind it. "Ya'll better get back in those cars, turn around, and go home to wifey!" he yelled at the cops.

"You're the ones who need to get on home! Get off that thing!" The other cop screamed. A bullet ricochet off the mole near where Juan's head had peeked around a moment before. Catorso and Patina came out of the hatch, guns drawn. They fired off a few shots as they climbed quickly down.

Juan waved his men towards him, and they gathered around.

"This thing's a tank," Suardino said. "We can roll right over these guys."

"Don't be stupid," Juan said. "It's as slow as hell and designed for burrowing, not squashing cars. No, we get in the car, lose these guys, get the plutonium and come back."

"They'll have a guard on the mole by then," Suardino said.

Juan glared at him. "We'll deal with that when the time comes."

"I'll cover you," Catorso said. He ducked his head out from behind the mole and fired a couple of shots towards the cops.

"Let's go!" Juan said, and the terrorists ran for the car while Catorso kept the cops' heads down with a volley of bullets.

As soon as he made it to the car, Patina fired shots to cover Catorso, who ran right behind them, barely avoiding the cops' return fire.

"Fuck, let's get out o' here!" Juan said.

The four jumped into Suardino's car, and a moment later it screeched past the cop cars, spraying dirt from the tires.

Paxton ran around the front of his car, shooting as he went. Enemy fire blew out one of his side windows.

"You don't know who you're messing with!" One of the terrorists screamed as he fired.

A bullet ripped into Paxton. Blood squirted, and he fell face first on the hood of his car.

Stone ran to Paxton. He looked alive. Anger contorted Stone's face. "Fuck. They're getting away!" He fired a couple of shots at the retreating car, but the terrorists took off down the road in a spray of gravel.

Stone pounded the butt of his gun on the car hood in frustration, then bent over and gently examined Paxton's wound. He was wheezing blood. "Don't worry, Pax, you'll be okay! I'm calling an ambulance." Stone punched in 911, reported the shooting and gave directions. "Be right back."

He grabbed the first aid kit from Paxton's car, ripped open the packaging of a thick, sterile pad, lifted Paxton's blood-covered hand off his wound, and placed the pad on the wound, then he replaced Paxton's hand and covered it with his own, applying more pressure.

A car sped towards them down the country road. It whizzed around the corner and stopped just short of them. Dom stepped out.

"Jesus, thanks for coming!" Stone yelled, his eye muscles tight. "Where were you?"

"Well, someone took their sweet time letting me know any of this was going on! Jesus!" Dom yelled back as he walked towards them. "How in the hell was I supposed to know unless someone tells me!" He stood on the other side of the car, breathing deeply as he surveyed the situation. His eyes rested on Paxton, still slumped over the hood. "Fucking Jesus."

"One of those bastards shot him in the neck," Stone said, still keeping pressure on the wound. "You just missed them. I called an ambulance. It should be here any second."

Dom put hands on hips and glared at Stone. "Why didn't you keep me informed? I should know what's going on at all times."

"If you haven't noticed, we're moving second by second with this case," Stone retorted. "We don't know what the next turn will be!"

"Yeah, well, you still have to let me know what's going on!"

"They're heading to Chimerton."

"Shit. We have to stop 'em!"

"We will," Stone said, "just as soon as the ambulance arrives."

"Go ..." Paxton gurgled.

Stone and Dom turned to the sound of a vehicle heading their way. An ambulance drove towards them and pulled up beside the car. Two medics jumped out and raced over.

Stone looked at his hand and lifted it off Paxton's. The bleeding seemed to have stopped. "Hang in there," he said, then turned to Dom. "Let's take your car. It has a lot more power than mine. Time is of the essence. You drive."

"Okay, but this is on your butt if something happens to it!"

"Let's just get there!" He nodded his gratitude to the medics, then raced to Dom's Lexus and jumped in. A moment later, they sped down the road on their way to the Chimerton nuclear plant.

"Listen, Stone ..." Dom said.

"Yo, Dom." The two looked at each other across the car.

"I think we need to get back on the right foot."

Stone nodded. "Yeah, we really should. But first we've got to stop these guys."

Dom nodded and pressed his foot harder on the accelerator.

"I'll call Von and see what's happening," Stone said.

She answered immediately. "Roberts here. What's going on?"

"They came," Stone said. "We tried to stop them, but they got away. They're on the way to Chimerton now. Paxton's been shot so we waited for the ambulance to come, and now we're off after them."

"Holy shit! O'Connor and a couple of helpers are on their way there right now."

"Okay, I hope they're armed."

"They are," Von replied, and then added, "Be careful."

"I'll try my best."

"I'm coming too, by the way. I'm sure it'll be okay if I take Nick's car! Right, Nick? The other guys can keep an eye on the prisoners here."

Stone considered trying to dissuade her, but figured he'd be wasting his time. "You'd better be careful too, then."

"I will."

"You'd better. Okay, now." He ended the call.

~

Brad, Barry, and Clem blazed down the road to Chimerton on the mid-southern side of Pennsylvania. They had to make tracks to get there before Juan and Suardino. They were geared up and armed with enough power for a small army.

"Which road is it, Brad?" Barry checked his GPS on the dash.

"Route 31 to 71 and then a left on Barnett Ave. Straight down till you see the stacks. You want me to drive?"

"No, you stay put. You gotta get ready to jump out and make tracks to the control room to secure it as soon as we get there. Game?"

"Oh, yeah, I'm game. We have to stop those bastards!"

~

Juan and his gang raced down small roads Suardino had found trying to stay one step ahead of Stone.

"Step on it, Suardino! We have to get there and claim our territory. That plutonium is ours!" Juan yelled,

The car pushed eighty-five miles per hour, weaving through the trees of Pennsylvania. Once they rounded the corner of Route 70, Suardino, Juan, Catorso and Patina saw the familiar stacks of Chimerton Nuclear Facility.

"There it is," Suardino said.

"Yeah, hurry up. Just pull up to the front."

"We'll have to get through some kind of security gate or something," Patina said.

"Fuck security! Get that grenade launcher!" Juan barked as Suardino stopped the car smack dab in front of what appeared to be the entrance. "Follow me!"

All four jumped out and bounded in the front door, guns at their sides. Sure enough, they found a security gate with two guards standing next to it. One guard stood at attention, minding his own business. The other waited right in front of the x-ray machine.

"Hello." Juan pointed his gun at the front guard's head. "Get down on your hands and knees and forget you ever saw us."

"Sir, you need to stop and put down the guns!" the man said.

The other guard bent over as if he planned to push a security button on the side of the desk.

"Don't touch that button," Juan yelled, "or this'll happen to you too." He shot the front guard right between the eyes.

The second guard straightened up, raising his hands.

"Got it?"

The guard swallowed and nodded.

"Good."

Patina tied up the man with duct tape and strapped him to the bag-check table, then they ran down the hall and into the control's personnel room. There, they scanned the map of the layout, got their bearings, and located the control room and the plutonium storage room.

"Hmmm," Juan said, reading the guards' duty roster. "Looks like we have a Mr. McGinnis on duty as assistant controller today, and Michaels is chief. Let's find that plutonium."

"This place is huge," Catorso pointed out.

"Yeah, tons of plutonium here. All for us!" Juan grinned like a rabid dog.

"I'm ready. Let's go," Suardino said. They disappeared down the hall, down two flights of stairs, through the basement, and took a left, following the map ripped off the wall from the guards' room.

~

Brad and gang pulled up five minutes later. When they saw the van parked right in front, they realized they were too late.

Brad took the mission into his own hands. No one had a better idea, so they walked in through the front door. They stopped, eyes wide at the sight of the dead guard.

"Clem, can you untie him," Brad said, referring to the still-living guard, "and find out what happened. Explain who we are and what we're doing."

"Will do!"

Brad and Barry continued on. Weapons drawn, they sneaked down the hall.

"The control room's this way," Brad said. "And the processing glove boxes are over there."

He led them to the left, down a small hall, and to the right. They flanked around and looked in the glass window of the control room. Inside, two men examined the collection of knobs, sliders, meters, and small computer screens on the large wall in front of them. On their right sat another control room also with a window. The sign on top read: BACK UP CONTROL B. While Brad looked through the window in Control A, Barry tried the handle of Control B, and a high-pitched alarm suddenly filled the complex.

Barry looked panicked. "Shit!"

They stood motionless for a second, unsure what to do.

One of the men in the control room yelled, "Breach!" Then he raced towards the door and opened it just in time to catch Brad's face as he and Barry turned around and took off. "Hey! Get back here!"

~

Juan and his gang stopped and stared at each other when the alarm blared. "Damn, they must know we're here!" Juan hissed.

"Juan! Suardino! Give yourselves up right now!" someone yelled from behind them.

"Is that O'Connor?" Juan asked.

Suardino nodded. "Yeah; fuck it."

"We need plutonium," Juan reminded his men, "but there's no time to get it now. Let's get to the control rods. We can threaten to blow the place up!"

Suardino frowned. "Isn't there any plutonium in the glove boxes?"

Juan frowned. "We'll come back and check it later. Let's get that O'Connor first!"

They ran back up the stairs and down the hall.

"Juan! Suardino!" O'Connor yelled. "I know you're in here! We'll protect this place no matter what!"

287

Juan stopped them outside a restroom. "Okay, Suardino," he said, "you know what to do. Now's the time."

"Roger, that. I'm on it." Suardino walked into the restroom, and swung his backpack off his back. Out of it, he took his makeup kit, complete with base, makeup, hair color, gelatin, face paint, brushes, and the like. He'd used this same kit on many other occasions—to lie, cheat, steal, to do dirty work. And to kill.

Suardino knew he'd only have about a minute, but he'd practiced putting on the make-up for Brad O'Connor and had gotten the whole process down to about fifty seconds. He quickly smeared on the five o'clock shadow, then drew on the outline of the birthmark with the eyeliner and filled in the lines with the purple home-made mixture of hand lotion and women's purple eye shadow. Next, he yanked on a brown, wavy wig, gave his mouth a quick touch-up and straightened the wig. He smiled. *Good job.*

CHAPTER 19

The man in the control room hadn't chased Brad and Barry, but they'd retreated enough for Clem to catch up with them after untying the guard and sending him for back-up. When they heard no reply to Brad's shouts, they retraced their steps towards the control room.

Brad spotted Juan and three of his crew as he rounded a corner. He ducked back out of sight, holding up his hand to stop the others. Where was Suardino?

"He's there, around the corner!" Juan yelled. "Get him! Show him who he's messing with!"

Damn, he must have seen me!

"You two draw them away," Brad said. "I'll hide in there," he pointed to a nearby storage room, "then I'll slip out and head in and up to the catwalk to try to protect the rods."

"Okay, Brad, you got it," Clem said, and he and Barry ran off, making sure they made plenty of noise.

Brad slipped into the storage room and remained there motionless, listening as footsteps thundered down the hallway after Barry and Clem. When they'd gone, he opened the door a crack, found the hallway empty and cautiously headed towards the control room. He assumed Suardino had a sub-machine gun, or worse, somewhere, and was waiting to pounce.

"Hey, wait! You can't go in there!" someone yelled from Control A. "I've seen you now, buddy!" A resounding shot rang out and a male screamed. "Stop it! What the hell ..."

Another voice yelled. "Juan! Go through the airlock!"

Brad knew that voice. *That's fucking Suardino! He's in the control room!*

"On my way," Juan shouted from behind Brad.

Brad raced down the hall. He figured that Juan and his goons were behind him, where they'd raced after Barry and Clem, and Suardino was clearly heading for the plutonium. He had to stop him. Barry and Clem would have to handle the others. He got to the control room and slowly entered. One staff member stood up from under the desk, his mouth and eyes wide in disbelief. "Wait a minute! I just saw you. He, you, just went in. What the hell is going on?"

Brad raced on through, heading for the reactor airlock and the protective suits.

"Twins?" Brad heard the other man suggest as he closed the airlock behind himself.

~

Juan Gabriel, in a fit of anger and frustration, raised his M-16 and pointed it directly at the controller's chest. Remembering the control duty roster, he figured it must be McGinnis, and the other one would be Michaels. McGinnis threw up his hands and froze.

Juan looked around, surveying the situation. Michaels stood in the corner, watching, not moving. "Get a gun on him, too!" Juan yelled, motioning towards Michaels.

Catorso obediently turned his gun on Michaels. Juan held up his hand to signal Patina and Catorso to pause.

"Wait a minute," Michaels said, taking a step forward. "There's no reason to get irrational now. I think we can work something out. Just tell us what you want, and we can take care of it. Anything is okay."

"Shut up, you filthy dog!" Juan screamed. "Keep your guns on him and the other guy, too, Catorso. You, too, Patina!"

"I wouldn't mess with him if I were you, Juan!" someone with a deep voice yelled through a crack in the door. "I'm armed and dangerous here."

Fuck! One of O'Connor's people. Likely the big one.

Out of the corner of his eye, Juan saw McGinnis lunge forward and grab something from the desk. Suddenly, something flew through the air. Before Juan could react, it hit him in the forehead, directly above his left eye. He grabbed his forehead; that hand came away filled with blood. He looked down at the object, an old military timer enclosed in a plastic shell.

"Fuck, you've had it now!" Juan yelled. He yanked the trigger of his M-16, and fell backwards, hitting the floor with a thump and spraying bullets all over the room. Several hit McGinnis in the arm and torso. McGinnis grabbed his arm, and tried to run out the door, tripping as he went. He fell on the ground, shaking, before he made it.

Juan glanced about the room. O'Connor's men had slipped inside at some point. Patina was sneaking up behind one of them, and another one crept up behind Patina.

"Patina! Watch out behind you!" Juan yelled.

Patina turned and shot the man once in the abdomen—one of the scapegoats; Patina thought his name was Clem. Juan ran over and spewed him full of slugs. "That didn't get you very far, did it?"

Clem fell to the ground, shooting wildly, "Ahhhh, you fucker!"

291

Meanwhile Patina disabled the other guy with a solid rifle butt to the head. Juan had no idea where the big guy had come from. Did O'Connor have friends they hadn't found out about?

McGinnis managed to right himself and tried to scoot out the door, but despite losing blood rapidly, Juan jumped up and began shooting blindly. *Fuck this shit!* "You people have pissed me off for the last time!"

He must have shot the main controller in the back, because the man lunged forward and fell onto the control panel. "Ahhh, what did you do that for?" Michaels yelled.

As he slid back off the panel, he grabbed at the switches for support. His hand found the water level valve, and he grabbed on to it, pulling it down while trying to pull himself up. Inadvertently, he turned it off, stopping the flow of water into the main core, an especially dangerous, and deadly, proposition.

An alarm sounded again. Different this time, a deep, *wonk, wonk,* and the emergency lights flashed on and off.

Juan looked around, and everyone looked up at the lights, as if in awe. "What the hell is that? Hey, what did you do?" Juan stepped up behind Michaels, gun trained on his back.

The man fell onto the ground, his glassy eyes staring up at the ceiling. Juan bent down and felt his carotid artery. "Gone." He looked around at McGinnis, who lay on the ground at the open door. "Hey, what did he do?" The blinding and deafening alarm annoyed and antagonized him. His plan was backfiring. "What's going on? Why is it doing this?"

"He might have turned off the water by mistake," McGinnis managed through teeth gritted against the pain.

"What does that mean?" Juan demanded.

"Just what you'd think: nuclear meltdown in a matter of minutes."

"Well, get in here and fix it! Turn the water back on." Beads of sweat bubbled up on Juan Gabriel's face.

"There might be time."

"Well, do it, fuck-face. Don't just lie there!"

The man groaned and struggled to stand. "Give him a hand for God's sake," Juan said, waving Patina over.

Patina half carried him across to the control panel, then propped him against the bench and stepped back.

"Let's see ..." McGinnis reached to the other side of the control panel and pushed two buttons: one green, one white.

Juan noticed that while his hand was busy at the top, his other hand reached toward some other button. *He's trying to push another alarm. Fuck that noise.*

"What in the fuck are you doing?"

"I'm turning on the water, like you said."

"Yeah? And trying to push some kind of security button, too?

"What are you talking about?

"I saw your hand," Juan stepped forward and held the gun on McGinnis' forehead. "Is the water on?"

"It is now," the controller said and pulled the switch down into the locked position. His eyes wandered back to Juan Gabriel's. Juan raised his gun, walked over, and placed the barrel right on the spot between McGinnis' eyes. They stared at each other.

Though the first alarm still screamed in the corridors, the buzzing and the flashing lights in the control room stopped.

"Good," Juan said. "I sure the fuck hope so. Now turn off the other one."

McGinnis reached below the console and flicked a switch.

The building fell silent.

Juan put the gun down.

No one spoke. All eyes were pegged on Juan Gabriel, who stood at attention like a cat waiting for a mouse.

CHAPTER 20

Brad, suited up, walked cautiously out onto the catwalk above the main core. The alarm inside the reactor almost deafened him, and he breathed a sigh of relief when it stopped. From his vantage point, he could see directly down into the workings of the nuclear power plant. He didn't like the place, not one bit.

Brad knew that Suardino would go to any length to stop him. But Brad had familiarity with the place on his side. He doubted Suardino knew what to do. He knew his mission: stop the EOD from reaching the plutonium access and unsealing the safety lock on the top deck of the catwalk. The problem was that once you unsealed the safety lock on the storage chamber, a small amount of radioactivity would be let loose into the air. Though small, it could be deadly if handled improperly. Brad figured that, unfortunately, like every terrorist, The Edge of Darkness members would gladly risk their lives for the good of the cause. No matter how irrational it was.

The catwalk was used for maintenance purposes, as an access to adjust valves, and for the eventual spent rod removal after use. The spent rods were processed in the glove boxes and eventually used for fuel and weaponry.

He glanced back at the door, wondering if he should go back, but realized it would be futile.

I've come this far, why give up now?

Unless Stone and his team arrived to save the day, the only way to end this game would be to kill Juan Gabriel and that goon Suardino, and that wouldn't be easy—especially since Brad wasn't a killer. But he couldn't let these guys win. He had to stop them.

~

Dom Darrera did seventy-five on the interstate freeway on route to Chimerton. Greg Stone sat next to him.

The car approached the turn-off for Chimerton but barely slowed, and nearly skidded off the slick cement, moist from recent rain.

"What are you doing?" Stone yelled. "Slow down, Dom, please! We need to get there in one piece!"

Dom was a man with a mission, and there was no stopping him. They saw the nuclear reactor dome in the distance, and kept racing towards it. Dom was about to turn into what looked like an entrance when he asked, "Is this it? Or what?"

"I don't know! Yeah! It's gotta be. Turn in!"

Dom yanked the wheel to the left, turned into a driveway—rolling them right with the inertia—and sped down it into a parking lot. He parked at the entrance to the building and both men jumped out immediately. They knew the scenario: terrorists stopped at nothing.

They raced through the front door and into the maze of the Chimerton Nuclear Facility. They saw the dead guard, but a commotion in the control room drew them further in. They followed the sound of voices, staying low and against the wall.

~

Brad hid in the west wing, right outside the storage room door. If they wanted plutonium, that was where they would have to come. He listened carefully for any sound of Suardino or Juan and his thugs.

The facility was designed so that the actual core was in the center, enclosed in bulletproof, double thick insulated glass. One could look in and see the nuclear rods being moved into place. Around the bottom sat coils, pipes, and tubing for water-cooling systems, and aluminum tubing for encasing bundles of electric wires. The catwalk, used by technicians to check the core and to lower the rods from a huge motor suspended from above, ran along the outside wall of the dome. The facility was not just a nuclear power reactor; it was also a plutonium extraction facility, used to obtain weapons-grade plutonium from the waste of used rods. Lead-lined storage rooms were located on both sides of the facility in the basement, the floor under the core.

Brad had to stop them getting into the storage area. Seven grams of the minute particles from ore found naturally in the earth was enough to make a small bomb, and thirteen grams would blow up an airport. The storage rooms here held tons, but Brad wouldn't allow any of it to become Juan's personal stash.

~

Juan moved in front of the door and stood, gun alert, guarding the prisoners. All he had to do now was wait for Suardino to return with the plutonium. Suddenly, he felt a tap on his neck. Thinking it was a fly, he went to brush it off, and discovered the barrel of a gun.

Juan spun around. "Well, blow me down, look who we have here. Dom Darrera. Detective extraordinaire."

"Yeah, right! I'll be just that when I take you into custody and haul you back to Greensburg."

297

"Oh, yeah." Greg Stone slipped through the door with a .357 Magnum trained right on Juan's head. "Don't make another move, Juan."

Juan stared into Stone's eyes.

I'll freeze this bastard.

Clanking and clamoring suddenly came from the containment room. They all looked towards the sound. "You hear that?" Juan said smugly. "That's my man, Suardino. He'll have this place in no time."

"Oh, yeah? We'll see about that!" Stone's gun dug deeper into Juan's temple.

~

Brad hid below the entrance to the catwalk and looked up. There, wearing a matching suit, his face unmistakable through the clear helmet, stood his nemesis: himself!

He looked again and could hardly believe his eyes.

The man looked exactly like him: Brad P. O'Connor. So it was true. That's how they did it. The hair, the eyes, the birthmark were faultless. The semi-automatic pistol he carried even looked similar to the one Brad held in his own hand. Brad felt a momentary rush of rage. He had to stop these sick bastards.

Since he hadn't seen Suardino with Juan, Brad figured that he must be the man in the disguise. He watched him climb the ladder up to a mid-level catwalk and put a small box right outside the control room door.

Fuck, that's gotta be a bomb.

Then Suardino ran up the stairs to the catwalk at the top of the containment vessel, looked around and disappeared from Brad's sight.

Brad sat tight, waiting for Suardino to try to get into the storage area. He crouched down, pistol ready. He'd used guns several times before, but he'd never wanted to kill somebody before today. Footsteps sounded on the catwalk: clank, clank, clank, clank, clank. Then all of a sudden, the clanking stopped. Brad stayed low for several minutes, and then peeked out from behind the corner.

He sneaked around the corner, gun in hand. He had to keep control. Juan and his gang knew he was there, and one wrong move could be the end. He climbed up to where the ladder met the second layer of the catwalk.

"Hey there!" Suardino called, his voice muffled from inside the suit.

Brad flinched as his own face popped around the corner.

"Stop!" Brad yelled.

The figure raced down the catwalk towards the control rods.

Brad ran after him, and the two Brads chased each other around the third tier of the catwalk, and then down the other ladder. Brad chased Suardino down the stairs, back through the airlock and into the control room, where a couple of cops had Juan and his two cronies on the floor while Von, Barry and one of the techs looked on. A couple of bodies lay on the floor, one of them Clem.

All heads turned at their entrance. Suardino Brad stopped and turned his gun on Brad as he followed him through the airlock.

Von gasped. "Wait. Which one ... Oh, my god." She looked from one Brad to the other. They looked virtually identical.

The two Brads faced each other, guns pointed at each other's heads, a challenge in their eyes, as if tempting each other to fire. They circled around each other.

Suardino Brad fired, then spun around, dashed back through the still-open airlock and up onto the catwalk again.

Brad flinched as the bullet flew over his shoulder. "Hey, what the fuck do you think you're doing?" he yelled as he ran after him.

Rapid gun fire whizzed past Brad's head, spraying the wall behind him and ricocheting off the metal catwalk.

"Brad!" Von screamed from the control room.

"O'Connor, get out here!" Stone yelled through the airlock.

A spray of bullets came again from the imposter. Suddenly a blast went off from deep in the reactor core, and sirens blared again.

"Breach! Get out. Everybody get out!" someone yelled from the other side of the airlock.

"O'Connor! Get your ass out here!" Von screamed through the airlock.

"Go! Go!" a male voice yelled.

Brad heard footsteps running out of the control room, but he had to finish this. Had to make sure the make-up artist didn't survive to destroy anyone else's life. He flanked the impostor, trying to stay out of sight but get close enough for a clean shot.

The place went up in flames, water poured from the security sprinklers and smoke billowed out from the fire. Brad had little time left. He shot at the figure he could now barely make out in the smoke, and ducked to avoid the return fire. The impostor raced back to the airlock, and Brad took off after him. He chased the impostor out of the airlock, through the control room, and down the corridor.

Both Brads ripped off their helmets as they ran into the front lobby. Brad chased the impostor out the front door, then stopped. The impostor stood there in front of the facility, facing him, gun aimed at his chest.

Everyone else was also there. The cops held their pistols on Juan, who wore a set of cuffs, while Barry had his trained on a couple of shadowy figures in the back of the police car. Von was helping Clem, who was clutching his stomach, into her car, while one of the techs, also wounded, hauled himself into the back seat.

When the Brads appeared, all eyes turned towards them. One of the cops swung around and moved his pistol back and forth from one Brad to the other, clearly confused by the appearance of a second O'Connor.

Staring into the eyes of each other, one O'Connor said, "Good job. You actually look like me!"

"No, you look like me!" the other said.

"Who the hell do I shoot?" one cop yelled.

"Wish I knew," the other cop muttered, taking his eyes off Juan to glance at the Brads.

Juan ran.

Brad swung towards him and fired. Juan collapsed in mid-stride.

"That's gotta be the real one!" the second cop shouted.

"You're right; it's the real me!"

Von stared, speechless, her heart pounding. He was right, that had to be the real Brad. Stone took a shot at the one they thought must be the fake Brad. In retaliation, the man sprayed them with gunfire, then ran back into the facility.

Everyone still standing ducked. The other Brad flinched; blood streamed from a wound in his arm. He turned towards the door.

"Don't go back in there, O'Connor! It's gonna blow!" Stone screamed as another blast came from within.

That Brad didn't listen; he ran straight back into the facility.

Another blast rocked the building, and one of the Brads screamed from inside.

"No one goes in," Darrera said.

Von bit her lip. He was right. Though she wanted to run in and help, it was too dangerous. All she could do was wait.

Gun fire echoed through the building

"Ahhhh! Get the fuck ... ahhh!"

"Hey!"

More screams.

Large bangs made Von flinch. It sounded like something falling on the stairs.

Those standing out front watched and waited in anticipation. No one said a word.

Smoke billowed from the building, but the *wonk*, *wonk* of the alarm finally stopped. Von guessed that the sprinkler system must have put the flames out.

No movement came from inside. They waited. Time dragged.

"We don't have much time," Stone said. "Radiation will start to leak."

"A clean-up crew will be on their way," McGinnis said from the back seat of Von's car.

Darrera knelt by Juan and pressed his fingers to his neck. "Dead."

Von glanced at the remaining members of his team, safely cuffed and in the back of the police car and under Barry's watchful eye, then she looked at the wounded men in her car. They seemed stable and the ambulance was on its way. One of the techs was dead, but the only one missing from their team was Brad.

"Where are they?" she asked.

Suddenly, a figure walked through the smoke of the lobby, still in the plastic radioactive suit, carrying a gun at his side. The cops immediately trained their guns on him, but he just wandered out the door and stood there. Von held her breath. She could hear the sound of sirens in the distance, coming their way.

"Shit, which one is it?" Darrera said.

"Hey, which one are you?" Stone yelled.

In a quiet voice, the man said, "It's me. It's the real Brad."

"Oh, yeah? Prove it!"

"My birthday is June seven. I live on Sheffield."

Darrera snorted. "Yeah, but the EOD would know that if they did their homework."

Stone turned to Von. "Von?"

"Sounds like him, but ..." She replied, unsure.

A Toyota Tercel drove up and stopped behind Von's car.

Stone turned and motioned for the people to get out of the car.

A man and a woman joined them.

The woman walked to the bottom of the steps and looked at the figure in the plastic suit. "Hi, Brad," she said.

"Sally. Tom," he replied, looking from one to the other. He nodded at the police. "They don't know whether to believe it's really me."

"Hi, Brad," Tom said, walking up to stand at Sally's side.

"Tell me my daughter's nickname, and I think we can agree it's you."

Brad smiled. "Pookie."

Eyes gleaming, Sally ran up the steps, hugged him tightly, and buried her nose in his neck, then she stepped back and looked at him.

"Sal, it's really great to see you," Brad said. "Sorry I worried you!"

"I'm just glad you're okay." She turned to the others and said with commitment, "It's him! The real Brad O'Connor!"

"Yep, definitely," Tom said.

The onlookers cheered and clapped.

Brad slipped an arm around Sally's waist and they walked down the steps.

"Sorry to interrupt your reunion," Stone said as he walked over, "but where's the impostor?"

Brad sighed. "Down. He fell. I didn't check if he was still breathing."

Stone nodded. "Just so long as he isn't gonna storm out of there shooting."

"I'm pretty sure he's past that."

Stone nodded. "Good. Juan Gabriel is out of the picture, too, and I'll put his little friends in safe keeping." He jerked his head to Juan's goons in the back of Darrera's car. "Oh, and squad cars are heading to their headquarters to clean up there, as well," he added before walking away.

The emergency vehicle sirens had grown louder, and now two fire trucks and an ambulance rolled up in front of the facility.

People in suits jumped out, helmets under their arms. "Okay, let's make sure the control rods are contained!" one of them yelled as he raced towards the door.

"I already did that," Brad said. "I closed the rod access hatch and locked the basement storage door. The sprinklers came on and the fire is out."

The man and his team stopped and stared at him, then he sighed with relief. "Thanks, Buddy. We'll go in and check it all out, anyway." He donned his helmet and led his crew inside.

Von waved the medics to her car. "Wounded. Over here." They raced over, carrying their equipment. She stepped out of the way to let them do their work and headed over to Stone. "How come they turned up?" she asked, nodding at Brad's friends.

"I sent a text when I realized we might need help with identification," he replied. "They happened to be together, looking at some property not too far from here."

Brad and his friends wandered towards them.

"I wasn't sure what was going on with you, buddy," Tom said to Brad. "I thought you were going a little crazy there." He put out his hand for Brad to shake.

Brad stopped and shook the proffered hand. "Yeah, you and me both," he replied. "I'm happy Von believed me. And Stone, too." He looked over at them both.

Stone nodded. "I wasn't sure if I should believe you, but that video you made really made me think. The Edge of Darkness over there sent us their own little video, too. Plus, this woman right here turned me around." He motioned at Von. "If it weren't for her, I might not be here right now."

"Stone, I think you deserve a promotion," Darrera said as he walked up.

"Ten-Four. *Muchos gracias*," Stone replied.

Darrera rolled his eyes, then smiled.

Brad turned to Von. "Thank you. Thank you for believing in me, for calling these people, for standing up for us scapegoats."

"How could I not? You made me believe in you. It's because of you that the other guys came through. You stopped those nut jobs from kidnaping the president and blowing up the White House."

"I had help. You, Barry, Tombo, the others."

"Yes, but it was you who made all the difference."

"I second that," Barry called from where he still stood guard over the remaining terrorists.

305

"Thanks, but I couldn't have done it without you." Brad looked into her eyes, and then they hugged. "I'll never forget you," he said as the hug came to an end.

"Nor will I forget you."

Sally put her arm around him. "Oh, Brad, I'm so proud of you. Look what you've done. You stopped a disaster. You're amazing. I love you."

He turned to face her and they stood there, eye to eye. "Uh. Yeah, I guess so."

And then Tom said from behind, "Do you guys need a ride?"

A Note from the Author

Did you enjoy my book?
If so, I would be very grateful if you could write a review and publish it at your point of purchase. Your review, even a brief one, will help other readers to decide whether or not they will enjoy my work.

Do you want to be notified of new releases?
If so, please **<u>sign up to the AIA Publishing email list</u>**. You'll find the sign-up button on the right-hand side under the photo at **<u>www.aiapublishing.com</u>**. Of course, your information will never be shared, and the publisher won't inundate you with emails, just let you know of new releases.

Acknowledgments

A very special thanks to writer and teacher David Melhuish, whose initial comment upon reading the first draft of Scapegoat years ago was, "That's an interesting idea; I've never thought about it." Of course, this kept *me* thinking about it until the novel was complete. I honestly don't think I would have kept going had I not received those words.

I would also like to thank fellow writer John Noon for his helpful and thoughtful advice on updates for chapter one which helped the novel become routed on its present course.

I owe my colleagues Michael Rupp and Terry Laskowski great recognition for their positivity, productive questioning, and useful discussions about writing and life after working hours over pizza and wine. Michael's adept checking and reviewing also is appreciated.

Perhaps the biggest thanks would have to be to wonderful writer, editor, guide, and writing teacher (at least for me) Tahlia Newland of AIA and Escarpment Publishing regarding her first statement about the novel: "I find that I want to know what's going to happen next, but ..." Tahlia pointed out problems that I wasn't aware of and taught me how to think about the writing process in a more professional manner, all the while maintaining never-ending attention to form and style. At the same time she lent incredible suggestions for becoming a better writer, and I think I have become so, a little anyway.

Lastly, I would like to thank my wife and best friend Nori for her patience and understanding while I spent valuable weekends and holidays behind the computer, and for her consistent pushing that I finally finish the novel and send it out. And I have. And I did.

www.ingramcontent.com/pod-product-compliance
Lightning Source LLC
Chambersburg PA
CBHW030625110726
47901CB00002B/324